THE SAPPHIRE

THE SAPPHIRE

BY
A. E. W. MASON

C. COMBRIDGE LTD.

This edition first published 1970
by C. Combridge Ltd
Wrentham Street
Birmingham

Printed in Great Britain by
Lowe & Brydone (Printers) Ltd., London

CONTENTS

CHAPTER I

IN THE FOREST

I CANNOT pretend that the world is waiting for this story, for the world knows nothing about it. But I want to tell it. No one knows it better than I do, except Michael Crowther, and he, nowadays, has time for nothing but his soul.

And for only the future of that. He is not concerned with its past history. The days of his unregenerate activities lie hidden in a cloud behind his back. He watches another cloud in front of him lit with the silver—I can't call it the gold—of the most extraordinary hope which ever warmed a myriad of human beings. But it is in that past history of his soul and in those activities that the heart of this story lies. I was at once near enough to the man and far enough away from him to accept and understand his startling metamorphoses. I took my part in that dangerous game of Hunt the Slipper which was played across half the earth. Dangerous, because the slipper was a precious stone set in those circumstances of crime and death which attend upon so many jewels. I saw the affair grow from its trumpery beginnings until, like some mighty comet, it swept into its blaze everyone whom it approached. It roared across the skies carrying us all with it, bringing happiness to some and disaster to others. I am Christian enough to believe that there was a pattern and an order in its course ; though Michael Crowther thought such a doctrine to be mystical and a sin. Finally, after these fine words, I was at the core of these events from the beginning. Indeed I felt the wind of them before it blew.

Thus:

My father held a high position in the Forest Company and I was learning the business from the bottom so that when the time came I might take his place. I had been for the last six months travelling with the overseer whose province it was to girdle those teak trees which were ripe for felling. The life was lonely, but to a youth of twenty-two the most enviable in the world. There was the perpetual wonder of the forest ; the changes of light upon branch and leaf which told the hours like the hands of a clock ; the fascination to a novice of the rudiments of tree-knowledge, the silence and the space ; and some very good shooting besides. Apart from game for the pot, I had got one big white tiger ten feet long as he lay, a t'sine, and a few sambur with excellent heads. I had the pleasant prospect, too, of returning to England for the months of the rainy season, and giving the girls there a treat they seldom got.

I parted from the overseer in order to make the Irrawaddy at Sawadi, a little station on the left bank of the river below Bhamo, but above the vast cliff which marks the entrance to the Second Defile. The distance was greater than a long day's march, but one of the Company's rest-houses was built conveniently a few miles from the station. I reached it with my small baggage train and my terrier, about seven o'clock of the evening. A small bungalow was raised upon piles with steps leading up to the door, and a hut with the kitchen and a sleeping-place for the servants was built close by. Both the buildings were set in a small clearing. I ate my dinner, smoked a cheroot, put myself into my camp bed and slept as tired twenty-two should sleep, with the immobility of the dead.

But towards morning some instinct alert in a sub-conscious cell began to ring its tiny bells and tele-graph a warning to my nerve centres that it would be wise to wake up. I resisted, but the bells were ringing too loudly—and suddenly I was awake. I was lying upon my left side with my face towards the open door, and fortunately I had not moved when I awaked. The moon rode high and the clear-ing to the edge of the trees lay in a blaze of silver light. Against that clear bright background at the top of the steps, on the very threshold of the door, a huge black panther sat up like a cat. His tail switched slowly from side to side and his eyes stared savagely into the dark room. They were like huge emeralds, except that no emerald ever held such fire.

" He wants my terrier dog, Dick," I explained to myself. I could hear the poor beast shivering under the bed. " But that won't help me if he crouches and springs."

My rifle lay on a table across the room. To jump out of bed and make a dash for it was merely to precipitate the brute's attack. Moreover, even were I to reach it, it was unloaded. So I lay still except for my heart; and the panther sat still except for his tail. He was working out his tactics; I was hoping that I was not shivering quite so cravenly as my unhappy little terrier dog beneath my bed. As I watched, to my utter horror the panther began to crouch, very slowly, pushing back his haunches, settling himself down upon them for a spring. And that spring would land him surely on the top of the bed and me.

I found myself saying silently to myself, and stupidly:

"Here I finish. This is where I get off. I hope it won't hurt. . . . People who have been mauled say that it doesn't. I shall know about that, however. He'll probably smash my face in. Beastly!"

But while my thoughts were stupid, my right hand was acting very cleverly. It slipped down to the floor on the far side of my narrow camp bedstead. It sought, found, and grasped one of my heavy walking shoes. Until that moment it seemed to have been acting quite independently of me. But as I felt the weight of the shoe, I took command of it. I sat up suddenly, yelled with all my voice and threw with all my strength. By good fortune my aim was straight. The heavy, nailed heel struck the beast hard between the shining eyes when he was on the very point of springing. No doubt the shoe hurt, but the panther even so was more startled than hurt. He uttered one yelp, turned tail, and streaked across the clearing into the forest, black and swift as some incarnation of Satan overtaken by the dawn. I was out of bed the next instant; I slipped a dressing-gown over my pyjamas, put on my shoes, and fixed a clip of cartridges in my rifle.

I fumbled over that proceeding. For now that the moment of danger had passed, I felt the animal's great pad slapping down on my face and wiping it away. I smelt its fetid breath. And I probably felt and smelt more acutely than I should have done had it actually leaped. However, the clip was shot into its sockets at last. Then I waited on the verandah in the hope that my panther might return. And I waited. And I waited.

I had an odd feeling that the forest was waiting for him too, listening for the tiniest rustle of its undergrowth, watching for him to charge out of that tangled wall. I had never known silence so complete. I was prepared, of course, for my camp servants to sleep through that or any other racket. It would have needed the last trump to rouse them and they might have overslept themselves even then. But the hush was so deep that I was aware of it less as a negation of sound than as a new form of activity. I tried my pulse ; it was now perfectly steady. I was not excited. There was not a drop of sweat upon my forehead. Nor do I think that I am particularly vain. But for the rest of that night I felt myself to be the axis of a world in suspense.

The panther did not return. My fox-terrier crept out, and still whimpering and shivering, nestled close against my side. The glamour of the moonlight took on a shade of grey. The clearing, the crowded boles of the great teak trees were bathed now in a spectral and unearthly light. Then darkness came, black and blinding, like a cloak flung over the head. There was no longer forest or clearing. There was nothing but one man with a rifle across his knees of which he could only see the speck of its ivory foresight. But during all these changes my sense of expectation never lifted. It changed, however, as the night changed. I no longer waited for my panther. My mind had lost sight of him, as my eyes had lost sight of the forest. What it was I waited for I had no idea. But it was for something big, forming somewhere out of the reach of knowledge. Nor did the morning help me. I marched into the little village of Sawadi merely conscious that I had passed the oddest night in all my experience.

On the stern-wheel steamer *Dagonet* I made the acquaintance of its Captain, Michael Crowther.

CHAPTER II

THE PACKET

DURING the morning Captain Crowther stood beside his helmsman at the high wheel on the roof of the steamer. The Second Defile with its monstrous, high cliff, its racing waters, and the unmanageable great rafts of teakwood floating down to Rangoon presented always a delicate problem in navigation. But Captain Crowther certainly knew his business. He edged his steamer in here, thrust a raft aside there, and by lunch-time the hills had fallen back and we were thrashing down the broader waterway to Schwegu. At luncheon Crowther took the head of the table and I found that a place had been laid for me at his elbow. He was a man of thirty-six years or so, and he had the sort of hard, leering, and wicked face the early craftsmen were so fond of carving on the groins and pillars of French cathedrals. I took a dislike to him at my first glance.

" You are Mr. Martin Legatt of the Forest Corporation," he said to me as I took my seat.

" Yes."

" I am Michael D. Crowther, the Captain of the *Dagonet* " ; and he spoke with so violent an American accent that I felt sure at once that he was an Englishman.

" Press the flesh," said I, extending my hand, and equal, I hoped, to the occasion.

The stewards placed great basins of soup in front of each of us. There were eight passengers besides myself, so far as I remember. Michael Crowther consumed his soup with a little finger crooked from a suburban past and almost an excess of good breeding. When he had finished—and he deserved every drop of it for his skill in wriggling so quickly through the Second Defile—he said :

" A solitary life yours, Mr. Legatt. Gee, I don't think that I could stick it for a week."

I had all a young man's inclination to make his ways look magnificent and unusual ; and the presence of the eight tourists was a temptation to embroidery. But Captain Crowther was the last man in the world to whom I would have tried to explain the magic which forest life then held for me. So I answered with a show of indifference :

" There are compensations, Captain. I don't suppose, for instance, that there is a single person on board who is feeling half the pleasure I am at this moment from simply stretching my legs out under a civilised dining-table with the knowledge that I have nothing to do all the afternoon except lounge in a long chair and watch the river-banks go by."

" Well, each man to his taste," Captain Crowther remarked. He was kind enough to look me over with approval. " I should have thought that a young fellow like you, however—why, holy snakes ! I reckon you never came across a bird from one end of the month to the other."

For a moment I was mystified, but the knowing wink with which Crowther supported his remark was a sufficiently explanatory footnote.

" Nary a bird," I answered.

The tourists looked up intelligently. They were going to obtain information at first hand about the forests of Burma. Two ladies of middle age sat opposite to me—the two inevitable English ladies to be met with on any steamer and any train within the world's circumference. One of them, the younger I suppose by a couple of years, said eagerly :

" Not a bird ! Now isn't that strange ? Would you say that that was particularly Oriental ? "

" My dear ! " the friend chided her by the right of, say, her two years' seniority. " After all, we have our birdless grove at Goodwood—or rather the Duke has his."

She was standing up gallantly for her country. Privately she might think it was down and out, publicly you couldn't beat it. Even if it came to a comparison of birdlessness, the gorgeous East had nothing on England. Wasn't there the famous Grove ?

The junior of the pair, however, objected to corrections at the dinner-table. She bridled and answered with a definite tartness.

" I have heard grave doubts thrown upon that story——" she began, but I thought it time to stop a rift which might in the end split a pleasant fellowship. I interrupted her.

" I am afraid that the birds of Captain Crowther's vocabulary are not the birds which nest in trees."

The ladies were puzzled ; Captain Crowther was

noisily delighted.   He slapped the flat of his hand
upon the table.

" That's a good one !   That's a witticism, that is,
Mr. Legatt ! "   He felt in his pockets.   " I keep a
little book to jot down the wise-cracks I hear.   ' Not
the birds . . . ' "   And pulling out his book he wrote
my poor little remark down, with a final stab of his
pencil at the end which no doubt it deserved.   " And
not a pal to hobnob with over a glass of something ? " he continued.

" A pal to hobnob with from time to time, yes, but
not a glass of something.   And talking of glasses "—
I turned towards the steward—" I would like a
whisky and soda."

" With me," said the Captain.

I sat up.

" Oh no, please ! "

" With me," Crowther repeated, waving a hand to
the steward ; and there was an end of the matter.   I
couldn't make a scene, of course, but I grew hot with
resentment and I talked no more until the end of the
banquet.   All   the   meals   upon   the   Irrawaddy
steamers are banquets, even the breakfasts which
are little trifles of four set courses.   I watched,
however, and noticed that the other passengers were
as uncomfortable as myself.   Michael Crowther was
behaving like a profiteer pressing drinks upon his
poorer friends in his new nickel-plated yacht.   I
should have to come to an understanding with him
before the hour of dinner.

All through the afternoon, however, Captain
Crowther stood by the high wheel driving his steamer
down the stream.   It was very pleasant on the great

triangular porch in front of the saloon. The chant of
the two men with the sounding-poles announcing the
depth of the water, the thud and thunder of the
great stern-wheel; the banks now falling back in flat,
green rice-fields, now closing up with jungle-clothed
hills, and perhaps a great white-legged buffalo knee-
deep in the water; a village here, a village there, and
always a pagoda; the red poles marking the channel
upon the one side and the white poles upon the
other; the long rafts where the steersman seated on a
high throne with an immense sweep in his hands
looked like the steersman of a Greek trireme in a
picture; all the accessories of sound and prospect
filled the long afternoon for me with enchantment.

But towards evening Crowther came down from
his sentry-box on the roof to the second wheel on the
porch. Here was my opportunity, but for the
moment I was too lazy to take it. The huge headlight in the bows was turned on. For the moment it
threw merely a grey and rather ghostly beam down
the river, a beam hardly noticeable except when it
struck a sand-bank. Then it became a radiance.
But the darkness rushed upon us, the sky blazed with
stars and the beam became a thick column of bright
gold along which myriads of white moths, like the
flakes of a heavy snow-storm driven by a high wind,
streamed to their death on the burning glass of the
projector.

I got up from my chair then and went to the
Captain. He was standing by the wheel, but the
First Officer was steering so that he was free. I
said :

"Captain, I want to be clear about this. I'm a

passenger on an Irrawaddy steamer, and if I ask you at some odd time to have a drink with me or you ask me to have one with you—that's all in order. But if you insist on paying for what I drink with my meals you're going to force me to drink nothing but water till we reach Mandalay, and I'm tired of water."

I expect that it sounded rather priggish, but most young men have a touch of the prig in them and I like the others. Captain Crowther was certainly taken aback, but he had no time to answer me. For at that moment we rounded a bend of the river and a petrol storm-lamp upon the bank lit up a little square of sand, a group of people in bright silk skirts, and a few booths backed by trees.

"Tagaung," said the First Officer. He rang the engine-room bell, set the indicator at half-speed and put his helm up. I had said my say and was glad to pass on to another subject.

"We stay the night here, I suppose?" I said.

Captain Crowther looked at me quickly and queerly. The First Officer grinned.

"No," Captain Crowther replied curtly.

"It looks as if there were a good many rice-bags waiting, sir," said the First Officer.

The First Officer was puzzled now. There was indeed a parapet of rice-bags built up on the shore.

"All the more for the next boat then," said Crowther sharply. "I'll wait half an hour here. I have orders to reach Mandalay as early as possible to-morrow, so I shall push on to Thabeikyin to-night."

The First Officer was utterly at a loss. His eyebrows went up to the roots of his hair. I thought indeed that he was on the point of protesting. But Michael Crowther stood with his underlip thrust out and a black look upon his face which would have stopped any subordinate from questioning his commands.

" Very well, sir," said the officer, and the *Dagonet* sidled up to the bank and was made fast. The great headlight was swung round towards the shore and lighted up the little settlement, the great tamarinds and fig-trees behind it and the groups in the open square. It was like a tiny scene upon a stage fantastically bright, set in a proscenium of ebony. A general scene of coloured movement to prepare us for the appearance of the principal characters. I walked aft and, leaning upon the rail of the ship, watched it ; the long prison wall of the brown rice-bags melting down to a garden wall and then here and there without any order, to a terrace parapet as though a bombardment had blown breaches through it ; a procession of men tramping down the mud-bank and up the gangway to the lower deck with the bags upon their heads, and then back again with no bags at all, purposeful as ants. I lifted my eyes to the illuminated square and I suddenly saw the principals take the stage.

Captain Crowther first. He came from the darkness of the huts behind the square and for a moment I doubted whether it could be he, so imperceptibly had he vanished from his ship, and so completely had my attention been engrossed by the busy spectacle. But it was the man. I recognised the shortish, thick-set figure ; I could see the gold badge upon his cap and count the gold stripes upon his sleeve. He was not alone. The First Officer's grin when I asked whether we were to stay the night at Tagaung and his perplexity when the Captain definitely answered " No," were explained to me. For here was Captain Crowther the centre of a small family group. A young and pretty Burmese woman in a gay tartan skirt of silk with a rose in her black hair, walked at his side. And she held by the hand a little girl whose hair was fairer than her own and her skin less brown. The pretty Burmese woman was pleading earnestly at one moment, and coaxing daintily the next with a small, appealing hand laid upon his arm. The little girl whom I took to be about eight years old, every now and then added her entreaties, setting the palms of her hands together in prayer, catching hold of the hem of his jacket and jumping up and down on her toes. There could not be a doubt of their relationship. The mother, though her feet were bare, had put the child into white socks and little brown shoes to emphasise that she was white, and their supplications were as easy to understand as they would have been had they been uttered within my hearing. They were all in the one word : " Stay ! "

I looked at Crowther. He was a picture of compunction and regret. He looked at his ship. He took off his cap and scratched his head and shook it. I could see his face clearly now. He was the most woebegone man one could ever see. A martyr to duty. He would stay if he could, but he was only a servant. He had his orders. He must go. On the next trip he would not be so hurried. Et cetera. And et cetera.

I should have thought it the prettiest little romantic scene of happiness deferred if I had not had a conviction that Michael Crowther was merely giving a performance. I had no belief in those orders. He had only to make an early start on the next morning and running downstream he could reach Mandalay before noon. The young woman ceased to plead, her face lost its vivacity and then crumpled like a child's when the tears come. A movement of irritation and a sharp order from the Captain checked her, and the next moment the child plucked at her skirt. It seemed to me that she was reminding her mother of something which, in her distress, she had forgotten. Certainly the trio turned aside from the lighted space. They were just visible still but they were amongst the shadows and I could no longer distinguish their movements or the expressions upon their faces. They stood thus for a few minutes and then Captain Crowther emerged again into the light, but alone. He walked quickly down the slope of the bank to the gangway and he carried a small package in his hand. It should have been a box and the name of the lady who gave it to him should have been Pandora. So many troubles and misfortunes tumbled out of it for all of us.

CHAPTER III

FIRST APPEARANCE OF THE SAPPHIRE

THE great headlight was switched on to the channel, the *Dagonet* shook and rumbled from stem to stern, the gap widened between it and the shore. I stood by the rail of the ship aft of the saloon. In a few minutes nothing of Tagaung was visible but the storm-lamp on the ground in the tiny square. It diminished to a spark. A cool wind blew through the ship. The spark on the shore flickered. I suppose that I had been more deeply moved by the odd episode than I was aware; and there's always, I think, a particular sadness, not of separations but of leaving people behind. Anyway, that little shaking flame in the heart of the darkness seemed to me the very image and symbol of a soul in great distress. I turned to find Michael Crowther at my elbow. He, too, was watching the tiny flame wavering, pleading, desperately calling. A bend of the river hid it from our sight.

I wondered what Crowther's reactions would be to its utter disappearance. I turned and looked at him. His face was one wide smile of gross content.

"That's that," said he, and followed his words with a great gasp of relief. He slapped the pocket of his jacket and I noticed that it bulged unnaturally. He winked cheerfully at me and strode forward through the saloon. He took the wheel himself, smiling like a man fresh out of prison, and between the white poles and the red he drove his steamer down to Thabeikyin. The river was low and now and again the steamer grounded with a bump upon a sand-bank and must go astern and wriggle itself clear.

" I'll dine afterwards," Crowther said to the steward when the dinner-bell rang ; and the dinner for the passengers was over when the ship was moored to the bank. Thabeikyin is bigger than most of the villages along the upper river. It is the port of the Ruby Mines sixty miles away over the hills at Mogok. It has a Government rest-house, a telegraph office and a row of shops along the river's edge. The other passengers accordingly trooped on shore, leaving the saloon to the Captain and the cool, dark porch to me. But I was not to enjoy my solitude for long. Crowther was laughing aloud whilst he ate. He was in one of those moods of high spirits and relief when he must confide or burst. Anyone with a pair of ears would have served, and mine were the only pair handy. He turned round towards the open door and called to me.

" Won't you join me, Mr. Legatt ? " he asked.

I rose reluctantly.

" If you'll take a liqueur with me," I answered.

" A double one, if that'll make you easy." Was there a hint of contempt in his voice ? There was. " You're a very sensitive, delicate-minded young man, aren't you?" he continued, and then shouted to the steward.

"At Mr. Legatt's expense," he shouted.

I was all at sea with this man. I spoke to him like a meticulous prig and he showed me that he thought me one, and there I sat with no more power of repartee than an owl. I ordered a cup of coffee and a glass of brandy for myself, and for a while Crowther forgot me. He wagged his head and chuckled and winked, and every now and then his hand stole secretly down to his side pocket and felt it. The side pocket still bulged. The little packet which I had seen in his hand at Tagaung was still concealed there. I had not a doubt of it and I became possessed suddenly by a quite unreasonable curiosity to know what it contained. I did not have to ask, however. For as I leaned upon the table Crowther nudged my elbow with his.

"Tagaung!" said he. "I saw you on the deck and you saw me on the beach. You can put two to two and make four, eh? Well, this time you've only to make three."

It dawned upon Crowther that he had cracked a joke.

"By Jiminy, that's a good one!" he roared, and he flapped his hand upon the table. "Two and two make three! I call that wit, Mr. Legatt. Cripes, I do! Just as smart as your birds in the trees, what? Two and two make three. Me and Ma Shwe At and little Ma Sein."

"Ma Sein's the child, I suppose?"

"That's so, Mr. Legatt. Little Miss Diamond. Pretty kid, eh?"

He cocked his head sideways at me, seeking admiration not so much for little Miss Diamond as for himself, who had been clever enough to beget her.

" Yours ? " I asked indifferently.

Michael D. Crowther was hurt.

" Well, what do you think ? " he cried indignantly. " Didn't I tell you she was a pretty little kid ? Of course she's mine."

One day or another, nine or ten years ago, young Crowther, newly appointed to the Irrawaddy Service with a single gold stripe upon his sleeve, had made the acquaintance of Ma Shwe At. He may have been the Junior Officer on one of the Bazaar boats, those travelling shops which, while carrying passengers, supply the river-side population. And Ma Shwe At may have come aboard to haggle merrily and daintily and very firmly for a strip of silk to make a new skirt or for some household implement. He may have been attached to a mail-boat which tied up at Tagaung for the night, and stepping ashore when his duty was done, have bought some trifle at her booth. I do not remember ever to have heard how the ill-assorted pair began its fateful courtship. It was difficult for me at the time to picture Michael Crowther without his arrogance and his leer, his loud laugh and his essential vulgarity. But no doubt youth had lent him its seemly mask and Ma Shwe At was flattered by the white man's attentions. A trip or two more up and down the river and they contracted a Burmese marriage, as the phrase runs. Marriage has no ceremonial in that country. The religion of Buddha sets no seal upon it and offers no obstacle to divorce. Both states are matters of consent between the parties. The worldly wisdom of the village headman and the wishes of parents have in practice an influence, but there is no binding authority behind them.

" Of course she's mine," Crowther repeated. He drank a little of his brandy. I should be painting an untrue picture of the man if I did not state clearly that at that time when he was at his worst he was always a temperate drinker. He just took a sip of his brandy and his mind slipped away from this trifle of his fatherhood. He nudged me again with his elbow.

" I'll give you a word of advice, Mr. Legatt. Watch out! You haven't got my authority, of course, behind you. On the other hand you have some looks I haven't got," he was kind enough to say. " These Burmese girls with their white teeth and the roses in their dark hair. Pretty little play-things, all right, all right! But passionate, too! Take care they don't get their hooks into you! The taste of the flesh, what?" And he drew in his breath with a long, sucking sound which was simply revolting. He drew a line with a stumpy forefinger on the cloth. " Toys on this side! The things of life and death on the other!"

Very sound advice, no doubt; but whilst he was speaking I was wondering with all the conceit of my youth how incredible it was that this blatant, leering creature should have inspired passion into any woman. But the vision of Ma Shwe At with her flower of a face crumpling into tears and ugliness rose before my eyes. It was not incredible. It was intolerable.

" Full of fun, too ! " Captain Michael D. Crowther continued. " The tricks of a kitten ! Make you laugh till your sides ache. But, by Jiminy——! " And he let himself go in a paroxysm of mirth, a gross and shaking figure. He rolled in his chair, he choked and he bellowed till the tears ran down his cheeks. If there had been any real heartiness or geniality in his laughter I might have called it Homeric, it was so loud and encompassing. But he was applauding himself for his cunning and congratulating himself upon his astonishing good luck.

" Of all the good laughs Ma Shwe At ever gave me," he explained, " the best she gave me to-night."

He pushed his coffee-cup and his glass away. He slipped his hand at last into the bulging side pocket which had so provoked my curiosity and drew out of it a little bag of pink silk with the mouth knotted tight by a pink silk string. He laid it on the table in front of him and it rattled as he set it down.

" This surely is my lucky day," he said. " Who could have guessed that just at this time—when we're on this trip—not the last one and not the next one, a band of dacoits should start in robbing the houses round Tagaung ? Fairly providential, I call it."

He fell to chuckling again and to pushing about the little bag with the tip of his forefinger like a cat playing with a mouse.

" Can you tell me what this little silk bag holds, Mr. Legatt ? "

I had an idea of what it held. For his words had given me a clue. But he wanted to tell me, not to hear me guess correctly. So I merely shook my head. Michael D. Crowther was pleased. He looked at me tantalisingly.

" Not a notion, eh ? "

" I can't say that.   I've got a notion."

But Crowther did not propose to hear it.   He interrupted me quickly :

" Well, I had better tell you at once and put you out of your misery, Mr. Legatt.   This bag holds all the little bits of jewellery and ornament which I have given to Ma Shwe At during the last ten years."

He looked at me for an exclamation.   So I made it.

" Really ? "

It was not very adequate, but then Michael D. Crowther's generosity had not been very adequate either.

" Yes," said he.

" And since there were dacoits busy in her neighbourhood Ma Shwe At gave them to you to keep safe for her ? "

He sat back in his chair and his shoulders heaved with his merriment.   It was a very dainty affair, that little bag, made from a piece of silk woven, no doubt, by Ma Shwe At herself, and then delicately embroidered with her name and fitted with a silk string to match ; all so that it might make a fitting tabernacle to hold the gifts of her lover.   It seemed to me shameful that after so many hours and so much loving care spent upon it, it should serve only for mocking laughter in the saloon of the *Dagonet*.

" Just made on purpose ! " Crowther exclaimed. " Don't that add to the joke ! "

" Yes, I want to hear that joke," said I.

Captain Crowther wiped his eyes.

"It's a corker of a joke. A pound to a penny you'll never guess it, quick as you are."

"That's very probable," said I.

"Well, it's this!" cried Crowther, and once more the humour of the situation overwhelmed him. "I'm never going back to Tagaung. I've resigned from the service. This is my last passage. I'm for home."

The news did take me by surprise. I pushed my chair back.

"You're going to England!"

"I am that, and by the first boat, sir. I've been here sixteen mortal years and I've got to run or I'll never get away." And I found myself looking at a stranger. The Crowther I knew had already run away. The triumph had gone from him. His laughter had died away. His arrogance had dwindled to a pin's point. Behind the sham and the shoddy I suddenly touched something real and big—fear. Fear was bright in his eyes. His voice was uneasy. His shoulders took black care upon them and threw it off again and took it on again blacker than ever. I was never to forget the startling change in him.

"It turns my heart right over when I remember the young fellows I've seen come out to the East slappin' their chests, going to found great business houses and make great fortunes, and in a few years the sun and the indolence and the ease have melted their bones to putty. Prisoners, Mr. Legatt! Prisoners of the sun!"

"Lots succeed," I rejoined.

Crowther nodded his head gloomily.

" The to-and-fro people. The men who can go up into the hills. A few of the others too, extra hardwood men. But for the ruck and run of us— we're the little grey flower Ouida used to write about. We flourish above the snow line. Look here ! "

He took out of his breast pocket a short stubby nigger-black cheroot.

" Do you see that ? A cheroot. A Watson Number One. Twenty for twopence. That's the proper emblem of Burma—not a pagoda nor an elephant nor an image of Buddha nor a pretty-pretty girl in a silk skirt—but just this, a cheap, ugly, strong black cheroot. For why ? Because once you've got the taste for it, the finest cigar out of Havana 'll be nothing to you but brown paper in a schoolboy's pipe. This is what you'll want. No, sir, I'm not going to wander up and down the Irrawaddy in the sunshine any more. I'm afraid. What with my commissions and my pay and a lucky speculation or two I've made a bit. Often there's a tourist on board who'll put you on to a good thing. So whilst Michael D. Crowther still remembers the flavour of a Havana, he's going to quit the cheroot."

He stopped, struck a match, lit his cheroot and inhaled deeply the smoke of it. I do not know what vague association of ideas made me ask idiotically :

" What does D. stand for ? "

He looked at me blankly.

" Eh ? "

" Michael D. Crowther," I said, throwing all my weight on to the D. Upon my word, he didn't know. His ignorance suddenly enlightened me. His over-emphasised American accent, his use of American colloquialisms, the Michael D. Crowther —they were all tokens of his enthusiasm for the great legend of American hustle. For myself, I have never been able to believe that when things had to be done the Americans are really much slippier than other races. People still make a song about it, but I have been to New York. You may see two gentlemen any morning hurrying along Fifth Avenue to keep an appointment. But it does not necessarily follow that they are so bolstered and crammed with business that they have not a moment to spare. It may just mean that they have been drinking a cocktail in the office. And I know no country where it takes longer to cash a cheque except France. However, Captain Michael D. Crowther was obsessed by the notion of an abnormally slick, swift race of men, whose methods he meant to transplant in London.

" I'm going to be a hundred per cent Englishman. Got me ? " he said. " I'm going to be an outside broker. I am going to rattle up that old Stock Exchange in Throgmorton Street till it's dizzy. See here, Mr. Legatt ! When you read a fine notice of a company put on the market by Michael D. you come along to me and you'll hit the sky. I've taken a liking to you."

I could not respond in the same hearty spirit but I did my best, for I was grateful for the odd little glimpse he had given me of another man whom, as yet, I did not know at all.

" That's very kind of you, Captain," I returned.

B

" But meanwhile, what of Ma Shwe At and Ma Sein ? "

Captain Crowther stared at me.

" What do you mean ? "

" You're going to leave them in the lurch ? "

" I bequeath them here and now to you," he replied with a grin.

His anxieties had slipped off his shoulders. He was back again in all the enjoyment of his impish vulgarity. " But you must make your own presents. I can't have you handing out mine as if you had paid for them, can I now ? It wouldn't be reasonable."

He turned his eyes again to the little silk bag. He took it up and untied the strings and dipped his fingers into it as if it were a lucky bag at a bazaar. He brought out a filigree bracelet. " I bought that at Mandalay." Then came a silver necklet. " I bought that cheap from a pedlar in Rangoon, so cheap that I reckon he stole it." A pair of nadoungs of gold, the plugs with which the women ornament their ears, followed ; then a jade pendant and an acorn of a deep red amber slung upon a gilt chain. " I bought those at Bhamo. Cost me a sovereign the lot." He drew out an anklet next, then an elephant, that, too, carved from amber, with a dead fly in the middle of it, and finally, tiring of his examination, he emptied the bag on to the cloth. It was, after all, a trumpery collection of trinkets hardly worth stealing from a girl by a man who proposed to go home and upset Throgmorton Street. But Michael Crowther gloated over it, pushing the shining, tinkling little gifts of his about as if he had recovered the lost treasure of the Cocos Islands.

Suddenly he bent forward. He made a wall about the heap with his hands. He sat with his mouth open and his eyes staring out of his head like the eyes of a fish.

" My Gawd ! " he whispered.

Then he scattered the trinkets here, there and everywhere with a sweep of the palms, and sat back. Burning on the white cloth by itself lay a big sapphire. It was certainly, if not the most precious, the most lovely stone which I had ever seen. By some miracle of nature it was a perfect square ; it was thick through ; and in colour it was the deep bright blue of tropical seas. Crowther lifted it reverently, stood up and held it against the lamp swinging above the table. It was flawless. Crowther's limited vocabulary of oaths held nothing which could cope with his amazement. He could only sit down again and stare, speechless.

" Well, one thing's clear," said I. " That's not one of your presents to Ma Shwe At."

Crowther looked at me as if he knew me for a born fool.

" I give her that ! Why, Mr. Legatt, that stone's worth money." He pulled at his moustache for a moment. " It comes from one of the native workings up to Mogok, I'll bet." He jerked his thumb landwards. Sixty miles away on the far side of the mountain chain lay the great ruby mines, where sapphires, spinels, zircons and all sorts of minor gems were to be found amongst the rubies. As you drew near to the town on that undulating road through the forest where the monkeys played, you passed on this side and on that, native claims with their primitive equipments. But, nevertheless, every now and then some stone of real value was retrieved by those native equipments from the earth. "Yes, that's where it comes from," Captain Crowther repeated, and his face darkened. "Only, who gave it to her?" He thumped the table with his fist and added to the natural unpleasantness of his face another degree of unpleasantness. "Who gave a stone like that to Ma Shwe At? By gum, I'd like to know that!" And his voice descended to a whisper or rather a hiss between his closed teeth. "Jiminy, but I would!"

He sat, obviously trying to remember the people who might have made the gift, and brooding over their names like a man with a crime to be committed upon his mind. He shook his head in the end and made a statement which, coming from him, paralysed me by its stupendous simplicity.

"Anyway, these Burmese girls have no morals," he said.

But his mood relaxed. He smacked his lips noisily. He had discovered a compensation for their deplorable deficiency, and he added:

"But I am bound to say they're lousy with sex appeal."

As soon as I had recovered my balance I remarked:

"The problem is, how are you going to return the sapphire to her?"

Michael D. had looked at me before as if I was a fool. He now recoiled from me as if I was a dangerous lunatic.

"But she give it to me!" he cried. "You were

on the deck when I was on the shore. You saw her. She give it me with her own hands."

I rose from my chair. I looked at him with dignity and cold disdain—or, to speak truly, with as much of both those manifestations as I could produce. It was the moment for one final annihilating phrase. Unfortunately Captain Crowther discovered it before I did.

" You're spluttering, Mr. Legatt," he said pleasantly.

I was, too. The man was just a common thief. But so many epithets were tumbling over one another in my mouth that not one of them would give right of way to the other. I stood and spluttered and was saved by a chirrup of voices from the beach.

The passengers were returning from their explorations. Captain Crowther hurriedly swept his trinkets together and dropped them back into the silk bag. He tore a scrap of linen from his napkin, wrapped the sapphire in it, and put that into the bag more carefully. Then he tied the pink strings tight about the mouth and back went the bag into his pocket. He went out of the saloon and in a moment or two I heard him giving a cheery welcome to his passengers as they climbed the companion from the lower deck to the porch. I had no further speech with him that night. After all, I argued, it was really no concern of mine whether he stole the sapphire or returned it to its owner. But my argument left me still uncomfortable and I did not sleep in my cabin until late.

Long before I awaked the next morning, the

Dagonet was rumbling down the river to Mandalay. I was slow in coming to the breakfast-table, for I did not wish to meet Captain Crowther. But I need not have been at so much pains. He was long since perched beside the helmsman at the upper steering house, and though the water was low he never touched a sand-bank. We reached the big town before noon and I confess to some disappointment at Michael D.'s proficiency at his job. I should have liked him to have run plump on a sand-bank in midstream in full sight of all the water-side people and to have wriggled there helplessly like a butterfly with a pin through its body, an offence to his Company and a joke to the rest of the world. But he ran neatly up to the river port. It was crowded, steamer upon steamer moored to the bank and just one small space half-way down the line. I did not think that Crowther could possibly sidle into it without doing a lot of damage. But he did. He might have been commanding an ocean-going mail-boat with twin screws, so easily did he gentle his stern-wheel machine up to the bank. There she was moored, her bows almost touching the stern of the steamer ahead, and her stern almost touching the bows of the steamer abaft.

" Not so bad, Mr. Legatt," said Crowther genially, as he descended to the porch. I was waiting for my baggage to be taken ashore. " Have a drink before you go ? "

" I think not," said I, towering frostily.

I caught a gleam of amusement in Crowther's eye.

" I believe you've got a come-over against me,

Mr. Legatt," he said. " You think I've not treated that girl up the river as a gentleman should. You do indeed ! I fancy you'll appreciate me better when you have more experience of this country. But it's clear you don't appreciate me at all now and I have a real respect for you, Mr. Legatt. I want you to have the same for me."

" That's quite out of the question," I returned, looking him in the eye.

Crowther poked his head forward very earnestly.

" No, Mr. Legatt, you're wrong there. I can prove to you that you misjudge me."

I laughed, scathingly I hoped.

" How ? "

" This way."

Crowther took the small silk bag from his side pocket and balanced it on the palm of his left hand. He made it dance a little so that the trinkets which it held tinkled.

" I'll hand this bag over to you with all its contents, here and now, on condition that you with your own hands return it to Ma Shwe At at Tagaung."

He was as impressive as a man working the confidence trick, but I was not to be taken in so easily. I shook my head.

" With all its contents—yes. But without the sapphire."

Captain Crowther drew himself up. He was dignified, he was hurt that anyone should hold so low an opinion of his probity. With the neatness of a conjuror demonstrating that there was no trickery in his magic, he untied with his right hand the string of the bag and opened the mouth.

" Please, see for yourself, Mr. Legatt."

" I don't wish to."

" You accuse me.   I ask you to be fair."

I had let myself in for this test.   I did not see what else I could do but obey him.   I shrugged my shoulders and dipped my fingers into the bag.   The first thing which I pulled out was a stone wrapped in a strip of linen.

" Will you open the wrapping and make sure that I haven't tricked you ? "

I had not a doubt now that it was the sapphire which I held.   The stone was square, about the right thickness and the right size.   Yet I felt that I had been tricked—tricked into making a fool of myself. I dropped the stone back into the bag.

" That's all right," I said reluctantly, and still more reluctantly : " I am sorry."

" Now will you take it back to Tagaung ? "

" I will not," I cried.

I was angry.   I was on my way home.   I had a few days' work waiting for me in the office at Rangoon which I must complete before I started.

" I'll have nothing to do with it," I added.

" One day and one night upstream," said he.

" Your affairs are no concern of mine, Captain Crowther."

Captain Crowther appeared to be perplexed.   He tilted his cap back with his right hand and scratched his forehead.

" Yet you seemed to take a very definite interest in them, Mr. Legatt.   Come !   Oblige me ! "

He was still holding the little bag balanced on his outstretched palm.   I could not help wondering what would happen if I then and there took it and agreed to return it. It was possible that Crowther had thought over his conduct during the night and come to a more honest mind. I might be wrong and hasty in my judgement. He had already surprised me once by his fear of this easy and indolent country. Why not a second time ? I was tempted. I could not, however, sail upstream until to-morrow. It would take me a day and a night to reach Tagaung, and there I should have to wait perhaps the best part of a week for a steamer to bring me back again. No, certainly not ! Besides, though I seemed to recognise a sign of grace in this proposal of Captain Crowther's, I wished that no link of any kind should bind us together. I thrust my hands into my pockets.

" You've a surer way to return those ornaments."

" How ? " Crowther asked earnestly.

" By handing them to your First Officer." I remembered the smile with which the First Officer had heard my remark to Crowther that I supposed that he was meaning to tie up at Tagaung for the night. " He'll recognise Ma Shwe At, and I shouldn't. Give the bag to him."

" With that fine sapphire in it ? Not on your life, Mr. Legatt."

" Seal up the bag then and trust it to one of your brother captains."

" To no one but you, Mr. Legatt. I don't want the whole world to think me dippy just as I'm stepping off on a new career. It's up to you or up to no one."

He shook the bag again at me till the ornaments

inside of it clinked and tinkled.   Then with a sigh of
resignation he dropped it again into his pocket.

"Here's to-day's good deed sticking out a yard
and we're both of us turning our backs upon it.
You were in such a taking last night, Mr. Legatt,
that I felt sure you'd oblige me this morning.
However, I can't say I'm sorry," and he suddenly
burst into a laugh and made a gutter-boy's grimace
at me.   My word, he had been laughing at me the
whole time !   He had seen my baggage being taken
on shore and carried up the beach.   He was confident that I would never turn round and go back to
Tagaung.

"Captain Crowther," I said, "I think that you are
the most detestable person I have ever met."

"Well, you do surprise me," replied Captain
Crowther.

It was odd, but it was true.   I must suppose that
he expected me to take him for a humorist.   He
was not speaking with any sarcasm.   He really was
surprised.

CHAPTER IV

PRISONERS OF THE SUN

I SPENT the first year after my return to England
in the London office of my Company, acquiring
knowledge of its internal economy, and enjoying
myself in the intervals. But the forest had set
its seal on me and I could never hear the wind
rustling the leaves in a town square without flying
back upon the carpet of my dreams to the vast
woodlands of the Irrawaddy and seeing the elephants
carry and arrange the huge teak logs. At the
beginning of the second year my father died, and
what with the settlement of his estate and the
new dispositions which his death entailed, I could
not hope to find my way back again to Burma for
another eighteen months. I was thus two years
and a half in England and chiefly in London. Yet
during all that time I neither met nor heard of
Michael Crowther. For all I knew he might be
entertaining the great world in Mayfair or occupying
a cell in Maidstone Gaol. I thought the latter
alternative the more likely. If he had rattled the
Stock Exchange, as he promised to do, he had done
it very quietly. But I could never quite forget him,
for from time to time I felt a foolish twinge of
remorse in that I had not taken him at his word and
carried the silken bag with its trinkets and its

sapphire back to Ma Shwe At at Tagaung. I did have the time, and I might at all events have sustained her pride by pretending that in the interval Michael Crowther had died. But that small opportunity had gone.

It was not, then, until the decline of the third year that I could with any honesty towards my Company propose another visit to Burma. I made my plans to leave England during the second week of December, being persuaded to that date chiefly because it would save me from the festivities of Christmas, an uncomfortable season for a man without a family. My luggage was packed days before it was to be collected by the Shipping Company's agents ; and on the afternoon of a dank, raw Sunday, the darkness beginning to fall and the air heavy with mist, I wandered out from my lodging into a small neighbouring street of garages and reconstructed houses much favoured by film stars. The hub of that street, however, is a mighty church, and as I passed its door the thunder of its organ called me in.

I stood at the back, facing the great altar ablaze with the golden light of its many candles ; and a tall priest with a red stole upon his shoulders mounted into a pulpit set aloft above the congregation against the farthest pillar of the nave. He preached in a high, clear voice upon a text from Hosea about the valley of Achor and the door of hope. So much I remember, and then my attention was diverted. For in front of where I stood, at the end of the last row of benches, separated from me by an open passage-way, sat Michael Crowther.

It was the last place in the world I should have
expected to find him. I could only imagine that,
like myself, he had wandered by chance into the
church as a refuge from the chill and gloom outside.
I noticed, however, that he sat very still, like a man
enthralled, and I wondered whether he had got
religion, as the saying goes. His head, with its
thick and bristly hair, stood out in relief against the
distant candles on the altar and never moved. His
face was turned towards the preacher so that I
could just see his heavy jaw thrust out as I had
seen it when he was feeling his way amongst the
sand-banks on the porch of the *Dagonet*. I made
up my mind to speak to him as soon as the service
was over. But I did not get the chance. For as
the offertory plates began to be handed along the
benches and the chink of coins to be heard, Michael
Crowther rose without shame to his feet, and stalked
past me out of the church. I said to myself:
" That's Michael D. He may not have rattled the
Stock Exchange, but he's true to type."

Towards the end of the week I travelled overland
to Marseilles and embarked for Rangoon with two
complete years ahead of me before I needed to
return. I spent the first year in the forests of the
Salween River. But at the beginning of the
second, I had occasion to travel again to the upper
waters of the Irrawaddy. I took the night train
from Rangoon to Mandalay, saw my baggage placed
in my cabin on the steamer and then, having still a
few hours to spare, I took the usual walk towards
the Zegyo Bazaar. I say " towards," for I never
reached it. In the street of shops which led to it,

a name upon a board caught my eye. The board stretched above a shop and I should probably not have noticed it at all but for the queer circumstance that at this very busy hour of the morning a boy was putting up the shutters. Once I had noticed it I could not turn my eyes away. For the name painted in bold white letters on a black ground was:

MICHAEL CROWTHER.

There might be two Michael Crowthers of course, and both linked with some sort of shackle to Mandalay. Coincidences are after all more usual in life than in fiction. Or the great assault upon the Stock Exchange had failed and its strategist had fled back to the lines he knew. It occurred to me that if that were the case, the sooner I pushed along to the Bazaar the less risk I had of being annoyed. To this day I don't know why I loitered. But I did. I waited amongst the creaking bullock-carts and the streams of passers-by: now a Shan from the hills with an enormous hat upon his head, now a group of girls with tuberoses in their black hair and silken skirts, and more gaiety in their laughter than even in their clothes, a monk in his yellow robe with a shaven head, a party of tourists holding above their helmeted heads white umbrellas which would have condemned them to the stocks in King Thibaw's day. I waited there in the blazing sunlight, and gradually and slowly I was bewitched by an intense and inexplicable expectation. The feeling was vaguely familiar to me. Yes, some where and when I had experienced it before. It could really have nothing to do with Crowther's name upon a board, I argued, for I had seen Crowther himself in the Farm Street Church and not a nerve in me had thrilled. Yet here was I in a street of Mandalay—enthralled. A man with a terrier dog at his heels pushed by me, and I remembered when this same sense of expectation had possessed and controlled me. It was in a moonlit clearing of the forest north of the Second Defile. There I had waited for a panther—and something else. Here I waited for Michael D. Crowther—and something else. There nothing had happened. Here Michael D. Crowther did. For as I stood and waited, he came bouncing out of his shop.

" Of all people, you ! " he cried, and I drew back with a little jump. It was perhaps the oddest circumstance, at all events at that time in our acquaintanceship, that though he was often in my thoughts, the moment I heard his voice I wanted to break away. " Now isn't that a piece of luck ? " he continued eagerly.

" Is it ? " I asked. " For whom ? "

Michael D. grinned.

" Cold ! " he said, wagging his head at me. " Oh, very cold and biting, Mr. Legatt. You know all the talk there is of Gandhi and his Untouchables. Well, when I read of the Untouchables I always think of you."

" Thank you ! " said I. " Good morning ! "

As I moved on all the truculence left him. He ran after me and caught me by the arm, and his hand shook as he held me.

" Please don't go ! " he implored, with so notable a change of voice and so humble a prayer in his eyes that I could not but stop. " I withdraw every word. My tongue ran away with me. It often does with witty people. But I've got to speak to you. I'll get a hat and give an order to my boy. I won't be a second."

He was back in his shop almost before the sound of his words had ceased. I thought : " What a fool I was not to slide past the shop with my head turned the other way ! " I asked myself immediately upon that : " After all, aren't you a bit of a prig ? Why shouldn't you stop and listen to him ? " And by the time I had put those questions Crowther had rejoined me.

He led me to a café. We sat in the open under an awning. In front of us across the road the wide, lily-starred moat slept about the walls of Fort Dufferin ; and as each of us drank a cool lime squash Crowther went back with a curious eagerness and flurry to the last conversation we had held four years before.

" You must have been surprised to see me here, Mr. Legatt ? "

It was a difficult question to answer. I sought unwisely to put him at his ease by suggesting that he had suffered no more than the common lot.

" Oh, I don't know," I answered. He was up in arms in a second. You might disapprove of him, but you must not forget him. Above all you must not find him uninteresting and become indifferent as to whether he failed or succeeded.

" You can't have forgotten all those ambitions of mine," he cried indignantly.

I in my turn was a little nettled.

" I really don't see why I shouldn't have."

He glared at me.   Then he chuckled.

" But you haven't, anyway."

I laughed and climbed down.

" No, I haven't."

" Then you must have been surprised to see me," he insisted with some petulance.

" All right.   I *was* surprised.   I ought not to have been, but I was," I acknowledged.

But Crowther was not appeased.

" And why oughtn't you to have been surprised, if you please, Mr. Legatt ? "

" Because I have been three years in London and never once in business or any other circles did I hear your name."

Here was something Crowther could not question. He sat back in his chair and nodded his head gloomily.

" I've been a great disappointment to myself, Mr. Legatt.   I had stayed in the East too long.   I was a prisoner of the sun after all.   Funny !   Governors and soldiers and big business chiefs can go back and hold their own—men really of the same calibre as myself.   I suppose that I am more sensitive than most people, what ? "   I was careful not to interrupt and to keep a very straight face.   " Yes, I had got the habit of the cheroot, and Havanas made me ill. I didn't realise it at first.   No.   I hired a little flat in South Kensington and stood in Piccadilly Circus and made a noise like Dick Whittington.   I looked up all the smart fellows I had any sort of link with. Queer thing !   Most of them were a good deal more cordial to me as a Captain on the Irrawaddy than as a man starting in their own line of big business. There was one, the head of a great financial family, who fairly sickened me, Mr. Legatt. I sent in my card one morning and I was shown into the holy of holies, and he sat back in his chair and looked at me without a word. I said to myself : ' That's good ! That's the way ! I'll make a note of that. He puts me at a disadvantage.' So I started in on him. I had come home to put a little pep into English methods, and he just looked at me. I could help him and he could help me; I said Michael D. Crowther was going to get to work ; and he looked at me. I reckon I lost my head a bit then, but he only looked at me, and I just had to come away. And he had never spoken one word. I tell you I wondered for a moment whether pep didn't really mean simply saying nothing. However, others put bits of business in my way. But here's the amazing thing. They were little bits of business, but I didn't bring them off. No, sir, I didn't succeed.''

He was now merely Michael Crowther, a woe-begone Englishman consoling himself by the recital of his experiences. He had meant to be the big noise ; he was not even the baby's gurgle. He had planned to hit the skies ; he had not even flapped up off the earth.

'' Other things besides the hustle made me shud-der. The east wind, the clear brown fog ten foot high and the miles of black soot on the top of it, the cars bearing down on you and hooting death at you, and above all the utterly damnable, chilly, disobliging loneliness of it all. I began to pine for the colour and the ease and the good humour of the life I knew here under skies which really laugh and a sun which really warms. I wanted to hear the copper-smith bird tell me a real summer is coming. Yes, Mr. Legatt, I had Burma in my bones, and the want of it made me ache from head to foot. I'd have given all the hooting motor-cars in Piccadilly for the creak of one bullock-wagon in Mandalay. The Havana cigar—you can have the crop. What I wanted was a Watson Number One ''; and as though he had forgotten it in the need to pour himself out from a bottle and hold himself up in a glass against the light, he pulled a cheroot from the pocket of his white drill jacket and lit it.

" I can understand all that," I said. " I am not so deeply rooted in England myself. What bewilders me a little is not your return, but your name over a shop."

Before now Michael Crowther had looked at me as if I was not all there. I hate to be taken for a congenital idiot when I am making a perfectly reasonable remark ; and mine was a reasonable remark—in spite of Michael Crowther and his question.

" Why should that bewilder you, Mr. Legatt ? "

" Because "—I was huffy but I meant to be fair— " because from what I remember of your navigation, you could have got another steamer by asking for it. Or if there wasn't a steamer, an agency to keep you going until there was."

Crowther's manner changed completely. There was a warmth in his voice, a gratitude in his eyes.

" That's kind of you, Mr. Legatt. It is indeed. When your self-esteem has had the bumps which mine has, an unexpected bouquet here and there is very welcome."

"What are you going to sell, Captain?" I continued. "Antiquities? You? You're the last man to be interested in dead and gone things. If I were you I shouldn't drop down to a shop."

Crowther remained silent for a little while. He looked straight across the moat to the machicolated walls of the Fort. I thought that he must be considering my advice. But I was wrong. He was merely considering me; happily, however, from a new angle. I say happily, because on looking back, I can see that our acquaintanceship took a turn at this corner. It is too early to say that friendship began here, but at all events we were on the road to it.

"I am going to sell nothing at all," he said. "We'd better have another drink. We have got time"; and when the cool lime squashes stood on the little table between us, he continued: "I have been brooding by myself so long over my story that I have come to think the world knows it as well as I do. Just wait a second!"

He put his thoughts into an order of words before he spoke them. He was not selecting what he should tell me and what he should keep to himself. Reticence was a word omitted from his dictionary. He was so interested in himself that everyone within his reach must know all about him and exactly.

"I was a failure. I hadn't made any friends. I was cold. I used to wander about on Sunday afternoons into the Park to listen to the spouters and then through the dead streets to get myself dog-tired.

Well, one dreadful afternoon, so damp that you felt your bones were wet inside you and as cold as the Poles and South Ken in one, I found myself in a queer little street, garages and oldy Englishy houses and a church."

I sat forward.

" Farm Street," I said.

" Oh ? May be. I never knew its name. But there were lights in the church windows, and there would be people in there and it'd be warm. So I went in. A man preached about a valley. He was a sensible sort of man—that's what made me listen. He said this valley bloomed once and was desolate for a few hundred years. You could work out the chronology for yourself if you liked—for himself he wasn't interested very much in chronology—that's what took me in the man—a very few hundred years would do for him—sensible, what ? —after that it bloomed again, a door of hope."

" The valley of Achor," I interrupted.

" Very likely," said Crowther. " I didn't catch on to the name." Suddenly he stopped and stared at me. " Say ! You know a lot about the Bible."

" I was there that afternoon," I said.

" You ? "

" Yes."

" In that church ? "

I nodded my head.

" A little more than a year ago. I saw you in the back pew."

" That's right. Now isn't that odd ? " He looked at me reproachfully. " You might have spoken to me, Mr. Legatt."

" I hadn't a chance to. You nipped out before the collection reached you."

" Instinct, Mr. Legatt," said Crowther smiling. " Nothing more than instinct. But in that case you can realise how hard that sermon hit me."

" I'm afraid that I can't," I answered. " I wasn't listening closely. I was watching you."

That seemed to Crowther very natural. No further explanation was required, and he went on :

" Then I must tell you something about it. The valley of Achor was a door of hope. It had bloomed once and hundreds of years afterwards a second time under the smile of God. That was the phrase which took me by storm. A valley all a-bloom under the smile of God. The valley of the Irra-waddy, eh ? Where everyone smiles—not only God. I suppose that every feeling I had, of darkness and failure and loneliness and cold, had been working up to this moment, had become so much tinder waiting for a spark to set it ablaze. And here was the spark—a phrase spoken by a preacher on a black, dreary afternoon in Farm Street—a valley under the smile of God. I went back to my little furnished flat in a back lane of South Ken like a man who has had a call—a call to lovely things instead of away from them. I sat in my dingy sitting-room with its ugly deal furniture and its bit of Brussels carpet, and I tell you, Mr. Legatt, I heard music. I was going to wind things up and go back."

He could hardly spare the time that evening to eat his dinner. He had the table cleared the moment the meal was over, and going into his bedroom rummaged in his big trunk. At the bottom of it lay Ma Shwe At's little silk bag with its embroidery and its pink string and its jingling trinkets. In his hurry to set his foot on the neck of London, he had tucked it away amongst his odds and ends and forgotten all about it. Now he carried it back into his sitting-room and rolled out the ornaments on to his red baize table-cloth, just as he had three years before on to the white linen of the *Dagonet*. They were all there even to the sapphire in its strip of napkin. The ornaments were tarnished and dull as pewter, but the sapphire glowed with a spark of fire striking up through the blue of tropical seas ; and the walls of his room fell away ; and a lorry which passed and shook the house was the rumble of his stern-wheel as it thrashed the water of the Irrawaddy.

" Jiminy! I was glad that you hadn't taken me at my word, Mr. Legatt, and carried the bag back to Tagaung. I knew that I ran a risk, but you carried your nose so high that I could almost see the vocal cords—now didn't you?—and I had got to show you you were thinking of yourself all the time like everybody else. But you gave me a jar, Mr. Legatt, I won't deny. You did stand hesitating whether you'd behave like a medieval knight in an opera or not."

Frankly I did not like his simile. I had no wish to be a knight in an opera, medieval or otherwise. I prided myself upon my actuality. I was a young man of my age with a fair share of hard common sense. I might have gone to Oxford or Cambridge. But I had gone to the forest instead. Homer and heroics meant nothing to me. Wild beasts and the

loneliness of great woods meant a great deal. I
was annoyed with Crowther absurdly. For I had
been on the point of starting back for Tagaung to
return to a Burmese girl I didn't know the presents
of a man I detested; and if there's one thing a
man's heartily ashamed of it's an experiment in
quixotics. I grew a little hot and uncomfortable.
I felt at a disadvantage with Crowther, as I had
done on one or two occasions before.

"You might get on with your story and leave
me out of it," I said tartly.

The momentary gleam of his old-time impishness
faded out from Crowther's eyes.

"No offence intended, Mr. Legatt," he cried
hurriedly. "I resoom. There were the ornaments
in front of me and I spent the evening polishing
them until they shone like a lady's nails before
she's dabbed the blood on them—the silver ring
which Ma Shwe At wore round her tiny ankle, the
filigree bracelets for her wrists. I tell you, the
warmth of her was there in my drab little sitting-
room with the red baize table-cloth. I could feel
her arms round my neck and see her dark eyes and
white teeth laughing at me an inch off my nose.
The taste of the flesh, eh?"

Crowther leaned back in his chair, his teeth
closed over his lower lip and sucking in his breath.

"You wouldn't know, but these Burmese girls
have got a trick of sending a little ripple down their
arms from their shoulders to their finger-tips, and
when their arms are round your neck at the time"—
he relapsed into his Americanisms and rubbed
his hands together—"oh boy, oh boy!"

I hope that the tip of my nose didn't rise priggishly into the air. But Crowther certainly hurried on.

" But there was ever so much besides. The fun of her, the chatter, and little Ma Sein dancing up and down on her feet as if she was a puff-ball."

Yes, I too remembered little Miss Diamond dancing up and down on the sand of the little square at Tagaung. I saw the tiny village, booths and square and pagoda, and the great tamarinds behind lighted up with the golden brilliancy of the headlight and rounded into a circle by the head-light's shape. I saw it as one sees a scene of marionettes through the spy-hole of a peep-show.

" I remember," I answered with a smile.

" And even that wasn't all." He turned sideways in his chair and leaned across the table, once more surprised by himself. " Do you know that I had been wanting her desperately all this time without knowing it ? There was an ache somewhere inside me, something missing, always missing, like someone you have dearly loved, who has been dead for a long while, but you don't think what it is that's missing until now and then some association brings you full-face with the knowledge. Well, Ma Shwe At wasn't dead. I hugged myself when I had worked back to that one vital fact. Ma Shwe At and Ma Sein—Mrs. Golden Needle and Miss Diamond —were still at Tagaung. Those presents were a promise—the preacher's door of hope. My mind took a hop, skip and a jump—there I was landing from the gang-plank. There they were laughing and waving their hands. The anklet was warm with the warmth of Ma Shwe At as I held it in my hand. I heard myself saying: ' Beloved Golden Needle, born of the lotus and the moon '—you know the sort of thing—' here is the treasure you asked me to keep safe for you.' "

" Oh ho ! " said I. Here was a Michael Crowther whom I did not know, proud of his cunning—that was old—but eager to make restitution—that was new.

" So you are going back to Tagaung ! " I said.

" To be sure. That's why I've opened a shop."

" That's why you've closed a shop," I corrected.

Crowther raised his eyebrows. He was always astonished if I did not follow at once the working of his mind. He explained compassionately :

" You haven't got it at all, Mr. Legatt. I'm not going to stay at Tagaung, nor is the shop for me. I've got money enough to wait until a good job comes my way. I'm going to bring Ma Shwe At and little Miss Diamond down to Mandalay, and then there's a shop here to amuse them. All these little Burmese girls love keeping shop. If you trotted into the big Bazaar over there you'd find lots of them selling silks and spices who could well afford to stay at home. They adore having a little business of their own. They make it pay too, I can tell you."

He laughed with a heartiness which I had never heard in his voice before. It had a ring of enjoyment like the laugh of a friendly man watching children playing cleverly.

" When do you go ? " I asked suddenly.

" This morning. On the *Moulmein*."

" So do I."

" I guessed that," he returned, and to my amazement I caught a note of wistfulness in his voice.
" You won't object, will you ?   Or call me down
if I offer you a drink ? "

It was my turn to laugh. Michael Crowther
could not live without explaining himself. Conversation was a mirror in which he saw a very
interesting person experiencing strange adventures
and developing in odd ways through unexpected
phases of life.

" I shan't object at all," I said. " On the
contrary !   I find you very much more human than
I did before."

Michael Crowther stared at me and slapped his
hand down upon the table.

" That's the most extraordinary thing," he cried.
" For I was going to say precisely the same thing
of you."

We settled our bill. Crowther's boy brought to
him the key of the shop, and said :

" Master's bag on board."

" Good," said Crowther, and we walked together
to the gangway of the *Moulmein*.

" The door of hope," said he.   " A sensible fellow,
that padre," and he went forward on to the lower
deck.

CHAPTER V

THE DOOR CLOSES

THE *Moulmein* was a Bazaar boat. It dragged, lashed alongside of it, a big double-decked lighter furnished with shops and stalls and occupied by steerage passengers. It put in at the smaller villages and stayed long enough for the villagers to make their purchases. It was, therefore, not until the forenoon of the second day after we left Mandalay that we tied up against the bank at Tagaung. No storm-lamp flickered a welcome; no headlight transformed the village into a golden spot of fairyland. It was a little place of thatched hovels enclosed by great tamarinds, and fig-trees, with a glimpse of a few bigger houses in a grove at the back. And a miserable, puny pagoda of bamboo and straw at the corner of the square indicated to all men the extremity of its indigence.

The *Moulmein* with its travelling shops was expected; for the central space was thronged. Michael Crowther stood at my side on the open deck, shifting his weight from one foot to the other and running his eyes eagerly over the crowd. A look of disappointment clouded his face.

" I don't see them," he said. " Do you ? "

" No."

" Yet they would naturally have met the Bazaar

boat. Even if they didn't want to buy anything, it's the place for gossip. Of course I wasn't expected."

He repeated that consolation as, leaning over the rail, he watched the men and women file along the gangway on to the steamer and across the lower deck on to the lighter beyond.

" I wasn't expected. That's it, of course." But he was uneasy. It looked as if the whole valley had turned out with the exception of Mrs. Golden Needle and Miss Diamond. Crowther turned to me. " Are you coming ? "

I had not meant to go ashore at all. But Crowther wanted support and bad news might be awaiting him. After all, young people did die in the villages of the Irrawaddy as elsewhere in the world.

" Yes, I'll come," I replied, and then, less carelessly, I added: " I certainly will come with you, Captain."

For when my eyes moved from him to the shore it suddenly struck me there was something unusual in the aspect of the place. There were no women left by the landing-place. That was to be expected. They were all by this time chattering and bargaining upon the lighter. But there was a large group of men, and these men, instead of sitting about on the sand indolently talking according to their habit, stood and watched the steamer in silence.

Crowther descended to the lower deck and I followed him.

" Of course I wasn't expected," he repeated.

But he was wrong. I had an impression that he

was expected even before he stepped off the gangway. But the moment he did, the impression became a certainty. For at once the group moved and according to a plan. It spread out, deploying into a line at the edge of the bank and as Crowther walked up the slope, the flanks of the line moved forwards and inwards, enclosing him and barring him from the village. They were all so far quite silent and their faces were quite impassive. Perhaps it was for those reasons that I felt the whole position to be dangerous. I was walking just behind Michael Crowther's shoulder. And from a slight hesitation in his movements, I realised that he, too, was disturbed. When he reached the top of the bank and could go no farther without jostling one of these sentinels, an old man with a thin straggling white beard spoke, smiling softly :

" We are happy to see the thakin again. It is a long time since the thakin was here and it does us good to see him. And now he will shake hands with us and go back again upon the steamer."

Crowther looked from one face to another.

" You expected me ? "

" A friend brought us word by the last boat that the thakin was coming to see us."

" To see Ma Shwe At."

Michael Crowther corrected the old man in a loud and rising voice, so that the name of his mistress rang out across the hovels and the booths. It was a call to her, wherever she was hidden, the call to the mate, heard in forest and jungle and trimmed garden, and wherever manners have not cloaked passion. But it was a cry for help too, so sudden, so poignant that it took my breath away. A dreadful terror of loneliness inspired it. I suppose that it was because I was behind Crowther and could not see his face. But I almost believed that someone else had uttered the cry, some unknown man breaking under the compulsion of pain and fear. Then he stood still, listening with both his ears, and it seemed to me with every tense nerve in his body, for an answer, however distant, however faint.

But no answer came—unless a quiet constriction of the circle about him could be called an answer.

"Ma Shwe At will not hear," the old man said gently. "It is four years since the thakin went away and in four years many things must happen. Ma Shwe At suffered and was unhappy. Ma Sein cried through many nights. But all that is over now."

"Over? But I am here to fetch them both to my home——" began Crowther.

The old man shook his head.

"Ma Shwe At is married to a man with many rice-fields. She is happy again. I beg the thakin to shake hands with us all and go away."

Crowther looked from face to face. There were young men there and there were old. There was no ill-will in their looks; but they pressed about him, not touching him but hampering him. He was shut within a round wall of living people. He could not have burst through that close-drawn cordon had he possessed the strength of Hercules, so near they stood and ready. But he didn't try. He drew back a step and his right hand flashed down into the side pocket of his jacket.

I gasped at his folly. He could not have made a more dangerous mistake. Even I knew that these pleasant, peaceable village folk would retaliate with the cruelty of children. From the beginning of the interview it had been obvious that behind the old man's smooth words was a quiet threat. Policy should have heard the threat, and as a rule Crowther had at his command a blatant but effective policy. He was now a prisoner. For in a twinkling a man upon each side of him seized his arm. Not one of the group but held a stick in his hand, although no one raised it. A boy plunged a hand into Crowther's pocket. Had he pulled out a pistol, Crowther—I haven't a doubt of it although not a stick as yet was raised—would have been beaten out of human shape then and there by wild men dancing in a frenzy. All that the boy did pull out, however, was a little soiled bag of pink silk tied at the mouth with a pink silk cord—a bag which rattled as he pulled it out.

The turmoil died down as quickly as it had spurted into life.

" Is that all ? " the old man asked.

" That's all," the boy answered ; and the old man took the bag and balanced it upon his palm, just as Crowther himself had done in the porch of the *Dagonet*.

" That small bag was worked by Ma Shwe At," said Crowther in a queer, broken voice. He could not but know how near he had been to a cruel and horrible death but the break in his voice was not caused by fear. " She gave it to me to keep for her.

There was a dacoity in the neighbourhood. It holds the presents I had given to her. I wish to return it."

" Ma Shwe At no longer needs the thakin's presents. I beg him to take them again."

Crowther put his hands behind his back.

" There is more than my presents in the bag," Crowther protested. " There is a jewel worth them all a hundred times."

The old man smiled.

" We are all happy that the thakin should keep it."

He gave the bag back to the boy who slipped it again into Crowther's pocket.

It was just then that the steamer blew its warning ; and Crowther, without another word, turned upon his heel and walked down the bank to the gangway. He looked straight in front of him. His face was grey and fixed like the face of a paralytic. I did not wonder. Apart from the danger which he had run, who within so short a time has endured humiliation so deep ? But humiliation was only one part of his distress. Possess a thing, it dwindles to nothing. Lose it, it grows into a world. Against his corroding failure and his four desolate years he had set the mirage of Ma Shwe At and the child Ma Sein. Than Ma Shwe At with her laughing face and small, flower-like hands, and Ma Sein jumping up and down in her glee, nothing was ever so passionately desired by the one-time Captain of the *Dagonet*. But he had lost them. The door of hope had closed.

CHAPTER VI

CHILDREN AT PLAY

A GOOD many pairs of inquisitive eyes watched Michael Crowther as he came on board. But he never returned a look. People were so much ship's furniture to him. He walked in and out amongst them, unaware of anyone, and marched through the saloon on to the deck behind it. He sat down there on a seat by the side of the rail ; and after I had given him a little time I wandered aft myself and stood beside him. He lifted his head and pleaded :

" You won't talk for a bit, will you ? "

" I didn't come along to talk," I answered.

" I know that. Thank you for coming."

I cannot put into words the dejection of the man. I had nothing to say which could help him. He had failed as the hundred per cent Englishman he had boasted himself to be, who was going to trample in hobnails over his inefficient countrymen. Now he had failed again as the orientalised European. I could not imagine a future ahead of him. The shop in Mandalay would be ridiculous as an occupation for him ; and he was not the man to take to drink. All I could do was to offer him the sympathy of a silent companionship.

It was he, therefore, who spoke first. The

Moulmein had edged out clear of the bank. Its great wheel was thrashing the yellow water into foam.

" That was a bad affair, wasn't it ? " he said with a rather pitiful bravado and an attempt at a smile. But he could not keep to that pretence. " The smile of God ! " he cried in a voice of such bitterness as I had never heard. Then his head drooped again and he clenched his hands so tightly together that the skin beneath the tips of his fingers was white.

" What am I going to do now ? " he asked in a whisper, and repeated his question : " What am I going to do ? "

I answered him foolishly. He was not thinking of an occupation but of how he was going to live through the succession of days until the day of his death.

" You ought to try to get another ship in the Irrawaddy Flotilla," I said.

" Perhaps so," he answered listlessly ; but he only knew that I was speaking and did not hear what I said. It was just as well. For no career in the world could have been so repugnant to him at this moment.

The steamer beat upstream past a wall of rice-bags and began to round a low bluff which reached out into the river. I saw Crowther rise slowly to his feet and grasp the rail with both his hands ; and I drew closer to him. I had a fear that he was going to fling himself headlong overboard to be beaten to death by the great stern-wheel ; he stood poised upon his toes in so tense an attitude. But his eyes turned towards the headland and at once were riveted there ; and from that moment, whilst it remained in sight, he had no thought but for what was happening on its broad, flat top.

" My God ! " he whispered, as though his throat was parched, and again, but on so low a note that the whisper died away and only his lips finished it : " My God ! "

His body relaxed, a great weakness overtook him so that his knees sagged, and though his hands still clung to the rail, they clung to keep him standing, not to give spring to a leap. If he had a thought of jumping overboard he had given it up and I could, myself, safely turn my eyes to the bank.

On the headland a group of children was playing a round game under the instructions of one of them ; and the noise of their young voices and shrill laughter floated across the water very happily. It couldn't be that Crowther grudged them their glee. It might be that they brought back to him with an intolerable poignancy the memory of Ma Sein dancing up and down upon her toes. But it seemed to me that a grief deeper than that of memory gave to his face its look of anguish. There had been some one final shattering blow to deal him, and God had not forgotten it.

The steamer was now abreast of the promontory and I distinguished at last the small significant circumstance which had caught Crowther's eye from afar and laid yet one more trouble upon his troubled soul. The game which the children played involved a winding in and out in the pattern of a dance. Many mistakes were made and corrected amidst peals of laughter. But the little girl who corrected

the mistakes and set all the players once more in
their order wore a sun-helmet upon her head and
white socks and brown shoes upon her feet. I
remembered suddenly that four years ago little Miss
Diamond had decked herself out just in that way.
She had worn a sun-helmet even after the sun had
set, even after darkness had come, and shoes and
socks into the bargain. She had been establishing
the whiteness of her blood. She had been showing
off to all with eyes to see and brains to understand
that she was the daughter of the white Captain of
the Irrawaddy Company. All the other little girls
might skewer their hair to the tops of their heads
and come to no harm even at midday. She, Ma
Sein, must wear a helmet even after dark to keep
off sunstroke. The others might run barefoot over
hard-baked ground and take no bruise. She must
wear socks and shoes according to the habit and
necessity of her race. Ma Sein had been eight years
old then, and the little girl now laying down the law
with unquestioned authority was older than that.
Twelve ? I was not very experienced in judging
children's ages, but twelve would be right or near to
right.

No wonder Crowther was clinging to the rail of
the *Moulmein* with his eyes fixed upon the group of
children. It was Miss Diamond who was the Beau
Nash of the ceremonies at Tagaung—the little
daughter whom he had come to fetch and whom he
was never to see again. She had cried all night, the
old man upon the river-bank had told us, but all that
was over now. It certainly was over. Ma Sein,
lording it delightfully over her friends, was enjoying

her game as though the tiniest memory of her father
had been obliterated from her thoughts.

Crowther suddenly turned his back and fixed his
eyes upon the seams of the deck so that this last
and unendurable vision might pass from them the
sooner.

" Tell me when——" he said.

" I will," I answered.

The steamer rounded the bend of the river.   The
land crept forward like a screen between the headland
and the ship.   The sound of the treble voices
ceased to pluck at his heart-strings.   In another
minute there were no laughing children to sear his
eyes.

" It's all right," I said.

" Thank you."

He sat down again upon the bench, but even so
hardly daring to look towards the shore.   We were
quite alone.   The luncheon-bell had rung as we
moved away from the bank.   The passengers were
all in the saloon.   And a curiously subtle change
crept over Crowther.   There was a gentleness in his
face, a submission in his bowed shoulders which
astonished me.   Michael D. had ceased to live.
And when he spoke, as he did to himself and not to
me, it was on a note of pure remorse.

" They were right. . . .   Of course they were
right. . . .   I made a mistake. . . .   I hadn't thought
of it."

The words were so much Greek to me.   I touched
him on the shoulder.

" Come and lunch ! "

Crowther shook his head.

" Not hungry."

" Please ! "

" No ! You run along. I'll stay here by myself for a little while."

I left him there and went forward to the saloon wondering what was this mistake which he had made and what it was that he had not thought out.

I got some part of the answer from the Captain of the *Moulmein*. Luncheon was half over when I took my seat at his elbow and in a little while he and I were alone. He said :

" You had an awkward moment down there at Tagaung, hadn't you ? "

" Yes," I answered.

" I was keeping an eye on you both," he continued. " But we shouldn't have had time to do much for Crowther. Crowther ought to have known better."

I pricked up my ears at that statement. It might hold the secret of Crowther's riddle.

" He might not have thought it out," I rejoined.

The Captain of the *Moulmein* smiled.

" He might, you mean, have refused to remember," he returned. I offered him a cigar, and after he had lit it, he resumed : " Crowther's story is, of course, known to a good many of us on these steamers. These Burmese marriages, as they call them, are not such simple affairs on the upper reaches of the river as you might think. They have their own primitive ethics. The Burmese girl who lives with a white man acquires prestige. It isn't a life of sin, as we should call it, in the eyes of her own people. Not a bit. She is the more honourable and—the important thing—more sought after in

marriage when she and her white man have agreed
to differ.   Odd, isn't it ? "

" Yes," said I.

" Well, Mr. Legatt, here's something still odder.
She's still more marriageable, her social position, if
one may use such a phrase, is still higher, if she has
a child by a white man.   It was fairly certain, then,
that Crowther, coming back to Tagaung after desert-
ing his girl for four years, would find her comfortably married to someone worth while."

All this topsy-turvydom was news to me, but I was
not fool enough to disbelieve it.   The Captain of the
Moulmein knew very much more of the people on
the upper Irrawaddy than I should ever know if I
lived to be a hundred.

" Crowther was only ignorant of that because he
wanted to be."   The Captain smoked his cigar for
a moment or two and asked :

" Did you notice some children playing on the top
of a bit of a hill just outside the village ? "

" Yes, I did," I answered, sitting up.   " Ma Sein
with the sun-helmet on her head was their leader."

" Ma Sein.   Is that her name ?   I didn't know.
Crowther's child, anyway."

" Yes."

" You were right, Mr. Legatt. She was their
leader.   She gave the law.   She was IT.   Prestige,
you see.   An odd thing, prestige ! Ma Sein will
have it all through her life, that is, of course, if she
remains on the upper river."   And with the utterance
of that proviso he climbed up to the wheel upon the
roof.

I had there the answer to my riddle.   The thing

of which Crowther had not thought—prestige. The mistake which Crowther had made—his forgetfulness of its importance on the higher water of the Irrawaddy. Yes, but I was not content, not by any means. If Crowther had forgotten the importance of prestige he had been roughly reminded of it on the beach of Tagaung. He could not have been unaware of it when he returned along the gangway and climbed to the upper deck. There he had sprung to his feet and poised himself for a leap. The more I recalled the scene the more confident I felt that he had meant to dive headlong over the rail and finish with everything. But he had not. He had caught sight of the children on their playground and he had changed his mind. Something had changed it—some gentler thought had touched him, some new concern for the happiness of that gay dancing little daughter of his, Miss Diamond, who had cried all night—" only that was over now."

" They were right. . . . Of course . . . they were right."

I had only heard remorse in his voice. But in that remorse there was renunciation, too. Could any facet of prestige shine with a light so revealing ? I wondered.

If I set out my speculations so fully it is because I am now sure that the picture of those children playing on the headland under the leadership of little Miss Diamond marked a moment of revolution in Crowther to which the incidents of four years had been tending. " Things had worked together," he had told me, to produce his little hour of inspiration when the words of the preacher in Farm Street had smitten his ears. Now other things had been added and amongst them this last little baffling circumstance.

I slept ill that night, but Crowther slept worse. The *Moulmein* was moored that night at Katha, the headquarters of the district, and Crowther went off by himself on shore and came back again when everyone was in bed. I did not in fact see him until my baggage had gone ashore and I myself was saying good-bye to the Captain. He waited on one side until the farewells were spoken. Then he came forward, his eyes heavy, his face ravaged.

" You're getting off here ? "

" Yes. I'm going up by train to Myitkyina."

" I'm sorry." He was silent for a second or two. " For myself, I shall go up to Bhamo on this boat and straight down again."

" To Mandalay ? " I asked.

" Yes."

" And then ? "

" I don't know. I haven't an idea."

He drifted along with me to the companion and suddenly turned round and faced me.

" They were quite right, Mr. Legatt, those men at Tagaung," he said, in a subdued and gentle voice. " I should have been a brute—shouldn't I ?—if I had taken Ma Sein away with me. I never thought of it until I saw her playing up there on the hill. But it was clear enough then. What would she have been back there at Mandalay ? A despised little half-caste bastard. Plain language, Mr. Legatt," he added, as I rather flinched at his description. " But that's what she would have been, and in a year or two every pomatum-smeared clerk would have been leering at her over the counter of her shop, thinking her easy fruit. But up there at Tagaung she's the Great White Queen." He even smiled as he spoke, finding pleasure and consolation and—yes!—even a trifle of amusement in the child's magnificence. For the moment Ma Shwe At and the humiliating end of his love affair with her were out of his mind. Little Miss Diamond held his thoughts and his heart in the hollow of her tiny hand.

" The Great White Queen," he repeated, and now he laughed openly. I shook him by the hand and went off down the gangway. I turned and waved to him once I was on land. The humour, however, had all gone from his looks. It seemed to me that again there was death in his mind and in his face. So there was, too, but it turned out to be not the kind of death which I expected.

CHAPTER VII

UNCLE SUNDAY

I DESCENDED the Irrawaddy a few months later, just in time to avoid the rains; and though Mandalay was intolerably hot, I stayed a day there in the hope that I should run across Michael Crowther. But the board was down from his shop and the shop sold. I made enquiries of the new tenant, a little Chinaman who was selling what Crowther, in his *Dagonet* days, would have called "notions." The Chinaman had no knowledge whatever of Crowther, for he had bought the shop from agents.

"Do you remember the name of the firm?" I asked.

"I lemember till I die," said he, and he allotted to the firm's female ancestry an extremely degraded rank in the animals' order of merit.

I felt that I was immediately upon the heels of my friend. Crowther might be sunk in woe, but woe wouldn't stop him from driving as hard a business bargain as he could. I drove in a ticca-gharri to the address in Hodgkinson Road, and called on Mr. Styles. Mr. Styles was a little round man, very hot, but not busy.

"What can I do for you, sir?" he asked.

"I want to find Michael Crowther."

The little man looked at me with a sudden interest and tilted his chair back against the wall.

" Do you, now ? " said he. " But I can't help you. For I don't myself know where he is."

" You sold a shop of his near the Bazaar."

" But that was some months ago, Mr.—— I haven't got your name, I think."

" Legatt," said I, and he brought the forelegs of his chair down upon the floor with a bang and stared at me open-mouthed.

" Mr. Martin Legatt ? "

" Yes."

He looked me over as if he already had a description of me in his mind.

" Yes," said he, satisfied at last. " Well, I'll tell you what you ought to do. You ought to run along to the bank in B Street. You see, Crowther was a close-fisted sort of fellow and bought little bits of land in Mandalay when it was a good deal cheaper than it is now. I know, for I've realised all of it for him——"

" All of it ? " I interrupted.

" Yes."

" And lately ? "

" Within the last few months."

" And yet you don't know where he is ? "

" I haven't one idea. But I'll tell you what," said Mr. Styles comfortably. " I think that when you do find him, you'll find he's barmy. Brain all gone to greengage jam, you know. Yes, the sooner you do find him, Mr. Legatt, the better. For an ex-captain of a steamer he's a pretty warm man, you know."

I went on to B Street, wondering why the announcement of my name should have so startled Mr. Styles, and discovered that it produced just the same effect upon the manager of the bank. He came hurriedly from his private room.

" Mr. Martin Legatt ? "

" The same," said I.

He took me into his office, seated me in a chair.

" I am glad to see you, Mr. Legatt," he said genially. " Upon my word, I am very glad to see you."

All this excitement and cordiality was very mysterious to me. The manager was a fair-haired, youngish man, who could hardly have reached his position without ability. Why, then, the hysteria ?

" It's very nice of you to welcome me like this," I said. " But I really only came to ask you where I could find Michael Crowther."

The bank manager—as far as I remember, his name was Halfin—Mr. Halfin, stared at me.

" You mean to say that you don't know where he is ? " he gasped incredulously.

" I do not," I answered.

" Well, that's very disappointing," said Mr. Halfin. " For I don't, either. You see, we hold a good deal of money of his on deposit. I think he realised everything, and it had been growing in value for some time."

" But didn't he spend a good deal in England ? " I asked.

Mr. Halfin shook his head.

" I think he cut things pretty fine there. Might have done better very likely if he hadn't."

I got up from my chair.

" Well, thank you, Mr. Halfin," I said.

" But you'll leave me an address, won't you, Mr. Legatt ? " he pleaded rather than asked. " I might want it in a hurry, for all I know."

I gave Mr. Halfin my address in London and the address of our office at Rangoon. But I do not like mysteries. So when he had neatly blotted his book, I asked :

" Will you tell me why you all go up in the air when you hear my name ? "

I see no reason why I should be taken for a lunatic more often than other people, but I do seem to find myself continually suffering from that misconception. Mr. Halfin gaped at me, and then reassured himself.

" You are joking, Mr. Legatt. Ha ! ha ! " and he joined in the joke.

" I'm not joking at all, Mr. Halfin."

" You mean to say that you don't know ? "

" I definitely don't know."

Mr. Halfin at last accepted my statement.

" Very well, then," said he. He became precise, formal, a creature of limitations and prohibitions.

" Yes ? " said I, encouragingly.

" I can't tell you, Mr. Legatt. Good morning ! "

By the merest chance, just outside the door of the bank, I ran into the Captain of the *Moulmein*.

" Here ! Stop ! " I cried, catching hold of his arm. " Why does everybody go off the deep end when I ask them about Crowther ? "

" Don't you know—— " began the Captain, goggle-eyed in a second, like the rest of them.

" No! No! No!" I exclaimed. " I don't know, and though I'm not off my head, I shall be unless you answer me."

At last the answer came.

" Crowther's left you all his money in his will. I know, because I was one of the witnesses, and Styles, the agent, was the other. The bank manager has got it with, I believe, a letter of instructions to be delivered to you after Crowther's death."

So that was the secret. I am bound to say that I was a little staggered myself.

" When did he make his will ? " I asked.

" After that trip up to Bhamo."

" And where is he now ? "

The Captain of the *Moulmein* pushed back his helmet and reflected.

" I did hear that he had been seen at Prome, down towards Rangoon—you know—the place with the Shwe Tsan-Dau Pagoda, but I haven't run across him for months and months."

And ask questions as I might, I could learn no more of Crowther than that. A total eclipse had hidden that shattered man, and I, a little annoyed that I should be so pestered by troublesome recollections of him, followed his example and vanished out of Burma.

I remained for the next eighteen months in England, dividing my time between the office in London and a house which I had bought near Woodbridge, in Suffolk. At the end of that time we were negotiating for a new lease with the Government of Burma, and it was necessary that a representative of the Company should go out and come to terms on the spot. I claimed the right to go. Internal questions of administration delayed the settlement of my business, and finding that I had a couple of months with nothing to do, I decided to spend them in the forest country which had never ceased to appeal to me. Thus once more I found myself with a brace of rifles and a shotgun, heading for the upper reaches of the Irrawaddy. I was twenty-nine years of age, heart-free and foolishly proud of my freedom. I could and did say to myself, adapting Crowther's derisive phrase: " I am one of the Untouchables." This was to be the last holiday of the kind which I should have for many years and I determined to make the most of it before settling down to the humdrum life which apparently awaited me.

I travelled on the old *Moulmein*. She had a lighter alongside and we stopped at many villages ; and I noticed that at each stopping-place now one, now two monks in their yellow robes, came on board with their sleeping mats, their beggar bowls and their acolytes, and squatted upon the lighter's deck. I was astonished at this unusual traffic and the Captain explained it to me.

"There's to be a great pongyi byan up at Schwegu. An old gaingok died there last year, and since he was a very holy abbot, they have kept him in honey —by the way, you don't eat honey whilst you are in Burma, do you ?—until they could collect enough money to give him a proper send-off. They've got it now and there'll be three days' gaming and play-acting and dancing, and the big fireworks at the end when the body's burnt."

A new idea occurred to the Captain. He looked at me curiously and smiled.

" Yes, you travelled with me nearly two years ago, didn't you ? "

" As far as Katha."

" Yes, and I met you afterwards in Mandalay."

" Outside the bank."

" That's right, Mr. Legatt, isn't it ? Take a walk ! "

He led me forward and pointed to a monk on the lighter who sat a little apart with his boy servant in front of him. His back was towards us and he was as immobile as a coloured figure in stone. His Talapot fan and his rosary of Indian shot seeds lay on the edge of his mat at his side. His eyes were fixed upon a great palm-leaf book which he held upon his knees, but whether he was reading it or lost in contemplation I could not tell. Certainly he never turned a page whilst we watched him. In a word he was as orthodox as a monk could be.

" There's a friend of yours," said the Captain.

I had an acquaintanceship, by now, with a good many Buddhist monks up and down the country, but I could not remember any one of them whom I had the right to call a friend. I shook my head.

" I'm right, Mr. Legatt," the Captain repeated with a laugh.

I moved to one side so that I might catch a glimpse of my friend's face. It was square and rather fleshless and in a vague way familiar. But even so I didn't recognise him until I began to ask how did the Captain of the *Moulmein* know that the monk was my friend. I had only once travelled on the

Moulmein and there had only been one man on board of her whom its Captain could call my friend. I ran down to the lower deck and crossed on to the lighter. I ran up the companion to its upper deck, and there, wrapped in the yellow robe, reading his great book, sat Michael Crowther.

I leaned against the rail by the side of him.

" Good morning, Michael," I said.

" Good morning, Mr. Legatt," he returned, lifting his eyes from his book and laying a finger on the passage at which his reading broke off. But he looked ahead of him and not at me. " I saw you come on board yesterday."

" You might have given me a sign."

" My name is U Wisaya now," he said, explaining in this simple way that with his new world I had nothing whatever to do.

But I was not to be put off so easily. I sat down on the deck by the side of him. I found that I was not so astonished by this new evolution of his character as I had expected to be. Michael Crowther was naturally violent. He swung between the extremes, but never hung between them. He would be at one or the other before you could wink. He was all England one day, and all Burma the next, and for anything I could be sure about, in a month's time he might have enlisted in the Foreign Legion and already have deserted from it.

" You may call yourself whatever you like, Michael. Uncle Sunday is a very good name too," I said comfortably. " But you'll excuse me if I talk the lingo you used to like. I'm from Missouri and you've got to show me."

Crowther, still keeping his finger on the paragraph of his book, explained.

" There was an American a good many years ago. Just a tourist. He came out sightseeing. The River, Mandalay, the Shwe Dagon and pagodas generally—that sort of thing. But he didn't go away. The country took him, the sun, the good-humour, the pleasant lazy life. He came up the Irrawaddy several times with me on the old *Dagonet*. He was always going back, but he never did. He shot for a season or two and then gave it up. He travelled out to the Shan States, then up the Chindwin to the jade mines. Just seeing the place —before he went away for good. But after the country, the religion took him—see, Mr. Legatt ? I knew that he was in a monastery down at Prome or Pagan ; and after you got off at Katha I began to wonder about him—yes, and about me. I had come to the end of things—see ? "

So Crowther, on his return to Mandalay, had liquidated his belongings and set off for Prome and from Prome again to Pagan, that dead city of pagodas. There his search had ended.

" The American was a full-blown pongyi and learned ! I was ashamed after all my years on the Irrawaddy to realise how little I knew," Crowther stated. " He talked to me. I was very unhappy. To be nothing at all—not even a separate conscious soul. That sounded pretty good, and worth a thousand existences if so many were needed to fit one. All life was misery. All passions dragged you further and further the Great Peace. To feel compassion for all living creatures, but to know no closer ties. He lent me some books. He preached to me the great Allegory. Do you know it ? "

" No," said I.

" You should," and a gleam of humour shone about his mouth. " There's a forest in it. A forest of glades and flickering lights and white, big, heavily-scented flowers, and golden-coloured fruits, and one rock path out of it, and a Keeper with a whip, Time. He lets no one rest in those glades. Lie down and the lash falls. All must run and run nowhere but where they ran before. The fruits have thorns which wound and the scent of the flowers cloys and the lights flickering between the trees dazzle, and fatigue comes and there's no end to it but to follow the rock path and the steady star, as at the last all men must."

I felt a little bewildered and no doubt my face showed it. For he turned to me with a real smile.

" You're thinking, Mr. Legatt, that you might hear just the same kind of allegory at a Revivalist meeting in the East End of London, aren't you, now ? "

" Yes," I admitted.

" But you're wrong. All men must at the last take the rock path and see the steady star and escape the lashes of the whip. There's the difference. It may be after ages in hell, a thousand lives as animal or woman, but in the end all—do you follow that ?—all—all without exception will make the great Renunciation and enter into the Great Peace."

Crowther was speaking with so quiet a simplicity and a sincerity so obvious that I began to wonder whether my easy judgement of him as a man who must rush from pole to pole and back again was correct.

" But who am I to expound the law ? " he continued. " I, a mere upazin and novice who has not yet mastered the two hundred and twenty-seven precepts of the Book of Enfranchisement."

He tapped the big palm-leaf volume upon his knees and at that moment a girl with a silk scarf about her shoulders and her lustrous hair secured with a jewelled pin passed him on her way to the bows of the ship. She was powdered with thanakah, she wore gold tubes in the lobes of her ears, she smoked a big green cheroot, and as she passed she gave that odd little kick of the heel which knocks upon the heart of so many Burmese gallants. But Michael Crowther did not see it. At the first glimpse of her up went his palm-leaf fan before his face in the orthodox way, so that no fleeting desire might disturb his meditations and set him back a mile or so on his rock path.

" She has gone, Michael," I said, and some imp nipped me till I asked :

" And what of the sapphire, Uncle ? "

Michael Crowther's body stiffened, and he remained silent, looking on the ground six feet ahead of him according to the rules. Oh, that American monk at Pagan had grounded his neophyte very well ! I began to feel remorseful at awakening old memories, but so far from taking my question amiss, he answered gently :

" I am glad that you asked that question, Mr. Legatt. The sapphire and all the other ornaments hang round the spire of a pagoda in the monastery grounds at Pagan, high up, and just under the swelling diamond-bud at the very top."

I felt ashamed of my question now. It is not, as the world knows, uncommon for the devout to give such votive offerings for the decoration of their temples. But I was still a little under the persuasion that I was merely a witness of one of Michael Crowther's more violent agitations ; and was not prepared for his consecration of these ornaments.

" I'm sorry," I mumbled.

" There is no need for regret," he continued. " I shall tell you the plan in my mind. I live a mendicant with my begging bowl and pledged never to handle gold and silver for any of my needs, I, U Wisaya. But meanwhile there is money in the bank at Mandalay standing in the name of Michael Crowther. There it will stand and grow."

" For what purpose ? " I asked.

" In ten years' time when I am admitted into the class of pongyis I shall take all that money and build at Tagaung a white pagoda decorated with gold——"

" To the glory of Ma Shwe At," I suggested with a smile.

" To the glory of our Lord Buddha," he answered seriously. " And when that is done I shall ask permission to remove the sapphire and the ornaments and I shall hang them high on the spire of my pagoda at Tagaung amongst the little silver bells. I shall rest in its shadow, hearing those bells ring with every breath of wind, until I pass on into another life if I needs must."

I understood now why Michael had bequeathed

to me his little fortune. The tenor of his letter of instructions was as clear to me as if I had broken the seal and read the words. If Michael died before he was a fully-fledged monk, I was to build his pagoda for him at Tagaung. To tell the truth I was a little moved by his trust in me. I had not covered myself with dignity during this conversation, and conscious of it, I was trying to fix the blame on Michael. But I had not discovered a pretext when the *Moulmein* swept in sight of the island of Schwegu with its golden spires gleaming against a background of dark trees like a city in a fairy tale.

But as we drew near to it, it became gaudy as a fair. On a wide, open space between the river and the town, booths with sides of matting and thatched roofs and projecting eaves had been built. There would be gaming and feasting and a play which would take the three days at the last to perform. At one side of the space stood a new pagoda of pasteboard and gilt paper, on the upper floor of which the abbot and his coffin would finally be burnt. Close by the side of this glistening outrage was a tiny temple in the same appalling taste which would carry the coffin on guy ropes up to the place of burning. A little apart stood a painted truck with a great rope of jungle grass at each end, on which the coffin in its tiny temple would first be placed for the tug-of-war—the great attraction of the festival. Anybody might join in and on either side, and anybody might leave off at any moment and take a rest. It would be very much like the race in *Alice in Wonderland*. At one end there would be cries of " We must bury our dead!"; at the other "You shall not take our friend from us!" The tug-of-war might last for three hours or for the whole three days, with an armistice at each nightfall. In the end, of course, the burial party would win, and those who had the luck or the foresight to be hanging on to the grass rope at that end of the truck would achieve great merit and shorten the number of the lives which stood between them and Nirvana. Around this open space rockets were planted ready to be touched off on the evening of the third day. They were aimed more or less at the gilt-paper pagoda and one of them no doubt would start the cremation; though to be sure several people might be killed first. There the whole construction stood in the blazing sun, as complete an affair of gimcrack and gingerbread as a primitive imagination could devise.

I glanced at Michael as he picked up his rosary and handed his mat to his acolyte. How in the world could he reconcile this showman's stuff with the simple faith he had been explaining? I was careful this time not to ask my question, but Michael answered it without so much as a look at me.

"All religions collect tinsel," he said, "just as all ships collect molluscs. The ships and the religions are not hurt. They just want cleaning from time to time."

I put it down to his fasting and his abstinence. But he was becoming uncomfortably quick in understanding the unspoken thoughts in a companion's mind. He walked along the gangway to the shore, his eyes fixed on the ground six feet ahead of him, as indifferent to the crowd which thronged the bank as to me. But his indifference affected me not at all. For once more the old spell was upon me. As I climbed back from the lighter on to the *Moulmein*, I was as certain as he was of his new Faith that I had not done with him nor he with me.

CHAPTER VIII

THE FIRST ASCENT OF THE DENT DU
PAGODA

THE decision, indeed, was taken out of our hands. It was made for us during the previous night whilst our steamer had been lying at Katha ; and by men whom Uncle Sunday would have pitied and I should have arraigned.

A few days before, whilst Michael was still sitting at the feet of the American monk at Pagan, two men came to the monastery. They had shaven heads and both wore the yellow robe. No one challenged them. They declared themselves to be students and novices, and they were both of an age in the late twenties. They had the right to lodge there, so long as they observed the Ten Commandments, just as they had the right to depart whensoever they wished ; and without question or complaint. They spread their sleeping-mats on the floor of the great hall and, rising with the others at the time when there was just light enough to see the veins of the hands, they lined up behind the abbot before the image of Buddha in the order of their degree in the brotherhood, and joined in chanting the morning service. They then helped in the household work, filtering the drinking-water so that no living thing might be destroyed when it was drunk, sweeping the floors and watering the plants in the enclosure ; all very dutifully and neatly. They then studied the book of Weenee which describes the Whole Duty of the Monk. This for an hour. Towards eight o'clock they took their begging-bowls, and in single file behind the abbot and again in their due order of precedence, they marched round the town, receiving, with a proper absence of gratitude, the food which the charitable, acquiring merit, heaped high in their bowls. Their last meal of the day eaten before noon, or, let us say, supposed to be eaten before noon, they passed the long afternoons in study and meditation. If a head nodded, who should notice it ? If eyelids closed, was not abstraction more complete ? Were not all thoughts fixed upon the Law and the Assembly and the attainment of Nirvana ? A slow and pensive walk for health's sake followed upon the afternoon. And while you contemplated such majestic opacities, would a voice in your ear call you back to earth or even the nudge of an elbow in your ribs ? Not a well-fed pongyi anyway. Towards evening, meditation lost its hold. From time to time the bow must be unbent or it will snap.

These two new-comers received monastic names. They were called in the secular tongue Nga Pyu and Nga Than ; and they were very, very glad to be called something else, since the prefix Nga has associations to which they were anxious not to draw attention. They were two very bad men but they became Pyinya and Thoukkya, excellent names for a pair of jugglers in a music hall or for novices in a brotherhood.

Their great moments were after nightfall, when the great doors of the teak stockade were closed and perhaps the abbot or the American monk, Nageinda, or one of the elders, would discourse. Pyinya and Thoukkya were second to none in their attention. And when the evensong was intoned at nine before the image of the Buddha, they were second to none in the humility of their voices. They would ask, thereafter, devout questions about the new white pagoda in the compound, which reared its two hundred glistening feet of spire to the golden, umbrella-shaped Hti.

" A great lady gave it ?   Surely in her next life she will have deserved to be a man ? " one of them would ask.

" Or perhaps she will enter at once into Peace ? " asked the other.

" Who shall say ? " would be the answer.   " The noble lady has acquired great merit."

" Is it true that a great diamond is set in the Hti ? " Pyinya enquired with awe.

" Gifts have the same value if they are equally proportioned to the means of the giver," U Nageinda answered.   " Thus, the sapphire and the silver ornaments of our brother U Wisaya confer no less merit upon him than the great diamond upon the lady."

" And those too are on the Hti ? " asked Thoukkya with a glance of admiration towards Michael, reading his book in a corner.

" They encircle the spire like a bracelet just below the Hti," said U Nageinda proudly.   He was still unregenerate enough to dislike any depreciation of his own particular convent.

Pyinya and Thoukkya wandered out on to the wide platform and, sitting on the steps, gazed upwards to the top of the soaring spire. There was still a scaffolding about it, for the great lady was decorating it with a string of electric-light bulbs, which on dark nights, to people on the river far below, would glow amongst the stars.

But the nights were not dark now. The moon lit up the enclosure, the two pagoda slaves who watched the night through whilst the scaffolding stood, and the palm trees, till all was as light as day.

" To-morrow the scaffolding will be down," said Pyinya in a whisper, lest he should disturb the serenity of the night.

" And the pagoda servants in their huts on the river-bank," replied Thoukkya.

" We shall see the pagoda in its beauty," said Pyinya joyfully.

" For a week, Brother," Thoukkya warned him with a regretful shake of the head. " Only for a week. Then there will be no moon."

Pyinya sighed, and then, like a man who has a happy thought, he smiled.

" But even if there is no moon, there will be the chain of electric lights from the top of the pagoda to the ground. It will be a comfort to us all to see it still."

Thoukkya was very sorry to dash the pious hopes of his fellow novice. But it was better that he should know the truth. Thoukkya had made discreet enquiries. Economy had been considered.

" The lights will not burn after nine," he said.

The two men gazed upwards to the Hti two hundred feet above the ground.

" The bulbs are hung upon a strong wire rope," said Thoukkya.

" A doubled rope," Pyinya added ; " so that when one of the lamps fails it can be lowered and replaced."

" Yes," Thoukkya agreed. " It is all very beautiful."

And both men, in spite of their concentrated meditations, had been very observant.

" It is a pity that we cannot see from so far below the great lady's diamond sparkling in the moonlight and thus understand the better the greatness of her merit," said Thoukkya after a pause.

" Yes, it is a pity," Pyinya agreed. " But at all events we know that it is there. Instead of regretting, shall we not hope that the workmen too have achieved merit by setting it irremovably in the Hti ? "

Thoukkya bowed his head.

" Yes, we must hope for that. But we know that workmen scamp even the most meritorious work."

" Alas and alas ! " said Pyinya. " But we shall learn the truth of all this when the moon has hidden her face."

Thoukkya looked upwards to the soaring spire and thought how strange the world must look, if you were perched upon the top of it.

" I am dizzy," he said. " I think that I am going to be sick."

" These long meditations," said Pyinya sympathetically.

It was nine o'clock now and behind them the lights

were being extinguished in the hall. The two men rose and went within and unrolled their mats; and but for the blaze of moonlight at the open doorway the monastery was given over to darkness and to sleep.

But in a week there was no moon and only a star or two entangled in the branches of a tree showed to any wakeful monk that there was an open doorway at all. But the monks, with the exception of two, were not wakeful. These two, certainly, made up for the rest, for they were very busy indeed. Very quietly—one might have thought that they had been trained in stealthiness— Pyinya and Thoukkya would slip on hands and knees through the doorway and meet in a corner of the enclosure behind a great banyan-tree. There a long bamboo pole, detached, surely by pious hands for a pious purpose, from the scaffolding before it was removed from the enclosure, lay hidden under leaves. It was twenty-five feet long, and for a couple of hours on two consecutive nights these devout novices worked upon it, splicing to one end a strong iron hook and strengthening the pole and making it easier to handle by coiling it tightly about with cord at intervals of three feet.

" It will be for to-morrow," said Pyinya in a whisper ; and the two men put their heads together for a little while.

" Muhammed Ghalli, the Indian, will meet us in the morning. It will all be easy," Thoukkya said in conclusion, and they crept back like shadows to their mats in the great hall.

The next night was as dark as any marauder

could have wished for. At two o'clock in the morning Pyinya and Thoukkya carried their pole to the foot of the pagoda. Seven small ledges, representing the sacred seven roofs of the great monasteries, broke the line of the cone at intervals of twenty-five feet, and from the topmost of them the final spire of gilded iron sprang with an ever-diminishing girth for fifteen feet and at that height expanded to its umbrella top. Pyinya dropped his robe and his waist-cloth on the ground. He rested the claw of his pole upon the lowest ledge near to the wire rope on which the lamps were hung. He was as lithe and silent as a lizard. With one hand holding the wire rope and the other grasping the bamboo, he crawled up, his toes clinging to the stone of the pagoda. On the first of the seven ledges he rested and breathed, his face and his body flat against the cone. So far the expedition had made no great demands upon him. A few minutes later a sound of breathing beneath his feet, a quiver of the wire rope at his side, and a rattle of an electric globe against the stone, and Thoukkya stood beside him.

It needed the strength of both to draw up the pole, steady the butt of it upon the ledge on which they stood and catch the hook on to the ledge above them. Then they mounted to the next stage.

The great cone tapered as they climbed. Both men blessed the darkness which hid from their eyes the height to which they had reached. They had emptiness now on each side of them as well as behind them. Their breath came in labouring spasms which threatened to burst heart and lungs ; their bodies ran with their sweat. Upon each one of them in turn came the almost irresistible impulse to let go, plunge down to earth with a shriek of fear, and so finish, meat, not man. Had there been one, so he would have died. But every now and then, a whisper or a touch kept them astoundedly aware that they were still alive, clinging like lizards to the spire. And above all their natural fears, there was this : At the very apex might there not be waiting a guardian spirit, the Nat of the pagoda, who would smite them with a colic, cramping their stomachs in an agony which no strength could resist ?

They stood on the last tiny ledge, clinging to the final spear of gilded iron which rose fifteen feet to the gold mushroom at the top. And as Thoukkya whispered in a sobbing voice : " I am finished. I dare not," they heard in a faint stir of wind the little gold bells tinkling above them, so near now, so near ! To Pyinya they were a call, an encouragement. They tinkled so prettily ! If there was a Nat up there, he was on their side. Very likely there was one. Very likely the great lady had offended it. Nats were very easy to offend and never forgot to let you have a nasty upper-cut in return.

" I'll go, Nga Than," he said. " Cling tight ! A few minutes and we can buy Rangoon."

The iron lance shook as he swarmed up it with knees and feet and hands. Every inch of his body seemed to cling close to it and support him. He mounted by the friction of muscle and flesh rather than by foothold and handhold. Thoukkya, gasping, and clinging with bruised hands on the tiny shelf below, suddenly heard above him a jangle of bells, as though they tossed in a storm. So loud they seemed to him that he glanced down in terror, expecting to see a lamp glimmer far beneath him in the compound, to hear a cry tear the still night. But no light shone, no cry was heard. There was nothing but the black emptiness below him and about him. His stomach was turned upside-down within him. Once let him feel solid earth beneath the soles of his feet and see it stretching out all round him—which he would never, never do—he would not even climb the smallest of garden trees for a diamond as big as an abbot's paunch. Thoukkya sobbed. He waited for a thousand years and then a scuffling noise sounded just above his head. He looked up; against the dark sky a dark bulk was just visible. Pyinya slid down beside him.

Thoukkya asked no questions. For around his companion's arm ornaments glistened. For a little while Pyinya leaned against the iron spear breathing and catching his breath like a man who has run a race and reached the end of his strength. Then he said :

"Let us go down, very carefully. For I am very tired." But Thoukkya was more tired by fear than Pyinya by exertion.

The descent, however, was easy compared with the climb. The coils of cord about the pole gave grips for hands and feet. So long as neither leaned back and dragged the hook from the ledge there was no danger for these men. But between the fourth

and the third ledge a small mischance occurred.
Pyinya knocked with his elbow one of the glass
bulbs on the wire rope. It clashed too hard against
the stone of the pagoda and tinkled down to the
ground in fragments. Both men stopped where
they were, their hearts in their mouths, one on the
ledge flattened against the pagoda, the other clinging
like a monkey. As each thin sliver of curved glass
leaped against the spire and was shattered again,
it seemed to them that cymbals clashed and loud
enough to wake the dead.

"Be quick!" Thoukkya whispered from the
ledge, his teeth chattering, his belly turned to water.
"Oh, be quick, Nga Pyu!" And indeed on such
a night sound travelled like voices over water.

"It is well," answered Nga Pyu. "It will not
be noticed until the lights are turned on to-morrow
night, and by then we shall be very far away."

They were at the base of the pagoda on the
ground. Thoukkya felt the soil with his toes. It
was incredible. He stretched out a foot gingerly.
Surely it would touch nothing. It touched soil.
He was like a man who comes down to the lowest
tread of a flight of stairs in the dark. The floor
jars him.

At the base of the pagoda they put on again their
waist-cloths and their robes. Silently they carried
the bamboo pole back to its hiding-place. They
waited in the darkness of the compound until the
violence of their breathing ceased. Then they
wriggled through the monastery doorway to their
corner of the hall and in a few moments were
asleep.

When the keeper of the monastery at daybreak beat upon his wooden gong and roused the monks, the two devout novices performed the sacred offices with the others. Only when all had scattered upon their household duties did they move quietly to the open gate of the stockade. They passed out, and with their eyes dutifully fixed upon the ground six feet ahead of them, but their ears most unmeditatively alert, they paced down a narrow lane to the river's edge. On the bank one man squatted, a large bundle by his side. The two novices paid no heed to him. They dropped their robes upon the ground close to him and bathed in the river. As yet no one else was abroad. The hovels of the pagoda slaves were still shuttered and a mist hung upon the water. There were just those three, the two novices bathing and the third man who spread out his bundle. In the bundle were two skirts of pink cotton, two white jackets. He wrapped in his bundle in their place the yellow robes, laid upon them a heavy stone and tied up all securely. He stood on the brink of the stream and looked this way and that. Then he flung the bundle in. The men of the pagoda mounted the slope. Nga Pyu and Nga Than warmly greeted their old fellow-convict, Muhammed Ghalli, the Indian, and dressed themselves in the usual cheap garments of the poor.

When Uncle Sunday returned from the burial of the Abbot of Schwegu he saw from the steamer's deck, with a throb of alarm, that the scaffolding was once more erected about the pagoda. He hurried to the monastery in a growing agitation. His

American friend, U Nageinda, was waiting for him and drew him aside.

"They were released convicts, of course," he said. "None but monks and convicts have shaven heads. It is a common practice for convicts on their release to take the yellow robe. Then, after a few days, they can go back to the world saying they had no vocation for the priesthood, and no one can point the finger at them. They are novices who have found themselves unequal to the monastic life."

"They stole, then?"

U Nageinda looked upwards to the spire.

"They were men of great strength and daring. The great diamond they could not reach. It is inset on the very summit above the overhang of the Hti. But your offering was suspended like a girdle below."

"And that they have?" said Crowther.

"Yes."

He sat on the ground, his hands clasped together and the fingers working, his eyes moody and his face like a mask.

"Nga Pyu . . . Nga Than . . ." he said very softly, and again: "Nga Than . . . Nga Pyu. . . ."

U Nageinda shook his head. He seemed to hear a note in that soft repetition of the names which was anything but monastic. He said gently:

"Let us remember that for so great a crime against our Lord Buddha and the Law, those two poor creatures may live for a thousand years in each of the eight Hells."

Apparently the words brought no consolation to

Michael Crowther. He sat by himself and brooded for the greater part of that day, and just before nightfall he got to his feet. U Nageinda observed the movement and was in two minds whether he should himself stir a finger or no. Each man must follow the steady star along the rock path of his own volition. To proffer advice was not within the four corners of his creed. Moreover, it could amount to nothing more than a plea that his pupil should not sully this newly-found soul of his by any passion, whether it be to recover a stolen thing or to avenge the theft. But his glance, lowered though it was, warned that such advice would be unprofitable. There stood Uncle Sunday hardening before his eyes into Michael Crowther, his head lifting, his shoulders squaring. But U Nageinda could help a little out of his long experience—if he would. He saw Michael take a step and he did. With a most unpriestly hurry he bustled to Michael's side.

" Our monks travel far," he said, " and they hear much, and they carry their tidings to other monasteries. Wherever you go you will find eyes and ears and tongues which will aid you. Use them so that you may come back to us the sooner."

Michael turned to the old American with a smile.

" I thank you," he said ; and he strode through the gateway of the stockade and was gone.

CHAPTER IX

ON ADAM'S PEAK

I HAVE described the rape of the sapphire in its order of time, although I only heard of it later, and of the perils and terrors which beset the robbers later still. But its proper place in the story is, I think, where I have put it. For in that way only a few circumstances in which at the time I saw no danger can carry their true meaning. In a sentence, I believed Ma Shwe At's anklets and Ma Sein's filigree bracelet and the sapphire still to be decorating the empty air two hundred feet above the earth; and my business finished, I returned to Rangoon on the date arranged under that belief.

I had left myself a clear month to do with as I chose. I could shudder over the *un après* at Monte Carlo, or simply luxuriate in Paris. I did neither of these things. It was clear to me that many years must pass before I could again find myself eastward of the Gulf of Aden, and I determined to realise a dream which on every voyage had beset me, whilst I still had the strength and zest for such adventures. I sailed for Ceylon. I spent a couple of days at the Galle Face outside Colombo, made my arrangements, hired a car and rode inland to Hatton in Dickoya, the little capital of the tea district. There a great wonder awaited me. I booked my room at the hotel and had hardly moved a couple of yards from the door when a clear, rather high voice suddenly called out on a note of welcome and surprise :

" Darling ! "

I knew the voice. A snake couldn't have turned quicker than I did towards it. There, on the opposite side of the road, her arms stretched wide apart, stood Imogen Cloud, her face one adorable smile. All Imogen's friends were darlings, and I, alas ! no more so than any other.

" Imogen ! "

I ran across to her, took her hands and laughed. " This is the world's birthday. Let me look at you ! "—and I held her away from me.

Imogen Cloud was always amusing to look at. In London, some queer little tip-tilted hat or another trickery of the fashion tickled one pleasantly. Here it was something else. The sun was low and Imogen wore no hat. The glossy ripple of her golden, shingled head and the vermilion of her lips were deliciously at odds with her small sun-browned face.

" Martin ! " she cried. " What are you doing here ? "

" What you are, I hope," I answered. " I am going up Adam's Peak to-morrow."

It was indeed that mountain, seen so often from the deck of a steamer afar and apart in the light of an evening sky, which had brought me to Ceylon. I had read all the descriptions of it upon which I could lay my hands. I was well grounded in its romantic and immemorial associations. It had become important to me. But I had never dreamed how real that importance was to become, or what unforgettable associations of my own I was now to add to those which history recorded in the books.

" Lovely ! " said Imogen. " So are we."

She slipped her arm through mine and took possession of me. How many friends of hers—again, alas !—had I seen swell with pride at the flattery of this annexation ! Also, she danced up and down a little as lightly as the eight-year-old Miss Diamond in the sandy square of Tagaung.

" Yes," she said. " I am here with Pamela Brayburn. We ran away from the fogs together." Pamela Brayburn was a girl of Imogen's age, twenty-two or thereabouts. They were both among the livelier spirits of the day : Imogen, the daughter of a West Country squire who had put his money into ships in the great age of shipping and had retired in time to keep it, and Pamela Brayburn, her cousin and the child of a famous judge.

" We shall start at midnight," said Imogen.

" And go to bed at nine," I added.

" Carefully putting on our bed-socks first," said she.

We were standing in the road outside the door of the hotel. I have a vague recollection now that I did see someone, a native of the island perhaps, a man of the East, anyway, slip by us from the direction of the servants' quarters. I was hardly aware of him, or indeed of anyone except Imogen. But the next moment my attention was attracted, as any small familiar thing happening in an unfamiliar place will attract it whether it's my attention or another's. I heard some words spoken behind me, and I spun round on my heel. The words meant nothing at all to me. They were as commonplace as words could be.

" Muhammed is already at Ratnapura."

That was all. Ratnapura had a sound of Ceylon even to one who had disembarked at Colombo only three days before. But I had never seen the place, and the name of Muhammed, of course, east of Cape Spartel was as one grain of sand in a Sahara. But the words were spoken in Talaing, the language of the old kingdom of Pegu, still the vernacular of a quarter of a million people in Lower Burma. We were after all four days' steaming from Rangoon. It seemed odd that I should hear this tongue immediately in this upland town of Dickoya. I only saw the backs of two men, however. They were moving away, but one of them was reading a telegram—a telegram, no doubt, from one Muhammed who had arrived at Ratnapura.

" Do you know those men ? " Imogen asked curiously.

" No. But they are from Burma."

Then an explanation of their presence occurred to me.

" The guide-books tell us that Hatton is the headquarters of the tea district. There are likely to be a good many coolies of all races here from the plantations."

" I don't think they are coolies," said Imogen. " They are more probably pilgrims for the Peak."

" Why ? " I asked, only interested because Imogen was, too.

" I rather think that I saw them in Kandy," said she.

There is a mark on the flat summit of the mountain which vaguely resembles the imprint of a giant's foot. Who first discovered it, no one knows. But the Buddhists claim it for a footstep of Gautama, the Hindus hold that Siva passed that way, the Mohammedans say quite simply that Adam made it. Thus eight hundred million Eastern men venerate Adam's Peak for one of three reasons and send their annual contingents to watch the dawn break upon that high shrine. It was very likely that the two Burmans were bound upon the same journey as ourselves.

" Of course, that's it ! " I agreed. " Why were you curious about them ? "

" I was thinking that we shall want a man or two, shan't we ? " Imogen replied. " I'm told that before morning it is very cold up on the top. One or two to carry wraps. If they're from Burma you might prefer to have them. They would make their pilgrimage and earn a little money at the same time."

" That's true."

It would be an advantage to have them. For I could talk their language and I could not do that in the case of a Cingalese. I turned about again to call to the men. But they had disappeared into some alley. We waited for a few moments on the chance that they might reappear and then walked on again.

" It can't be helped, my dear," I said. " After all, if we take a guide from the hotel, he'll know the way and be reliable besides."

But I did not finish the word " besides." I broke off with a cry.

" Imogen ! "

" Yes."

She stopped and faced me, puzzled, as indeed she well might be. For I have no doubt that my face spoke my consternation as loudly as my voice.

" Martin ! What's the matter ? "

Imogen was wearing a coat and skirt of a thin tussore silk with a white silk shirt open at the neck so that her slender throat rose free. Round it was fastened a light platinum chain, and dangling as a pendant to the chain was a large square sapphire, a quite flawless stone of a deep and lovely blue. I had not noticed it until this moment. I don't think, indeed, that it could have been noticeable. It must have lain against Imogen's breast underneath her shirt, and some movement must have now revealed it. But there it hung, darkly gleaming, with just that spark of fire in its depths which had burned in the stone that Crowther had rolled on to the table-cloth of the *Dagonet* from Ma Shwe At's pink silk bag. Of course, it was not the same stone. I told myself that over and over again. It could not be. That one hung far out of reach on the spire of a pagoda a couple of thousand miles away. And Crowther sat at the foot of it reading in his big Book of Enfranchisement. But this sapphire about Imogen's throat was its very twin, even to the fire-spark like some tiny lantern shining

sharply in the deep of Indian seas. It was its twin
—yes—discovered, very likely, in the same native
claim on the road to Mogok—but not the same. I
would not have it so—no, not for the world.

"Where did you get that sapphire? . . .
Please!" I asked, a little breathlessly.

"Darling!" she answered. Some trifle of concern
caused by my agitation clouded her face for a
moment. Her fingers closed upon the stone.
Even though I knew it to be merely the sister stone,
I hated to see Imogen touch and hold and claim it

"Darling, I bought it."

"Where?"

"At Kandy."

"When?"

"A week ago."

"You are sure?"

"Of course I'm sure. You don't think sapphires
like this are lying about in heaps. I saw it in a
jeweller's shop under the hotel, and since there
was no generous young man within range of my
flashing eyes, I gave myself a present."

I drew a breath of relief. It was not so long ago
since I had parted from Michael at Schwegu; and
Michael within that time had assuredly not recanted.
Besides, Crowther's stone was unset. I remembered
that clearly. It was still unset when Crowther
had discovered it still wrapped in its strip of napkin
at the bottom of his trunk after his return from
Farm Street. Imogen's sapphire, on the other
hand, was set simply and beautifully in a perfectly
plain, thin, square frame of platinum. No, they
couldn't be the same stone. I was catching at every

possible argument, you see, which would dissociate the sapphire which Crowther had stolen from Ma Shwe At from that which now gleamed against Imogen's breast.

" I am very glad," I stammered. " I mean that I should have adored to have given it to you—if you would have taken it. But I'm glad that it was bought at Kandy. . . . Oh, you must think me a perfect idiot."

I was furious with myself. The sight of that duplicate stone—on no account would I allow that it could be anything but a duplicate—hanging from Imogen's neck had given me a sharper shock than I was ready to meet. Crowther and his sapphire had been growing to be elements rather too disturbing to suit me. I didn't want to meet them at every corner of the road. I was all for an equable level life if I could get it—or rather if I could keep it. Storms of the soul, whirlpools of passion which sucked the heart down in dizzy spirals and then flung it up and up into thin air—anyone might have my share of these raptures who wanted it. I did not want to be disturbed by Crowther and his sapphire. The jewel had brought nothing but unhappiness to little Mrs. Golden Needle and Miss Diamond, to Crowther himself, and it had seemed in a queer, sinister way to be trying to entangle me. As though some malignant spirit lived in its blue loveliness—that spark of fire, for instance, shooting out always its tiny ray. I had been getting obsessed by it in Burma. It was setting a spell upon me ; and all the way to Ceylon I had been growing more and more conscious of relief, like a man throwing off a malady. Fear—yes, I will be frank—fear had begun to fall away from me as we dropped down the river from Rangoon ; and each new day upon the sea was another door to freedom. Miles away Crowther and his sapphire, and more miles with every hour. And now, suddenly, here in Ceylon, was the very image of that stone, resting lovely and menacing against the breast of the last person in the world whom I wished unhappiness to threaten. Oh, yes, I was troubled, and no doubt my face showed it. It was as if the original sapphire spoke :

" You don't get away from me like that ! See where I am ? Here's a friend of yours going to do some work for me now."

Not if I could help it !

But it was Imogen who spoke and not the sapphire. She used those very words. She glanced at me. No doubt I had spoken rather strenuously. She tucked her arm again through mine and gave it a little squeeze.

" You can't get away from me like that. I shall want to hear about this sapphire," she said.

" When we are back in England."

Imogen shook her head decidedly.

" Before that ! "

" I am going to refuse," said I.

" Martin, darling "— she was apparently arguing with an unreasonable child—" you can't keep jewel-stories to yourself when there's a young woman at your elbow."

I knew that it would be difficult when the young woman was Imogen Cloud. Did I say that she

was lovely ? She had a broad, low forehead, eyes
of a golden brown which grew bigger and bigger the
longer you looked at them, with long eyelashes
which had an upward curl at the end of them and
were set there to entangle hearts. Her eyes were
set wide apart, with a delicately-chiselled nose
between them. She had a short upper lip, rows of
white teeth and a little firm chin. She was slender
and supple and just the right height ; tall enough
not to look small, and small enough not to over-
tower you ; and her ankles and wrists were sculpture
at its best. But a description of her features is no
more than a catalogue. It is perhaps more illuminating to say that young men went down before
her like so many ninepins ; that the middle-aged
at the sight of her thought of the fine things which
they had done and wished that she could know of
them ; and that the aged, in the same position,
thanked their stars that modern hygiene had turned
senility into a legend of the past. The truth is
there was a grace of soul in her which matched
the grace of her limbs. Though she had a quick
eye for a foible and a sense of humour which made
play of it, she was kind. Those who talked with
her understood very soon that she considered them.
But I make no further excuses for the deplorable
exhibition which I made later on that evening.
We dined together, Imogen, Pamela Brayburn
and myself. Imogen did not harry me until dinner
was finished and we were smoking over our coffee.

" Now," she said.

" No," said I.

" What ? " asked Pamela Brayburn.

" Nothing," said I.

Imogen turned to Pamela.

" Martin's all up in the air about this sapphire I bought at Kandy," she said. " He has got a story about it and wants to keep it to himself."

" I haven't got a story about it," I declared in desperation. " I have got a story about a quite different sapphire."

My declaration did not help me at all. For Imogen rejoined :

" Then we'll hear the story about the different sapphire."

" Not now," I answered. " It's a very long story—very, very long and tedious. Some afternoon when we're half-way across the Indian Ocean I'll tell it you."

" I don't think that we can all go home on the same ship unless we're told this jewel-story to-night," said Pamela Brayburn. She was a brown-haired girl of Imogen's age and no doubt attractive. At the moment I resented her.

" Very well, we'll go on different ships," I returned.

Pamela looked at me. I might have been a nonesuch. She smiled at Imogen.

" I think Martin's stupid," she said sweetly.

What can you do with people like that ? Argument was out of the question. There was a big clock upon the wall and I pointed to it.

" It's nine o'clock," I said. " The difference between enjoyment and fatigue to-morrow means two and a half hours in bed now with your clothes off."

Pamela looked at me broodingly, and turned with a nod to Imogen.

" He's a sexual maniac, I suppose."

" I'm nothing of the sort," I cried hotly, and stopped. I was not going to be betrayed into behaving still more like an idiot than I had been doing for Pamela Brayburn's amusement.

" But, Martin, darling," Imogen asked, " how can you expect us to go to bed and sleep with that untold story upon our minds ? "

" You must put it out of your heads altogether," I explained with perhaps an accent of the instructor. For I saw Imogen's cheeks dimple suddenly. " And the best way is five minutes' general conversation and then to bed."

" Yes," said Pamela.

" Yes," said Imogen.

And they both waited, with their eyes round and serious upon my face, for me to begin. They were baiting me—these two girls. If they had been tigers in the jungle they wouldn't have dared to do it. But I couldn't say that. It would have sounded boastful and it wouldn't have been general conversation. I had to think of something which would set the ball rolling and so I made as lamentable a remark as any man gravelled for lack of a subject could have let slip. I said :

" Is not the peacock a beautiful bird ? "

The reaction of my companions was immediate. Imogen clapped her handkerchief to her mouth and rolled and shook in her chair. Pamela openly screamed her delight so that everyone in the room looked at us. It was the end of my resistance. I began to think that I was after all making too much of a coincidence. I had no wish to infect the girls with my forebodings. So out the whole story came, the history of the sapphire and Ma Shwe At and Ma Sein at Tagaung and the evolution of Michael D. into Uncle Sunday.

" I think that I should like to meet your Uncle Sunday," Imogen said in a very quiet voice when I had finished.

" I hope that you won't," I exclaimed fervently.

Imogen's eyes rested for a moment upon my face.

" But you think I will," she replied quietly.

" No ! I don't ! " I cried.

But did I ? Was the violence of my denial due to an unacknowledged fear that she would at some destined time meet Michael Crowther and be swept up into a web of peril and misfortune, at the heart of which the deep blue of a sapphire softly gleamed ? I cannot tell. All I know is that I felt a chill creep along my spine and I shuddered. Somebody was walking over my grave. " Let us go," I said, and I got up.

We met again in the dining-room at a quarter to twelve, drank some coffee, and started as the clock struck midnight. We took a guide from the hotel to show the way and carry the wraps, and we drove in my hired car the first fourteen miles to Laxapana. There we left the car and walking up a glen with a river rushing down it like a Highland valley, we mounted by the rock steps and jungle paths towards Oosamalle at the foot of the final peak. It was a clear and moonless night with the sky one soft blaze of stars ; and above us and below us in the

zigzag paths were little bands of pilgrims, their
lanterns flashing in and out amongst the trees,
their voices chanting as they went.

"I have never known anything so lovely," said
Imogen.

She and Pamela Brayburn had given their warm
cloaks to the guide. They were both dressed in
shirts open at the throat, shorts, stockings gartered
below the knees, and stout shoes. They had the look
of a couple of schoolboys. Our guide carried the
lantern just ahead of us, Imogen behind him and
I at the tail. Here and there the steps cut in the
solid rock were steep and disappeared into caverns;
here and there were chains. The mountain-side
was alive with lights and vocal with hymns. The
hymns floated down to us airy and delicate as though
they were sung by the spirits of the Peak, and rose
up from the valley reverberating like the music of
water. We left the trees beneath us. The Peak
towered straight above us now, a huge blunt mass
of rock, hiding from us half the starlit sky. We
traversed a ledge with a chain for a hand-rail; a
scramble up over broken rocks; at the end a rough
ladder clamped to a cliff face, and we stepped over
a low brick wall on to the flat summit of the
mountain.

I never saw anything stranger or more memorable
than the top of Adam's Peak. To men with their
blood thinned by the tropics, the air at that height
was cold as an Arctic night; and on the flat, square
surface, of a hundred and fifty feet, great bonfires
flung their sparks and flames into the darkness.
They blazed at the corners, in front of the wooden

canopy which sheltered the sacred footprint, and here and there in no sort of order upon the platform. Above, the stars bright as diamonds crowded the skies ; around us stretched the empty black of the night ; and this little square, eight thousand feet above the sea, was one flickering crimson glare in which shifted and crossed and halted, as though engaged in some fantastic dance, a throng of coolies in rags, Mussulmen in snow-white robes, Buddhist monks in yellow gowns and three Europeans—ourselves. For there were no other Europeans but ourselves upon the Peak that night.

The two girls hurried towards one of these fires, Pamela taking her cloak from the guide as she hurried. The men about the fire made way for them. I held Imogen's thick sable coat for her and as she thrust an arm into a sleeve, the red light played not only upon her face but upon a blue jewel gleaming darkly against her throat. I buttoned the coat close about her neck.

" Better keep warm," I said.

" And hide the sapphire," she added with a slow smile.

" Yes, I meant that too," I said, and I turned to Pamela Brayburn. She was already muffled to the ears.

" We shan't have long to wait," I said, and I suddenly felt Imogen's hand cling to my arm. I blamed myself for a fool. In my haste to hide the jewel at her throat I had really alarmed her, and no doubt to a girl fresh from the guarded ways of England, the throng of strange, dark people upon that lonely summit might well have been alarming.

" It's all right," I said.

This bonfire was towards the eastern corner of the platform and there the crowd was thickest. I drew Imogen and her cousin away. Along the southern parapet there were empty spaces, and we walked across to one of them. From this parapet the mountain dropped in a precipice ; to our left a spur projected and that spur was gemmed with the lights of moving lanterns and articulate with hymns.

" You are not giddy ? " I asked of the two girls. Pamela stood a foot or two behind, Imogen was at my side, her knees touching the low parapet.

" No," she said.

But where we stood, we looked down a sheer wall. Our guide was with us. He stood beside us, so that we were all four looking down the mountain-side.

" That is the more difficult path," he said. " Those who come that way acquire a greater merit."

" Where do they come from ? " I asked idly.

" From Ratnapura ! " he answered, stretching out his arm. " It lies far away in the jungle."

Ratnapura ? I had heard the name, and as I was remembering where I had heard it, a great wave of crimson colour swept across the mountain-top and someone stumbled against Imogen. Stumbled so roughly that she was lifted off her feet. Fortunately, too, she uttered a cry, and as she pitched forward I flung my right arm across the front of her waist and held her. I set her again upon her feet. The man who had stumbled was on his knees on the ground behind us. But before I could lay a hand on him, he had mumbled some words and slipped away into the darkness. But I had caught the words. They asked for pardon ; they talked of an accident. But they were spoken in the Burmese tongue.

I should not have followed the man if I could. I should have stayed with Imogen and her cousin in any case. But I could not have caught him even if I had pursued him. For at that moment a great clamour rang out from end to end of the rock and there was a rush towards the eastern corner. A faint and tender light was welling out of the east. A moment or two more and the sky was broken. Broad bars of cloud edged with gold stood out against a glowing crimson radiance. Prison bars above the mountains of Kandy. The whole effect was violent and lurid. Not a soul upon the Peak but turned his face towards them and so stood immobile and silent whilst the sun rose and the daylight came.

I looked at the rock surface on which we stood. There was not a fissure nor a ridge which could make a man stumble. Then I turned again and leaned over the southern wall. I heard Imogen shiver behind me, and I felt the clutch of her hand. But there was no one near to us now.

" There's no danger," I said.

And there was none. But the cliff plunged sheer for hundreds of feet to a sloping eave which overhung the ground below. Had Imogen fallen from that parapet she must have been dashed to pieces in the fall !

Behind me she gasped and uttered a cry. I had been holding her away so that she should not see. Even if she had now seen, I turned about and stood between her and the wall so that she should see no more. But she was not looking down the precipice. She was looking straight outwards to the west and her eyes were filled with wonder instead of fear.

I, too, gasped when I saw what Imogen saw—the miracle of the shadow. It was flung out across the white morning mists in the shape of a perfect cone. It was gigantic and lay across the world, its apex touching the distant clouds. It was transparent, for the mists thinned away underneath and green jungle and brown rock and the sparkle of the sea swam into view. There it rested whilst the sun rose behind our shoulders, a pyramid of gauze so exactly edged and pointed that it might have been carved out of stone. Then at a certain moment it began not so much to fade as to foreshorten. It came back on us as we watched it from the wall ; and quicker with each second which passed. It was as though the Peak drew it in and consumed it impatiently. In the end it rushed like a shutter which a spring releases and was gone. Below us stretched rock and shining forest, and far away the sparkle of the sea.

Imogen caught Pamela with one hand and me with the other.

" I am glad I saw that," she cried. " The shadow ! Everyone has talked of it. But I couldn't imagine it was anything so wonderful ! "

" Nor I," said Pamela.

The shadow had been lifted too from Imogen. The bonfires had died down and though the air was sharp the sunlight lit up the platform from end to end. The pilgrims, their pilgrimage over, were crowded about the ladder. We moved to the chain which guarded the sacred footprint, in the very centre of the flat summit.

" Well, I'll say this for his nibs "—thus Pamela irreverently referred to Gautama or Siva or Adam—" he didn't pinch his feet."

Since the foot was five feet long and thirty inches broad, we could all agree with her.

" And I'll say this for myself," Pamela added. " If the whole of him matched his feet, he still couldn't want his breakfast more than I do ! My mother gave me two pieces of advice when I left home. ' Darling Pamela,' she said, ' first, never go without your breakfast, for if you do your gastric juices will eat you like alligators; and secondly, if you find yourself with four kings in a little poker game on board a liner, throw your hand in for the dealer has four aces.' "

" I should like to meet your mother," I said.

Pamela shook her head.

" You would not. For if mother heard that you had taken two weak, lonely girls up to the top of a mountain without so much as a sandwich in a newspaper, she'd drive you screaming from the house."

I nodded my head two or three times.

" You'll eat those harsh words before the morning's out."

" They'll be something to eat, anyway," said Pamela.

We laughed. Imogen seemed quite to have forgotten her moment of danger. Pamela Brayburn, it seemed to me, was forcing her humour in order to obliterate that moment and, judging from the steadiness of Imogen's face, was successful.

" Shall we go ? " she asked.

The enclosure was emptying fast, and we could hear, already far down the hill-side, the cries of the pilgrims returning to the valleys.

" In a second," I answered. In spite of Pamela's appetite we might as well be the last to go. But Pamela raised no objection. We were all, I think, determined that no other accident should imperil Imogen, and a little alarmed, too, by a sort of composite recollection of all the legends which attribute curses to jewels. However, dawdle as we might, we were still not the last to leave. The guide climbed down the ladder first, Imogen followed him, next came Pamela, and I last, taking very good care that no one should pass me. In the same order we made our traverse across the ledge and descended to the tree-line. Half an hour lower down the interminable steps were interrupted by a path and a glade with one or two enormous images of stone scattered about it. I never learned how they came to be there. It looked as if a thousand slaves of a bygone king when Rome was young, being bidden to carry these images to the mountain-top had got so bored with their task that they had thrown them down and preferred there and then to die. However, I recognised the place of these monstrosities in the long chain of purpose when I saw Imogen and Pamela spreading their cloaks on the ground in front of one of them. The slaves might not have known what final cause made them cease to do, and die, but I hoped that looking down from Paradise they now saw Imogen and Pamela leaning their backs restfully against a huge stone gentleman and understood the wise order of events and were content. Trees made a pleasant shade above our heads. Outside the ring of their foliage every pebble flashed like glass. Within our view and call stood a row of huts and along the path in front of them passed family after family of pilgrims, happy in the consciousness of the great merit which that day they had achieved.

" Breakfast," said I rather proudly.

" Such as ? " asked Pamela, turning up her nose.

I had selected the breakfast and the guide had carried it. I thought very well of it. Without a rejoinder I spread it out in front of them. It consisted of sardines, a loaf, chicken, *pâté de foie gras*, fruit, and a bottle of champagne. And when we had finished them, we, too, were conscious of merit. Pamela reclined on her elbow smoking a cigarette, and nodded her head at me.

" You may meet my mother after all. When I was a baby she always said to me : ' *Pâté de foie gras* is more nourishing than Glaxo.' " Then she stretched herself.

" Think of all the other tourists ! " she cried with an infinite compassion. " Poor people ! I shall express my pity to them over and over again in no uncertain terms."

" You will be popular," said I.

" They'll hate me," Pamela returned, with a glow of satisfaction.

Imogen was lying stretched upon her back, her head resting upon her hands, her face upturned to the shading trees. She looked more like a slim schoolboy than ever.

" We might drive down to Kandy this afternoon and begin the good work," she drawled.

I sat up and looked at her. She had tucked her sapphire well out of sight. I had an intuition that she was really anxious to get away from the neighbourhood, however carelessly she spoke. She had, after all, been within a hand's breadth of a quite horrible death. Nothing could be more natural than that she should wish to put a wide distance between herself and the spot where an accident so nearly fatal had happened.

" I'll drive you both down," I said, and from under her half-closed eyelids her eyes shot me a glance of gratitude. " You have a maid with you ? "

" Yes."

" She can take your luggage by train."

So it was arranged and we descended the rest of the steps and tramped down the glen to the car by the bridge across the tumbling stream. I had left a second bottle of champagne hidden amongst the cushions ; and thus, more conscious of our high merit than ever, we reached Hatton by eleven and Kandy before the night fell.

Over dinner that night we debated plans. At least I debated and they decided. I suppose that if people in love can possibly make a mess of their love-making in the early days of their courtship, they generally do. I followed that rule.

" Couldn't we keep together ? "

That was good and asked with a modest eagerness. But I must spoil it all by adding :

" We must, of course, give a day or two to Kandy."

" You can 'ave Kandy," said Pamela, adapting the unforgettable aphorism of the lamented money-lender almost before I had finished.

" We are going to Anuradhapura by car in the morning," Imogen said in the same breath. " You see we've already spent some time in Kandy."

Imogen had the nerve to say that.

" Ah, yes," I said slowly. " Yes, I see."

" We've got to have a look at that old brass palace and the big man's bo-tree," Pamela continued.

" Of course you have," I agreed, as heartily as I could.

To tell the truth I was terribly hurt. The two girls had been looking up the guide-books whilst they changed for dinner. They had made their plan ; they had come down prepared to declare it at the first moment and rather aggressively. And their purpose would have been plain to a blind man. They did not want to see any bo-tree. The brass palace could be a mass of iron junk so far as they were concerned. No, they wanted to be free of me. So they put quite definitely as many miles as possible between us. Very well ! They certainly should not be prevented. I had no wish to be their parasite.

" I am sorry," I said, rather proud of the indifference of my tone. " But we shall meet, no doubt, one day in London."

There was a definite interval of silence. Pamela looked at Imogen and Imogen looked at Pamela. Pamela lifted her eyebrows. A question : " Shall

I ? " Ever so slightly Imogen shook her head. I
was not going to distress myself. They had tried
me out for a day and found me wanting. They
were quite entitled to. There was no need for
Pamela to ask of her friend whether they oughtn't
to be civil. Not the slightest, and Imogen was
perfectly right to answer " No." I had no wish to
be let down easily by Pamela Brayburn. In the
end it was Imogen who spoke.

" But, Martin, you'll be coming to Anuradhapura.
You can't come to Ceylon and not see one of the
Buried Cities, especially when I ask you to come ! "

A little too late that final clause. Still, it was
rather like her hand on my sleeve. But I shook it
off. No cajolements for me !

" No doubt I shall roll along there some time," I
replied. " I have promised to put in a couple of
days with a friend here."

There was not a word of truth in what I said. I
had no friend in Kandy, and if I had had one I
should have broken every promise to him at a real
nod from Imogen. I was aching to go on to
Anuradhapura. But I did not get that real nod. I
just got a conventional politeness. She said :

" Very well, we'll wait for you there. You'll be
two days here, you say."

" Two or three," I answered. " You'll want three,
I am sure."

Now Imogen was offended, although, upon my
word, I couldn't see the slightest excuse for offence
in my words or my manner. I was careful to be
studiously polite. But none the less we passed a
stiff and uncomfortable evening. They retired

early, as indeed after this long day was to be expected. But I did not expect the outburst of indignation from Pamela which followed upon our formal " Good night."

Imogen was half-way up the stairs, and Pamela just behind her. I was standing in the lounge, wondering whether after all Crowther wasn't right, and to cease to exist as a separate entity wasn't the final ideal one could aim at. Suddenly Pamela stopped. She turned, she came running down the stairs, her face in a flame. She ran straight up to me and stamped her foot.

" Can't you see an inch before your nose ? " she asked. " Can't you guess what happened this morning ? "

" What happened this morning ? " I repeated, and as I stared at her blankly, she flung at me :

" I think you are the world's perfect idiot."

I was staggered. I could think of no rejoinder but one which Captain Crowther had used to me. I said :

" You do surprise me."

And like Captain Crowther I really was surprised.

CHAPTER X

I SULKED about Kandy for three days. I did every proper thing. I saw the sacred Tooth and I visited the Peradeniya Gardens and I drove along Lady Horton's road under the arches of high bamboos. I admired the lake and the library and the opulence of the flowers and the fire-flies at night and the blue of the afternoons. At intervals of five minutes I said to myself with determination : " I wouldn't have missed this for worlds. The only way to see things really is to be alone." And at the end of the third day I could have wept.

On the morning of the fourth day I awoke with a curious exhilaration. I explained it to myself very reasonably.

" That means that I am looking forward im-mensely to seeing at last the famous Brazen Palace at Anuradhapura."

I dressed quickly, ate my breakfast more quickly still, ordered my car to be brought round and strolled out of the hotel. There I suffered the worst shock of my life. For on the stone parapet which bordered the lakes, at a point just opposite to the door of the hotel, sat Uncle Sunday—no, I am wrong —sat Michael Crowther—no, I am wrong again—sat

Michael D. I was so dumbfounded that I had to pass through these successive phases of recognition before I could place this odd apparition in its proper class. It was Michael D. at his worst. Michael D. in a mufti which dubbed him Michael D. as surely as a king's sword dubs a squire a knight.

I had never seen a panoply so outrageous. Yet no passer-by was even annoyed by it. I had to remember that the miracles of the West are the commonplaces of the East. He wore a sun-helmet, of course, like the rest of us, but nothing else like the rest of us. He was clothed in a jacket of dark tweed so thick and heavy that it made me perspire to look at it, a white cotton shirt very open at the throat, with enormous wings to the collar which covered the lapels of his coat. The Moore and Burgess shirt was caught in at the waist by a cricket belt of the I. Zingari colours and below the belt white drill knickerbockers decorated his knees and thighs. He wore, with the white knicker-bockers, thick, dark woollen stockings and—horrible, most horrible—white canvas shoes with patent-leather toe-caps and patent-leather fancy strappings.

At the first glance I could not believe my eyes. At the second I did not want to. For the first time I rejoiced that Imogen was eighty miles away at Anuradhapura. For the second time I feared that neither distance nor effort could keep her out of this man's orbit. I was going to do what I could, however. I set off at a brisk pace down the road as if I had not recognised him—a foolish manœuvre, for I should have to come back for my car, and

Michael D. would still be waiting on the parapet above the water.   So I stopped in front of a jeweller's window and pretended to examine its contents. Out of the tail of my eye I saw my car brought to the hotel door and my baggage placed in the back of it.   Then I strolled back.   Michael D. sat still, quietly and absolutely certain that I should be compelled to approach him.   I had no such intention.   I grew hot over his conceit.   If he imagined himself to be a magnet, I knew that I was the silver churn.   He could not attract me.   I took my seat in the car and then he rose from the balustrade and crossed the road to me.   It gave me a little pleasure that he had to make the move.   It encouraged me, too.   I said to myself : " You take me for a pongyi's acolyte, do you ?   I'll show you."   But I saw his face now, and both my resentment and my satisfaction became, in a second, trivial and mean.   For it was not Michael D. who looked at me, but Uncle Sunday—Uncle Sunday all the more Uncle Sunday because of his absurd clothes—and with so poignant a distress in his sharpened face that pity must go out to him.   I had not the heart even to be witty about his dress.

" I was waiting for you," he said.

" So I saw," I replied.

I sat in my seat for a moment.   There was nothing for it.   I nodded my head and got down from the car.

" I shall be a little while," I said resignedly to the porter.   " Please look after the car."

We walked away from the lake across the green square to the precinct of the Garden Temple, and sitting down upon a stone bench amongst the pagodas and the banyan-trees, Crowther told me of how he had returned from Schwegu to find his votive offering stolen from the high spire at the monastery door.

His story was a dreadful shock to me. I heard it with a distress not to be stilled by any argument that there might be two sapphires of exactly the same shape and size and colour. The sapphire which Imogen possessed was the sapphire from the pagoda spire at Pagan. I was convinced of it and on the top of that conviction a cloud of dim fears moved across my mind. I had as yet no details. I had drawn no deductions. I had not reasoned. I was simply frightened. Imogen had been drawn into the orbit of the sapphire. And my fear, although I am not more sensitive than other people and very probably not as sensitive as most, showed itself to me in a succession of the vague, rather meaningless and altogether alarming pictures which are apt to afflict the dreams of children. Before I could put a question to Crowther, he added as a corollary to his story :

" You will understand, then, Mr. Legatt, that I am obligated to repair that sacrilege."

I was on edge. I turned upon him. It ought, of course, to have been his smug concentration upon himself which made me turn. But if you are on edge, it's the trumpery irrelevance which suddenly makes life impossible.

" You mustn't talk like that, Michael D.," I shouted violently.

" Long ago I dropped the D.," Crowther answered meekly.

" You can't," I insisted.   " You're obligated to keep it, so long as you're obligated to anything."

Crowther was penitent. There was less of Michael D. in him than there had been at any time.

" I should, no doubt, have said obliged.   I think that probably the clothes I am wearing—I bought them without much thought at Rangoon—have lent some of their vulgarity to my speech. What I meant was that I felt bound to restore my offering to its place."

I had cooled down by then.

" Believe me, Michael, I should be very pleased to hear that you had restored it," I said cordially.

Michael was moved by my warmth of tone, but utterly misunderstood it.

" A kind thought confers merit upon the thinker," he replied.

" It wasn't kind.   It was purely selfish."

For the last shape which my fear had taken was oddly enough the shadow of Adam's Peak, and it seemed to stretch not westwards to the sea, but northwards to a buried city in the jungle, and was now less a shadow than a pointing finger.

I asked for details of the theft and I got them. They made my heart jump into my mouth.

" There were two convicts in the monastery ? " I asked.

" Yes.   Nga Pyu and Nga Than."

" Burmese, then ? "

" Yes," said Crowther.   " But there was an accomplice who was not."

I sat up stiff on the bench.

" What's that, Michael ? There was a third, then ? "

" Yes."

" And a foreigner ? "

" An Indian. Muhammed Ghalli."

Of course, there were millions of Muhammeds, I said to myself, and I kept on saying it until the words meant nothing at all. Millions of them ! Millions of them !

" You are quite sure there was a third accomplice ? " I darted at him hopefully.

" Quite. He was with the other two in the same prison. He was released with them. He went up the river on the same steamer with them to Nyaungu. He had the clothes they changed into on the river-bank. They were together in Prome and took the train from there to Rangoon. They sailed from Rangoon on the same ship for Ceylon."

I began to think with a little burst of relief that Crowther was romancing. He was as detailed in his story as Robinson Crusoe. Surely vigils and fasting had made him fanciful. The objection to my theory was that neither vigils nor fasting have any place in the routine of a Buddhist monastery.

" How do you know all this ? " I asked.

Crowther smiled.

" There are many monasteries and many monks moving from one to the other. There are many visitors and much talk during the afternoons. If we want to know anything it is not so difficult."

" I see. A secret service ready made."

I had no doubt of the explanation. The ramifications of the brotherhood were everywhere. There were thousands of pairs of eyes with the time to watch and of ears with the time to listen.

"They came to Ceylon, then! Yes—the three of them, Nga Pyu, Nga Than and Muhammed Ghalli," I agreed.

"After I landed," Crowther continued, "I traced them up from Colombo to Kandy by the same means."

"Yes?"

"At Kandy they sold what they had stolen."

I turned to him quickly.

"To whom?"

"To the jeweller under the hotel. You were looking into his shop window a few minutes ago."

I thought that I saw a flaw here in the link of his story.

"But how could you know that all the ornaments were sold to him? The monks could hardly help you there. They buy nothing. They have no money to spend at jewellers' shops."

"I didn't need them," Crowther replied. "I saw the filigree bracelet and the amber acorn myself, displayed in the window. I went into the shop. He had all the presents I had given to Ma Shwe At. I bought them all back."

I jumped up in an excitement of relief.

"All! That's fine!" I cried.

"All that I had given to Ma Shwe At," he repeated, spacing his words to signify that he meant just what he said and no more. "The sapphire had been sold."

My heart sank again. The sapphire was not one

of Crowther's presents.   They were all insignificant
—images in amber, bits of jade, trinkets of filigree
silver.   The sapphire was the one thing of value
amongst the lot.

" To whom had it been sold ? " I cried.   " No
doubt you asked."

" Oh, yes, I asked all right ! " Crowther returned.
" He sold it to a young English lady.   She had
another young lady with her.   She said to him that
she was going to give herself a present."

There could be no longer, then, the least doubt
in my mind that the sapphire which had shone on
Imogen's throat was the sapphire from Tagaung.
I had never really disbelieved it.   But I did not
want to believe it.   No doubt I was allowing myself
to be tormented by the merest fancy.   But I could
not help myself.   I was sure that there was misfortune in that stolen jewel, and if Imogen possessed
it, the misfortune would be hers too.   There would
be attacks which would look like accidents—nay,
had not one example happened already ?   I could
after all put two and two together.   Two Burmese
ex-convicts and an Indian named Muhammed
Ghalli for a third—two of them at Hatton and the
third coming up from Ratnapura to the foot of the
precipice below Adam's Peak.   Might not the next
one succeed and be fatal ?   I had got to be sure
that Imogen had Crowther's sapphire—sure beyond
the slightest possibility of a doubt—so much
danger shone in it, so much menace made its setting.
Common sense, of course, declared that the question
whether Imogen possessed Crowther's sapphire or
its twin sister made no difference whatever.   Imogen

ran precisely the same risk in either case. But I had in front of me Crowther—the bumptious, thieving, ignoble Michael D. evolving through failure and disappointment and loneliness and misery into Uncle Sunday of the yellow robe. Common sense had a very tiny unconvincing voice to my hearing in that precinct of the Garden Temple under the great trees. I had to be sure about that sapphire. I got up.

" Let us go to the jeweller."

Michael nodded and we walked quickly across the space of green to the hotel and down the slope beside it. The jeweller was a stout, bespectacled, comfortable, greasy Cingalese, with long hair dressed high on his head and held so by a big tortoise-shell comb. He described Imogen sufficiently. I made a last effort to dissociate her from the jewel.

" How was the sapphire set when you sold it to the young lady ? " I asked.

The jeweller explained that he had bought it without any setting at all.

" It was plain—like a sweetmeat that you pop in your mouth. I myself mounted it according to the young lady's wishes. I fixed a tight plain band of platinum round the rim and hung it as a pendant to a platinum chain."

No wish, however urgent, could argue against that statement. Imogen's sapphire was the sapphire given long ago by Ma Shwe At to the Captain of the *Dagonet* that it might be kept safe from the dacoits.

" Thank you," I said, and after buying a small trinket in gratitude for the man's amiability, I went out of the shop and sat with Michael on the balustrade above the water.

"There were two men who spoke Burmese at Hatton," I said slowly.

"Two men," Crowther repeated. He was not very interested.

"Yes. I took them to be coolies from the plantations or pilgrims."

"Did they wear turbans?" Crowther asked. He was kicking the heels of his appalling shoes against the stone parapet as he sat bent forward, with his elbows on his knees. But he was still really unconcerned.

I looked at him sharply. The point to me suddenly became of crucial importance. Burmans wore long hair, skewered up on their heads. But turbans, no! If these two had worn turbans they would have been wearing them to hide a stubble of new hair on a shaven scalp. They would be the ex-convicts for a certainty. But had they worn turbans? I tried to visualise the scene—the hotel at Hatton, the broad street outside, Imogen with her arms stretched wide—Imogen without a turban, the two of us standing side by side—I could feel the pressure of her hand in the crook of my elbow—one man pushing past us, the other saying: "Muhammed is at Ratnapura," my turn-about, and the two men walking away, their backs towards us and one of them reading a telegram. Yes, they had worn turbans. I had not seen their faces, but their backs —yes.

"They did wear turbans," I replied. "Thank you, Michael! That's a very important point."

" I don't think it's important at all," Michael rejoined, still knocking the backs of his shoes against the parapet. They would not stand very much of that usage, but I did not stop him. They were an offence against the world and the sooner he kicked them on to the dust-heap the more merit he would acquire.

" They talked of a third man," I went on. " An Indian, already at Ratnapura—an Indian Muhammed."

" You are not following me, Mr. Legatt," Crowther explained with a quite human testiness. " What does it matter whether the Burmese were at Hatton and the Indian at Ratnapura ? "

" It matters a very great deal to me," I said.

" But the Burmese had sold the sapphire. We have been to the shop where it was sold. We know it. They and the Indian are now out of the picture altogether."

" I wish they were," I answered gravely.

" You have your wish," said Crowther. " The important question is : Who is the young lady who bought it ? "

" That's an easy one," said I.

Crowther turned incredulously towards me.

" You can answer it ? "

" Of course."

" You know her, perhaps ? "

" I do."

It was his turn now to jump with excitement, mine to remain impassive.

" And you can sit there as cold as an icicle," he began, staring at me in his indignation.

We were completely at cross-purposes. He was occupied only with his self-imposed mission. He thought only of the restoration of his offering to its high place on the pagoda spire in far-away Pagan. I was troubled with a more immediate problem.

" You have given me very bad news this morning, Michael," I said.

That stumble on the top of Adam's Peak took on a very ugly look in the light of what he had told me—all the uglier because there had been no excuse for the stumble. I had looked at the spot where it had occurred immediately Imogen was safe. There was no break in the smooth surface of the rock—not a pebble to stub a toe upon. Had those two men been on the Peak with us that morning? Was one of them the man who stumbled?

" Two men on the Peak waiting for their opportunity." I put the case aloud for my own benefit rather than for Crowther's. " The third man coming up from Ratnapura and he, too, waiting—at the foot of the precipice below the overhang. . . . They knew the stone could be marketed. They had sold it once. They could sell it again—if they could steal it again. A crude way of stealing it? Yes. A rather childish way? Yes. And murder? Yes. But that's Burma. . . . And it nearly came off."

I shut my eyes and in that hot sunlight shivered. The next moment I was sitting up stiff and straight with one question clamouring for an answer. Had Imogen understood at once what had been made clear to me only now? I saw the two girls side by side in the hotel on the evening after the ascent. I heard them speaking almost in one breath and

according to plan.   They must go to Anuradhapura
first thing in the morning.   To see the Brazen
Palace ?   As if it was likely to uproot itself and fly
away ?   No.   To put as quickly as possible as wide
a distance as possible between the robbers and themselves ?   Yes.   Surely, yes !   And I had taken
offence !   The world's perfect idiot, said Pamela. . . .
Well, Pamela was right.   I jumped down from the
parapet.

"I'm off," I said, and I crossed the road to my
car.

Crowther ran after me.

"But you'll tell me the young lady's name?" he
pleaded.

"I will not," I replied.

"Where she is, at all events?"

"Nor that," I cried and I slipped behind the wheel
into the driving-seat.   "But listen to me, Michael !
I want you to have that sapphire back.   I want
it tremendously.   There's only one thing in the
world which I want more.   I'm going to try to get
it back for you.   And I think I can—and at once,
too."

I shut the door of the car with a bang.   Crowther's
face cleared as magically as a summer's day.   He
must not thank me, of course.   That would have
been altogether improper and absurd.   I should be
acquiring enormous merit for myself by restoring
to him the stolen jewel.   I might save myself a
hundred existences by this good deed.   But he had
thanks on the tip of his tongue and was in quite a
bother to keep them unspoken.

"I am going north," I continued.   "I'll meet you

the day after to-morrow in the morning. At some
quiet place.''

I did not want Michael Crowther to march in
upon Imogen and Pamela and myself at Anuradhapura. For if I would not allow that he was a
magnet to me, he might very well be one to Nga
Pyu and Nga Than and Muhammed Ghalli ; and
in his reach-me-downs a conspicuous magnet, too.

" I'll be at the Rock Temple at Dhambulla,'' he
said.

The Rock Temple, as all the world knows, is a
famous resort of tourists. If you travel to Ceylon
you must visit it or endure derision upon your
return and some scepticism as to whether you ever
got beyond Paris on your journey out. It would
be, therefore, a natural place for me to journey to.
I could meet Michael Crowther upon its terrace
without arousing any attention.

" It is to the north ? '' I asked.

" Half-way between Kandy and Anuradhapura,''
said he.

" You have been there ? ''

Michael nodded his head, or rather bowed it.
For there was a reverence in his gesture.

" Once. It is very wonderful. It stands high
above the forest and aloof.''

" The very place then,'' I cried. " I'll meet you
there at eleven in the morning.''

I shot the clutch in and started. The best of the
day had gone and I had eighty-four miles to cover.
I was in a desperate hurry now, for I had suddenly
become aware that I must reach Anuradhapura
before dark. The Brazen Palace was a very long

way from the top of Adam's Peak, no doubt, but a fact overlooked till this moment had disclosed itself whilst Michael was speaking and with every minute took on a more enormous importance. Nga Pyu and Nga Than and Muhammed Ghalli had money. They had sold the stolen sapphire. They were rich. If they wanted to travel swiftly, they could. If they knew where Imogen and Pamela Brayburn had sought refuge, they would. And away in the north of the island were those two girls alone and defence-less against them and confident that the eighty-four miles between Kandy and the Buried City meant safety. I drove down from the hills in a panic to the flat country and on through a land of shining green.

CHAPTER XI

THE MAGIC PIPE

BUT I did not, after all, see the Brazen Palace; nor the great moonstone at the steps to the Queen's door; nor the oldest tree in the world. A tyre burst on account of the great heat when I had been an hour upon the road, and at four o'clock in the afternoon I was still some thirty-odd miles this side of Anuradhapura. The road ran through the heart of the jungle between shrubs of scarlet lantana. Creepers with great flowers like painted trumpets laid their stranglehold upon the trees, and butterflies more richly blue than Imogen's sapphire flickered in squadrons through the sunlight and the forest gloom. The car was running silently and to my surprise I heard suddenly from somewhere upon my left, but very near at hand, the music of a pipe. It sounded oddly in that lonely place and perhaps, had there been no further reason, I should still have slowed down my car in spite of the hurry I was in. But the music had a singularly delicate and airy pitch. There was an enchantment in it, a purity and—I have no other word—a singleness, and in addition a compulsion, so that I must go gently and listen as I went. Thus, I thought, Paris must have piped upon Ida. I peered into the forest but the undergrowth was so thick and so blazed with colour that my eyes could not pierce the screen. I drove on again and after a few yards the road swung round to the left in a wide curve, and I lost the music. But I came upon a long, low, rest-house, set back behind a white gate in a green twilight. The tallest tamarinds I had ever seen sheltered it and only here and there through the thick foliage broke a lance of gold. No halting-place more charming could be imagined ; and as I looked at it, I used Pamela's phrase :

" You can 'ave the Brass Palace. It's here that I should find Imogen."

On the instant a voice in front of me cried : " Stop ! " and there, in the middle of the road, stood Pamela Brayburn, with a kodak in her hands. I stopped the car, slipped out of my long dust-coat, got out, and crossed to her.

" You are staying here ? " I cried.

" Yes."

" You and Imogen ? "

" Yes. We took a car and came here yesterday."

I was immensely relieved. The two girls were safe. The shadow which had hung over my spirits vanished as swiftly as the shadow of the Peak.

" But I might have missed you ! " I cried.

" And whose fault would that have been ? " she exclaimed unpleasantly.

" Mine ? " I asked. " I like that ! I was to join you at Anuradhapura."

Pamela drew in a long breath.

" Heaven keep me from falling in love, if it's going to make me such a simpleton ! " she prayed earnestly.

I felt that I was growing red. I think that I shouted at her.

" Who says that I am a simpleton ? "

Pamela hardly let me finish the sentence.

" No one, little boy," she rejoined. She seemed to be exasperated. " No one has any need to. It's sticking out like an ectoplasm at a séance."

She changed her style then and attacked me.

" Why didn't you come with us to Anuradhapura ? " she cried.

I was indignant. Pamela was too unreasonable for words.

" How could I ? " I exclaimed. " You made it impossible. The moment I suggested that we might spend a day or so at Kandy——"

" Looking at an old horse's tooth ! " she interrupted irreverently.

" —You both cried in one voice : ' We're off the first thing in the morning to see the bo-tree '."

" We neither of us could have said anything so ridiculous," said Pamela.

" Well, words to that effect," I answered. " It seemed obvious that you wanted to be rid of me."

Pamela shook a finger at me triumphantly.

" That's vanity—that is," she said. " But men are terribly vain."

I laughed—sardonically is the right word.

" Men don't examine themselves in looking-glasses all day."

" They daren't," said Pamela. " They'd cut their throats if they did."

I laughed. It only amounted to a snigger after all, and it seemed even as a snigger rather contemptible even to me. Pamela leaned towards me with a superfluity of kindliness.

"Did you ever," she asked, "see any of those pictures which newspapers are always publishing of men in the eighties and early nineties—men with big sprawly beards and short frock-coats and stiff straw hats—boaters you call them, I think."

"Awful!" I said, falling into her trap.

"Yes, awful," she agreed. "But are you quite sure that the awfulness ended with that era? To put it plainly—may I put it plainly?" Her voice was full of honey.

"Yes," I said.

"Looking at things objectively, aren't men awful now? Spats, for instance. Will you consider spats, Martin, as a method of adornment? Big feet in shiny boots and glaring white spats to wrap them up and crinkly trousers above them? Are you really sure, looking down through the ages, that men aren't always awful?"

I felt myself to be a fit subject for pathos. For whenever I was not worried out of my life by Imogen, I was quarrelling with Pamela. But I had the better of her in this argument. I could afford to laugh disdainfully.

"My dear Pamela, you must go to Burma," I said. Pamela answered rudely.

"To get my wits polished," said she sarcastically.

"To learn a very bitter home truth," I rejoined. "You will have to be re-born a man as a first step towards entering into the Great Peace."

"Then give me the Great Hullaballoo!" said Pamela.

I must admit that as I looked her slim figure up and down, I recognised a certain attractiveness in her appearance which made me doubt the desirability of Buddha's rules. However, it seemed that there was nothing to be gained by pursuing the controversy. I had put Pamela in her place—or I had not. I should get no change out of it anyway. I started off briskly upon a different topic.

" Anyway, Pamela, I hope that you enjoyed yourselves in Anuradhapura."

"We didn't," Pamela answered uncompromisingly. " We haven't enjoyed ourselves since you deserted us at Kandy——"

" Well, of all the——" I could not go on. Pamela's serene distortion of the truth took my breath away.

" Except," she continued, " for one hour this afternoon when a conjurer with several cobras in a bottle turned up here and made them dance for us."

" Cobras ! " I exclaimed. I have hated all snakes all my life, anyway.

" Cobras de capello," Pamela repeated firmly. " They were charming. He blew a little pipe and they wiggled their heads about and they lay flat on the ground when he told them to, and he beat the ground close to them with his stick and they never moved. He was a magician."

I stood up straight.

" I heard his pipe, I think, just before I came round the corner there."

" Then he was repeating his performance for the

chauffeur and the servants behind the bungalow,"
said Pamela. " He had finished with us an hour
ago."

I looked back along the road. Yes, it bent round
the bungalow to its front. I could not hear a sound
of the piping where I stood. No doubt he had
repeated his performance in the service quarters
behind.

" An hour ago ? Where's Imogen, then ? " I
asked.

" She went to lie down in her room as soon as the
snake-charmer had finished," Pamela answered.
She looked at me, her eyes hard with accusation.
" Imogen didn't sleep last night."

" Oh ! "

But I must suppose that I expressed in that
exclamation distress and not contrition. For again
she shook a finger and there was steel in her voice
now as well as in her eyes.

" Of course she didn't."

My heart made a foolish jump. She had missed
someone, then. Who ? It was not for me to say.

" Why didn't she sleep ? " I asked, as innocent as
a man could be.

Pamela flung up her hands.

" Have you no idea why we bolted from Kandy ? "

Yes, I had an idea to account for that—an idea
which had only lost its terror since I had found the
two girls safe in this forest bungalow. But I could
not see what in the world that could have to do
with Imogen's inability to sleep at Anuradhapura.

" Then you did bolt ! " I cried.

" Then you knew we had bolted," cried Pamela.

" No, I didn't," I returned hotly. " I may be an idiot but I don't cart my friends. I hadn't a suspicion that you were bolting until this morning. Even now it's only a suspicion."

Pamela looked at me for a few moments.

" Very well. If you'll drive your car into the enclosure and secure a room—we're alone here now, but some other party of tourists may come along at any moment—I'll tell you."

I got into the car again, drove between the gate-posts and handed over my baggage to the keeper of the rest-house, whilst Pamela followed me.

" It's just as well that you should know before Imogen joins us," she said. We sat down in long chairs on the verandah. Pamela drank lemonade, I something with lemon in it and no " ade." We sat in cool shadows. Far away great rocks like huge uncut blue jewels cropped up above a sea of green and gold. The very peace of the scene was enough to take the heart of terror out of any tale however terrible. And the danger was over. I stretched out my legs on the long wooden arm of the chair. Pamela was here. Imogen was asleep. I was at my ease. But I was sitting up straight before she had half finished her story of what had actually happened on Adam's Peak and I was on my feet when she had reached the end.

" You told us over dinner at Hatton of the marvellous resemblance of Imogen's sapphire to the sapphire of your friend, Crowther. But you weren't comfortable. You were afraid, and fear's horribly contagious. Although we both made light of the resemblance we were a little frightened, too. And we had more reason to be frightened than you. Yes, we had. For you had pointed out before two men in the street who were talking Burmese. And we had seen those two men outside the shop in Kandy where Imogen bought the sapphire. Now they were outside our hotel at Hatton. We were alarmed."

I interrupted her here.

"Yet Imogen wore the sapphire the next morning when we climbed the mountain," I said.

"I know. You see she had worn it always, ever since she had bought it, and not to wear it now was to own to fear. And Imogen didn't want to do that. It wasn't bravado. It was a feeling that once you acknowledge fear, you're likely to crumble altogether. Can you follow that ? So she wore it. No doubt she thought, too, that since you were with us we should be safe "—Pamela put her nose in the air— "the poor simp ! "

"Well, you were safe," said I indignantly.

"Hansard reports at these words, sardonic cheers from the Opposition," Pamela continued. "Do you remember that when we stepped out on to the Peak we stood in front of a great bonfire to warm ourselves ? "

"I do."

"Has it dawned upon you—but it must have ; you're as quick as a little snake, aren't you ? Then it must have dawned upon you that as Imogen slipped on her cloak—and honest to goodness, I've never seen a cloak so clumsily held in all my long life—the sapphire was showing at her throat."

" I did notice that," I exclaimed. " I buttoned Imogen's coat high under her chin on purpose."

" But too late," said Pamela.

It was then that I began to sit up in my chair.

" What do you mean ? " I asked.

" Opposite to her on the far side of the bonfire," Pamela explained, " were the two men who spoke Burmese. Something of a shock, eh ? " Pamela nodded her head at me. She was serious, like one who has seen a great danger just avoided. " You see ? The two men outside the shop at Kandy when Imogen came out with the chain round her neck, then outside the hotel at Hatton, then on the top of the mountain—and your story of the sapphire. Imogen hadn't a doubt that your friend's sapphire had been stolen and sold and was to be stolen again. But even then she was only afraid. She hadn't a suspicion as to how for the second time it was to be stolen."

For a moment I did not answer. I saw the broad surface of the mountain-top, the flames of the bonfires licking the black air, the waves of red colour lighting up the throng of dark faces and white robes. I drew Imogen and Pamela again to the empty space at the precipice's edge. I cried :

" Then the pilgrim who stumbled against Imogen——"

" He was one of the two. He didn't stumble at all. He was making sure of her and of the sapphire. If you hadn't been there close beside her, he would have made sure."

" How ? "

" He took her by the ankle and flung her forward off her feet."

" What ! " I cried.

" Nothing could have been more deliberate than that stumble. The man wasn't trying to save himself. His hand closed round Imogen's ankle as tight as a band and she was thrown—up and out."

And the third man—the man from Ratnapura, was waiting below the overhang at the foot of the precipice. I did not mention the third man to Pamela, partly because I did not wish the two girls to visualise any more clearly than they already did the cruel murder from which Imogen had been saved, but chiefly because I was marvelling at Imogen's courage and spirit. Of the three of us, she was the only one who had a suspicion—and she was certain—that an attempt had been made upon her life. She must have seen herself whizzing downwards, must have felt in all her nerves the smash of bone and flesh upon the pent-house slope of rock, the destruction in a moment of her grace and beauty.

" And yet Imogen never said a word."

There she had stood whilst the dawn broke and the shadow ran out over jungle and sea, and hung there, and raced back again into the mountain. There Imogen had stood without a glance behind her, and so far as I could remember without a tremor of her hand upon my arm.

" Oh, Imogen was in a panic," Pamela explained. " But we were alone up there, Imogen, you and I—just the three of us on a terrace crowded with fanatics. She dared not be afraid. She *had* to keep her head."

" Bless her, she did ! " I answered.

How long had we stayed after the attempt upon the Peak ? An hour ? An hour and a half ? We had certainly not started down until the day was broad. Then there was a rickety ladder against a cliff to be descended and a traverse across the face of the rock and a pathway of rough, steep rock steps through a cavern of trees, which made a twilight even of noonday.

" Even afterwards she didn't make a sign, didn't say a word, of the ordeal she had been through ! "

I pictured her again lying upon her back after breakfast, the smoke of her cigarette floating upwards under the trees.

" There was no use in talking about it," said Pamela. " Talking about it meant fear, and fear mustn't be. That's Imogen's creed. Once be afraid and you have nothing under your feet. You're a straw in the air. You must show yourself you're not afraid and then perhaps you won't be. That's why Imogen wore the sapphire up the mountain. You must show everybody else, too, that you're not afraid, otherwise you will be. That's why she wouldn't let me ask you to come along with us to Anuradhapura. You must come on your own suggestion entirely."

" You didn't give me much encouragement," I grumbled.

" You were too prickly for words," Pamela rejoined calmly. " And after all, in my day young men didn't want encouragement. We couldn't keep them off with a gatling gun."

"Said she modestly," I added.

But I was not proud of my performance or my perspicacity at our dinner in the Hatton Hotel. I was anxious to get away from the subject altogether.

"Well, however much you may blame me, you were all right at Anuradhapura," I said comfortably.

"Were we?" Pamela asked. "Oh, I am so glad to know that!"

"Weren't you?" I asked anxiously.

I could never be sure whether to take her words as a statement of fact or a provocation to battle.

"Then why are we here?" she demanded, and with a sweep of her arm she dramatised the isolation of the bungalow. "What do you take us for, Martin? Shy nudists?"

"I do not," I said firmly. "I can't accept the 'shy'."

Pamela laughed. Then in a quieter voice she explained: "We were followed to Anuradhapura" —and I jumped.

"By the same men?"

Pamela nodded.

"The two men of Kandy and Hatton and the mountain. I don't suppose we were difficult to trace. The servants at the hotel in Kandy knew. So did the people at the garage where we hired our car. Imogen saw them at Anuradhapura from the balcony outside her window the night before last.

They were standing on the grass outside the hotel. The light from a lamp fell upon their faces."

Imogen had turned out her light and had called Pamela into her room. Together they had recognised the two men, watched them from the darkness as they whispered together on the plot of grass below. The hotel was outside the city with a tiny park in front of it, and beyond this open space a high grove of rain-trees.

" I would have liked Imogen to throw the sapphire and the chain out to them and have done with it," Pamela related. " But Imogen wouldn't give in. She clasped the chain about her throat."

The two girls had stayed in the same room that night, behind their locked doors, and kept watch in turn until the daylight came.

" It was no use complaining," said Pamela. " We had no real evidence of the attack on Imogen on the mountain ; we couldn't even prove that we had been followed. We should just have looked like a couple of bright young spirits advertising themselves in the usual way. We had noticed this rest-house on the way to Anuradhapura. We went sightseeing in the morning as if we were settled in the place for some days. Then in the afternoon we bolted again."

The rest-house was certainly a place of secrecy and peace. And yet was it not a trifle too secret—too peaceful ? Here was the afternoon waning and never a glimpse of Imogen. I was beginning to be tormented by anxiety.

" How many men followed you to Anuradhapura ? " I asked.

Pamela stared at me frowning.

" Two, of course. I told you two. The two outside the jeweller's shop and outside the hotel at Hatton."

" Yes, but there was a third," I said.

" A third—accomplice ? " Pamela asked, holding her breath.

" Yes. A man who was to come up to the foot of the Peak from Ratnapura—who was waiting at the foot of that precipice."

Pamela started back in her chair. Then she rejected my statement.

" Too childish a plot ! " she said.

" Yes," I agreed. " Too childish and too cruel. In fact, thoroughly Burmese."

And whilst Pamela, her face pale, her forehead drawn, sat in startled silence, I said to myself : " Yes, but the third partner in this crime was not a Burman "—and suddenly I seemed to hear again the airy music of a pipe. I heard it only in my memory. For there could never be a deeper silence than the silence which here held bough and bird and the wind itself in thrall. In another hour the jungle would be shrill with cicadas, and the murmur of innumerable insects would throb with the thunder of a drum. But now there was silence and more than silence. There was suspense. Once, years before, in a clearing of the teak-wood by the Irrawaddy and again in a street of Mandalay I had been conscious of it, a sharer in the expectancy which hushed all nature.

" Tell me ! " I said. " Who was this conjurer with the cobras."

" I don't know."

" A Cingalese ? "

Pamela shook her head.

" No. He wore a turban. He told us that he was an Indian from Coromandel."

It was then that I started to my feet.

" An Indian ? Did he give you a name ? "

" No."

The two Burmese at Hatton and Muhammed Ghalli at Ratnapura. The two Burmese at Anuradhapura and Muhammed Ghalli at the forest bungalow. Snake-charming—not so rare a gift! Cingalese, Indians, Egyptians—who that has ever travelled hasn't seen one of them at his work ?

" You are so still," said Pamela uneasily.

" Don't you think," I asked—and I tried to give to my voice the most level and commonplace of notes—" don't you think that we might rouse Imogen ? "

Apparently I had not succeeded. I did not look at Pamela lest my face should betray the terror of my heart. But I heard her draw in her breath in a long, fluttering sigh.

" You know her room, of course ? " I said.

We both stood up, and with a pitiable mimicry of nonchalance we walked into the passage of the house.

CHAPTER XII

FEAR AND IMOGEN

O N our left as we entered the bungalow was the big living-room. Once beyond it the corridor ran to right and left, like the cross-bar of a capital T. Pamela turned to the left, and facing us at the end of the building was a closed door.

"That's Imogen's room," she said. "Mine is just this side of it beyond the living-room."

We walked to it. My shoes were soled with crêpe rubber ; Pamela's light feet made no noise whatever. At the door we halted. It was so still that the sudden hum of a dragon-fly, flashing in from the verandah and out again with a gleam of metal, startled us both like artillery. Pamela stood for a moment with her hand at her heart, catching her breath ; and I leaned back against the wall no better off. Pamela, indeed, was the first to recover.

"Imogen may be still asleep," she said in a whisper ; and very carefully she turned the handle of the door and pressed. But it did not open.

"It's locked," she said in the same low voice, and she leaned an ear against the panel. I saw a look of bewilderment overspread her face and she turned the handle back, so that the latch fitted again into its socket, without a sound. She drew back a step or two, and as I joined her she said :

" I don't understand. Imogen's there in the room, but she might have been running a mile."

Could there be a statement more alarming ? She might have been running a mile. That might mean unconsciousness, pain, terror—anything but natural sleep. In my turn I stepped forward, but my heart was beating so noisily that I could hear nothing else. I called quietly, my mouth against the panel of the door.

" Imogen ! Imogen ! "

I was answered by a sob and even that was subdued, as though someone listened, someone who was blind, and dangerous. I flung my shoulders against the door, but the lock held, and above the rattle and thud Imogen's voice rose in a broken scream.

"Don't, Martin ! It's no good ! Please ! Please ! "

There was such urgency and such panic as I had never heard in human voice. If Imogen had held fear at arm's length on Adam's Peak, it had got her by the throat now—and by the limbs. For there had not been the sound of a movement within the room. I swung round to Pamela.

" Which way does Imogen's window look ? " I whispered.

" To the back of the bungalow.." said Pamela.

I was aghast. It was from the back of the bungalow that the thin, faint music of the snake-charmer's pipe had reached my ears.

I called again through the door :

" Hold on, my dear, for a second," and again

Imogen's voice ran up and down the scale of terror.

" No, Martin. You can't do a thing ! "

I beckoned to Pamela. We hurried back along the corridor and on to the verandah and round the corner of the rest-house to the rear of it. A great hedge of lantana shut us off from the outbuildings. In front of us was a window with its shutters closed. I moved forward and touched them. At the touch they fell apart. They had not been bolted from within—therefore not bolted at all ; and the window was open. I looked into the room.

There was a bedstead on my right hand with its mosquito curtains folded on the top of the frame ; and no one had rested on the bed. There was the usual furniture, a sun-helmet on a table, a mat by the side of the bed, a brown teak floor—and Imogen. I shall never forget the sight of her. She was standing upright against the wall opposite to the bed, with her arms a little outspread and the palms of her hands pressed against the panelling to keep herself upright. She had thrown off her hat. She was wearing a dark blue coat and skirt, with a white shirt, beige stockings and blue shoes to match her dress, and the shoes and her ankles were pressed tightly together, to occupy as little room as was possible. Her eyes were wide open and fixed upon some spot on the floor a yard or so in front of her. She was in a trance, if terror can cause a trance. For from head to foot she was bound fast by terror.

As the shutters opened she cast one swift glance towards them. Then her eyes went back to the floor.

F

"Martin," she whispered. "Don't move, Martin! It'll strike if you do. He warned me. Move and it'll strike!"

And there was nothing at all on the floor.

I sprang over the window-sill.

"Imogen——" I began.

"Keep away! Keep away!"

She had leaned a little forward and her voice rose to a scream. So I took a stride and stood deliberately on the very spot on which her eyes were fixed. For a second she giggled like a schoolgirl —I never heard a sound more distressing—and then, without any warning, slid sideways down the wall. I was just in time to catch her as she fell.

I carried her to the bed and laid her upon it. Then I unlocked the door and called to Pamela. Pamela bathed her forehead whilst I got some brandy from my flask; and in a few minutes Imogen opened her eyes. She looked at us both as if we were strangers. Next she made a mocking little grimace at us and reaching out her hand smoothed it down my arm and gave me a squeeze. Apparently she was now satisfied that she had done enough for us. For she turned over on her side with her back towards us, stretched out her slim long legs and immediately was fast asleep. I searched the room—it was easy enough with its bare floor and scanty furniture—and I found nothing. There was nothing there to find. Pamela pushed me out, managed, somehow, to undress her Sleeping Beauty and get her into bed. Imogen slept without a break in her slumber until the sun was high on the next morning. There had been no need for either of us to keep a watch. For the platinum chain with its sapphire pendant had gone.

" For good and all, I hope," I said to Pamela Brayburn as we breakfasted together in the cool of the morning. I had no thought for Michael Crowther at that moment. Never before or since have I uttered a prayer more sincere.

" I, too," returned Pamela, but her voice trailed off as if she hardly believed that good fortune so marvellous could befall us. " Imogen will tell us when she's up."

Upon Pamela Brayburn in her turn the shadow of the sapphire had spread its canopy.

CHAPTER XIII

THE INDIAN

WHAT had happened? Imogen, lying in a low and restful chair, told us a part of it on the verandah after luncheon. All that she knew she told, but it was not all that there was to be told; and we who listened had to put the rest of it together as best we could, in the belief that the commonplaces of one race are the miracles of another. Imogen's long sleep had restored the colour to her cheeks and the buoyancy to her spirits. And if once or twice she flinched in her narrative, she recovered her spirits the next instant with a shake of the head which reminded me of a swimmer coming up into the sunlight after a deep dive beneath the water. She smoked a cigarette whilst she talked. Her mind was smoothed out. She, at all events, was now free from the shadow of the sapphire.

Imogen had stayed on the verandah after the snake-charmer's departure. She and Pamela had discussed the performance, wondering whether the cobras were tame and whether their poison-ducts had been extracted; and what qualities a little rod of nagatharana could have so to frighten them; and if the dark, porous snake-stone which had been shown to them was a genuine antidote for a snake-bite. The Indian was an old, unbelievably lean, tall man with a grizzled beard, who wore nothing in the way of clothes except a loin-cloth and a turban ; and certainly there were twin scars upon his wrists and upon his breast which only the fangs of a serpent seemed able to account for.

" We were perhaps twenty minutes talking about these things," said Imogen. " Not more. Then I got up and went away to my room. I was very sleepy."

She opened the door or, more exactly, turned the handle and threw it open. The door was set in the wall opposite to the wall against which the bed was placed, and at the inner end of the room. It opened inwards and downwards, that is, towards the window. Thus, if you entered the room you had a wall upon your left, the window at the end of the room on your right, and the bed upon the right of the window at a diagonal with the door. Imogen, then, flung open the door and walked in. She had her solar topee in her hand and she laid it on a round table which stood against the upper wall opposite to the window. The window was open, but the shutters were closed, and since that side of the bungalow was in shadow and the eaves of the roof were wide, little more than twilight crept through the lattices into the room. Imogen, coming straight from the verandah and the prospect of a green ocean of forest shining in the sun, was for a second or two blinded. She stood still for the darkness to clear away, but it had not quite cleared when she began again to move. She took two or three steps towards the window in order to open the shutters. And something flickered behind her and quite noiselessly.

Imogen felt her heart jump into her throat. The Indian had been waiting for her, hidden behind the door. As she turned she saw him close the door and slide the bolt into its socket. She did not scream, although she was about to scream. For as her mouth opened something else flickered in the dusk of the room and Imogen's heart whirled down within her. In the uncertain light it might have been taken for the neck and flat head of a swan ; and it hissed as an angry swan will hiss. It was almost white, too, but it had the sheen of hard scales rather than the softness of down.

" Miss Sahib not to scream," the Indian said softly. " Or I make cobra punish her."

Imogen could not have screamed now. Her throat was dry, her nerves paralysed by terror. She had felt her heart leap into her throat as the Indian bolted the door ; it stood still now in her horror of the snake. The passage of a minute had altered the world. She had walked lightly from the verandah, quite free from the anxiety of these last days. She had opened a door and fear bound her limbs, and death was an inch from her throat.

She was not aware that she had moved, but she found herself upright against the wall, between the window and the door, her small feet in the blue shoes making themselves smaller, the palms of her hands pressed against the panels to keep herself from falling. Had the cobra slithered an inch towards her across the floor, she must have fallen, and in falling must have screamed.

But the reptile merely swayed its head from side to side, a venomous flower upon a white stalk. In the gloom its eyes were bright as diamonds and held her, so that her eyes, too, must swing from side to side in a horrid slavery. Suddenly the sound of the Indian's pipe, playing a music which was plaintive and yet had a cadence curiously voluptuous, was heard in the room. The music was low. It reached me in my car because I was just passing on that winding road the corner of the bungalow whence the music floated. The Indian was kneeling upon one knee facing the cobra and close by Imogen's side. From the fold of his knee his little stick of nagatharana stuck out ready for use. And he piped. And Imogen, her wits all scattered, swung her head from right to left and from left to right in a synchronism with the head of the dancing cobra, brown eyes riveted upon diamond eyes glittering evilly beneath the expanded hood.

" I remembered, in a meaningless way," said Imogen, " what I had read in books on the voyage to Ceylon. That the cobra—even the king-cobra with the silvery neck and head which this one had —was a coward ; that little vedda boys would think nothing of capturing one and taming it ; that cobras had been kept by Cingalese as house-dogs, fatal to thieves and harmless to the inmates. But with those little eyes glancing like fire-flies in the twilit room, yet never, like fire-flies, vanishing, I could not believe."

The piping stopped. The Indian snatched his

little stick from the grip of his knee and stretched it out. The cobra ceased to sway. It seemed to the girl clamped by her danger against the wall, that its eyes dimmed. It sank and uncoiled and with a thud its head hit the teak floor. It lay stretched out, a knotted branch fallen from a tree but a branch with eyes.

The Indian spoke in a low voice :

" The Miss Sahib will raise her hands gently and unclasp the jewel from her throat and drop it in my hand."

Imogen obeyed him. He held the stick in his left hand over the snake's head, and the palm of his right hand was cupped at Imogen's side. Into that cup she dropped the sapphire and the Indian tied it in a knot of his loin-cloth, using but the right hand.

" I leave my cobra to guard the Miss Sahib," he continued.

" Oh, no," Imogen moaned, and at the sound of her voice the eyes of the reptile brightened.

" The Miss Sahib no speak, no move and no hurt. In a little whiles I call my servant and he follow."

He chanted in a low sing-song some hymn or order which Imogen did not understand. Then he slipped out of the window as if he were a snake himself. He left the cobra behind him on the floor of the room— Imogen swore to it. When he opened the shutters, and let in for the flash of a second the afternoon light, she saw the snake like the bough of a silver birch— plain as plain could be against the rich brown of the teak planks. It remained there and never moved— just as she never moved. Imogen swore to it. It was on that same spot—again she swore to it—when

near upon an hour later I threw open the shutters.
It was there when she warned me not to move.   It
was there till the very moment when I stood on the
exact spot where it was supposed to lie.   I have
known a man ride his camel knee-deep into the
waters of a mirage before the water vanished and he
rode over a desert of pebbles.   In the same swift
magical way the cobra had vanished from Imogen's
sight.

This was her story.   At what point had the
Indian lured his cobra back into his wicker-work
bottle ?   Had he left it behind him and called to it
to follow ?   Had he taken it away with him, and
yet left her with the vision of it stretched on the
floor like a branch and its diamond eyes claiming
hers, binding her hand and foot in the paralysis of
fear ?   None of us could answer these questions.
We talked a little of the famous rope-trick and
whether any living being had really seen it and of a
wagon-load of illusions.   But when we had com-
forted ourselves with our Western superiorities and
proved that that which had been could not be, I
retained, nevertheless, very vividly the terrible
picture of a girl crucified by fear, her small white
face and startled eyes fixed, as though they had been
moulded in wax a second after an agonising death.

Anyway, the sapphire had gone, and if I could
manage it it would keep gone.   Crowther could
chase it if he liked.   That was his affair.   But we
three here in the rest-house in the jungle were
emancipated, and were going to remain emancipated.
Imogen, it was true, had lost a lovely jewel and

friends of hers might have been expected to show some regret at her loss. I had no such feeling. The stone was compacted by an earthquake on a night of eclipse. It was accursed. Its setting was misery, not platinum, and the spark which gleamed in it was the very soul of malevolence. In other words I was elated to know that never again would Imogen wear it about her slender throat. She had bought it and paid for it—that was true enough. But on the other hand I had not a doubt that she would have given it back to Michael if he had talked to her for five minutes.

But even that conversation was not going to happen if I could help it. I should have to tread delicately, of course. A certain amount of diplomacy would be needed. But whilst we had been talking I had thought of a plan.

"About to-morrow," I said. "There's one place you've got to see, of course—the city on the mountain, Sigiri. It's on the way from here to the south. I must tell you about it. There was a King——"

"Darling," Imogen interrupted plaintively, "we, too, have a guide-book."

"Then that makes it all right," I said heartily. "I'll leave you both to go up by the gallery whilst I roll along to see a friend of mine, and come back again for you."

I saw the two girls sit up straight. They looked at me intently. I lit a cigarette with great indifference.

"Yes, that's the plan," I said.

"I suppose it's the same friend you had to put

in two days with at Kandy," Pamela suggested sweetly.

" Not at all. I have lots of friends," said I.

Pamela went off to her bedroom and came back with her Murray's Handbook.

" It's the map we want," said Imogen.

The unfolding of the map made me uneasy. For on a bare white space in print distressingly clear, there were marked, fairly close together, Sigiri and Dhambulla. Imogen put her finger on a spot.

" That's the place, I think," she said cheerfully, and then she turned to me. " For how long do you propose to leave us at Sigiri, Martin ? An hour ? "

" No," I answered.

" Less than that ? "

" More than that. About two hours altogether," I said indifferently.

The two girls stared as though I had committed some enormity. Then they bent their heads again over the map.

" That's the place," said Imogen, dabbing the tip of her finger on the map as if she were smashing a mosquito.

" Yes," Pamela agreed, " he's got a date at Dhambulla with a coloured lady."

" I have nothing of the sort," I cried.

" But you're going to Dhambulla," cried Imogen.

I suppose that an intellectual would have found a way out of the ditch I had jumped into. My reply was simply fatuous. I said :

" Well, I might look in at Dhambulla."

After that they played animal, vegetable, mineral with me until Crowther's name was yielded up.

" You have seen him ? " they both cried with one voice.

" At Kandy."

" It was his sapphire, then ? "

" Yes.   It was stolen from the top of the pagoda."

" And he has come after it ? "

" Yes."

" And what time is your appointment to-morrow ? " asked Imogen.

" Eleven o'clock."

" We'll go with you to Dhambulla," said Pamela. I had to make the best of it.

" I'm delighted, of course," I said.   " My business won't take a minute.   I'll leave you both in the car —it's a bit of a climb to the terrace——"

" As steep as the gallery at Sigiri, Martin ? " Imogen asked innocently.

" I don't know.   I haven't seen either one or the other," I replied firmly.   " But it's steep, and I'll run up and tell Crowther the sapphire's stolen again and then the three of us can roll along to Sigiri."

Imogen and Pamela exchanged glances of amusement.

" But, darling Martin," Imogen said sweetly. " You don't think that you're going to put it over us like that, do you ?   We're both going to see the Rock Temple and we're both going to see your Mr. Crowther."

I wanted to keep them both apart from Michael Crowther.   I did !   There was no longer, of course, any reason for uneasiness.   The only link which could have caused them trouble—and, indeed, it had

caused trouble enough already—was broken. Still,
I did not want them to meet.

" Oh, Crowther's nothing to write home about,"
I grumbled.

" But, Martin, we don't want to write home about
him," said Imogen gently. " We're just going to
meet him to-morrow on the terrace of the Rock
Temple at Dhambulla."

" But you haven't an idea what you're going to
meet," I exclaimed. " I know him of old, so it
doesn't matter to me what he looks like. But he's
too awful "—and I gave them a description of
Michael as I remembered him kicking his heels
against the parapet of the lake at Kandy. I thought
my description to be sufficiently humorous, but not
a smile illuminated their faces; and when I had done
Pamela declared :

" My mother used to say to me : ' Pamela, darling,
when the moment comes to select one of your
innumerable suitors, always remember that if you
choose a man wearing an I. Zingari belt, you have
chosen a gentleman.' "

I threw up the sponge.

" Very well. We start at nine."

Anyway, the sapphire had gone. Nothing could
alter that.

CHAPTER XIV

A COUNCIL AT THE ROCK TEMPLE

THE way led upwards over bare shelving slabs of gneiss. As we mounted, the blue hills of Kandy came into view in the south, a coronet of sharp peaks encircling the royal city. We wound about the mountain and climbed a short flight of steps with a lantern fixed upon a pillar at the side. Now a slender satin-wood tree with delicate foliage sprang here and there from a crevice in the slabs like a plume of lace. We came out again upon the crest of the ridge and the vast jungle streamed away before us to the north. It was broken by great rocks with the bloom of plums, and by vivid patches of fresh green where some primeval village hid ; and across ten miles of it the huge rounded pebble of Sigiri rose like an island from the sea. A few trees grew now on that high summit where once a king had built his capital, and the line of the long gallery, which alone had given access to the gates, ran plainly along the pebble's side like a fissure in the rock. Now the steps which we mounted broadened and rose in a welcome shade of trees.

" Listen ! " said Imogen, and we stopped ; and we heard a wild elephant trumpeting far away in the jungle.

We crossed more slabs and passed between the white-washed pillars, and beneath the brown-tiled canopy of the temple's gates. A bell hung within a stand upon our left. A bo-tree stood in a stone enclosure protected by a parapet. A long wall, above which two high tamarinds rose, enclosed the five temples and the terrace in front of them. And as we stepped on to the terrace a man rose from a stone seat in the wall and came quickly towards us.

"Crowther," said I.

He had changed his dress since I had last seen him. Gone were the white knickerbockers and the vivid glory of his belt and the worsted stockings. He wore a thin grey suit and brown shoes, a silk shirt with a small collar and a restful tie. He was vastly improved but not improved enough to appease me. All the resentment under which I used to labour on his steamer on the Irrawaddy had returned to me during the last two days. I blamed him for all the anxiety and the peril to which Imogen had been put ; and I was quite logical in my censure. If he had been honest with Ma Shwe At he would not have deserted her without a word, he would not have taken back his trumpery presents, and the sapphire would never have gleamed darkly on the white table-cloth of the *Dagonet* or been stolen from the spire of the pagoda at Pagan. I was altogether against Crowther this morning, and with a foolish hope that I could keep the girls apart from him, I stepped forward as he approached.

" At all events you don't make me hot to look at you, Michael," I began grudgingly. " That's a blessing "; and, of course, Imogen and Pamela were already one on each side of me.

" This is Miss Pamela Brayburn," I said reluctantly, " and this is Miss Imogen Cloud who bought your sapphire at Kandy—— Oh ! "

The " Oh " was an exclamation of annoyance. Although the sun was high above the rock, we were standing in the shade of one of the great trees and Crowther had taken off his helmet. I had meant to say all in one breath :

" This is Miss Imogen Cloud who bought your sapphire at Kandy and it was stolen from her yesterday at a rest-house and I wish you good morning."

But I found that I could not say it. I wanted to believe that since, in his pursuit of his sapphire, he had discarded his yellow robe, he had passed completely out of another phase of his violent career. But now I could not believe it. He had taken his hat off. I suppose that we have all known men devoted to one calling, to whom the slow sculpture of the years has given dignity, breeding, even beauty. But I have never known anyone in whom the change has been so swift, so definite, so obviously permanent. There was no trace left of Michael D. Even with the stubble of new stiff hair upon his crown he had the look of a saintly, ascetic and prayer-worn Cardinal. I said gently :

" I am sorry, Michael. I have no good news for you. The sapphire was stolen yesterday from Imogen and by the Indian."

Crowther looked down upon the ground. He

made no movement. He uttered no word. His very impassivity made the fullness of his disappointment clear to us as no outcry could have done.

Imogen broke into an account of the robbery. Crowther listened to the end with his eyes set hungrily upon her face.

" Yes," he said with resignation. " Muhammed Ghalli is bad. He is known. He has great powers and uses them wickedly. It will be long before he finds his way out of the forest to the rocky path."

Imogen looked puzzled, as well she might. She had never heard of that allegory which Michael Crowther had related to me on the deck of the lighter, lashed to the side of the *Moulmein* steamer on the way to Schwegu.

" But if you still had the sapphire," he asked, " you would have given it back to me in return for the price you paid ? "

" I would have given it back to you gladly," Imogen answered quietly. " But I would not have taken a farthing of the price I paid."

A very disarming smile took all the severity from Michael's face.

" The wish will be counted to you, Miss Cloud," he replied.

I intervened at this point hurriedly. I had a fear that he was going to point out to her that as a reward for her goodwill she might find herself a man in her next life, and by this change of sex ever so much nearer to her great Release. And I did not think that this point of view would commend itself to her at all. I said :

"Look here, Michael. I've got something to say about all this. Let's sit down!"

We sat down on one of the stone seats cut out of the wall. There was just room for the four of us. We were high above the world. In front of us the temple carved out of the hill-side. On our right hand rose the monstrous pebble of the Lion Rock of Sigiri where for eighteen years, in the last days of the Roman Empire, a parricide reigned splendidly and well. And below us to our left and our right spread the vast green ocean of the jungle. I began to argue.

"What I think is this. Your sapphire, Michael. It's a symbol of renunciation. A symbol of your renunciation. But in the end it's just a sapphire found in a native working near Mogok. It has no real sanctity of its own and no history. That's what I mean. It's not a great diamond stolen out of the forehead of an image of Krishna, for instance. It has no romance, no curse upon it "—that, by the way, I did not believe—" it's just a very beautiful sapphire. Do you follow me?"

"You are my friend," replied Crowther, and it was a very disturbing reply. It might just mean that "the obligations of friendship compel me to listen to any idiotic remarks you may feel disposed to make." Or again it might mean that whatever a friend says has a decided worth. I preferred the latter alternative and resumed:

"Secondly——"

Pamela broke in with a wail:

"Martin, you are not going to preach a sermon, are you?"

I crushed her with a look.   At least, I meant to ;
and since she did not meet my look but was gazing
at Michael Crowther, I claim that I did.

" Secondly," I repeated firmly, and went on :
" The sapphire, however lovely, is not one of the
premier stones.   It does not compete with the
pearl and the diamond and the emerald and the
ruby.   It   is   of   the   second   cru.   Allowed ?
Allowed ? "   I turned from one girl to the other
to bear me out. Neither answered, and indeed
I noticed traces of impatience in Pamela Brayburn.

" Well, then, since your sapphire, Michael, is
first of all a secondary stone——"

" No, no," said Pamela wearily.   " It was secondly
a secondary stone.   If you must be dogmatic,
Martin, you should also be correct."

I was exasperated, but Imogen took a side now.

" Pamela's right, Martin.   It was firstly a stone
without associations."

" And even that," Crowther added with a smile,
" is not quite correct.   For it has very definite
associations for me."

" Very likely," I cried with some triumph.
Here was my chance to get a little of my own back.
I wagged my finger at him.   " But not the sort of
associations you ought to be thinking about nowadays."

" Oh ! "

" Oh ! "

Two shocked feminine voices protested in one
breath.

" Martin ! "

Imogen was gently reproachful.

" Not nice."

Pamela was quite definite about my bad taste.
I ought never to have told these girls as much as
I had done about Crowther's murky past. That
was my fault. My good or bad taste was my
affair.

" I wanted to come up here alone," I exclaimed.
" I wanted to talk to Michael without any interruption. And I am going to say what I meant to
say in spite of you. Michael can buy another
sapphire and string it up on his hti. Michael has
money. Michael's going to build a pagoda at
Tagaung and live by the side of it."

I was very much in earnest about this. I did with
all my heart desire that Ma Shwe At's sapphire
should vanish as utterly as if it had been flung by
somebody blindfolded into the middle of the sea.
There was a shadow to it. Its deep clear blue
which had no clouds meant clouds for those who
handled it. I was afraid of it.

" Buy another, Michael. Buy one like it. It's
merely a matter of looking about a bit."

Imogen scanned my face with anxiety.

" But, Martin, darling," she remonstrated with
the upward inflexion of extreme surprise, " you
are not on the map at all."

" I won't be baited," I said, digging my toes in.

" Baited ! You're not a horse," said Pamela
scornfully, " although there is an animal I could
mention, if I had not been well brought up."

They were both siding with Michael, of course,
against me. I might have known that they would.
This was my unlucky day.

Then Crowther himself intervened.

" For me," he said with a smile of rare sweetness, " there can be no other sapphire. Firstly "—and his lips twitched again—" it is a symbol of renunciation. You yourself, Mr. Legatt, used the phrase and it is so, believe me !—a true description. But that jewel is the symbol, not another jewel like it. Secondly, there is that bad thought of mine to build a pagoda for myself."

I threw up my hands. I could not keep pace with the variations of Michael's belief.

" So that's a bad thought now ! " I exclaimed.

" It always was a bad thought," Michael answered ; and at this point Pamela must chip in and add to the confusion.

" It certainly was," she agreed serenely. " My mother used to say to me : ' Pamela, dearest, if I had got to do one or the other, I'd build an aquarium.' "

Uncle Sunday beamed upon her.

" Did she say that ? " he asked admiringly ; and for the first time in our acquaintanceship I saw Pamela Brayburn disconcerted. She had not an idea how to take the question. Was Crowther chaffing her ? But his manner was too simple and sincere. Was he asking seriously a literal question ? But the question was too idiotic. Pamela was unaware that in Michael's creed the destruction of life was a great sin, and the preservation of it a great merit. An aquarium preserved fish from being gobbled by bigger fish or caught in nets or hooked on lines—a highly deserving business. Michael was asking his question in absolute innocence. I am bound to say that I had noticed already that his

new religion had killed his sense of humour. He
continued quite eagerly :

" And did your mother build many ? "

" What ? " Pamela asked, still more at a loss.
She looked towards me for help. I grinned at her
with pleasure. I wasn't going to get her out of her
trouble.

" Build many aquariums ? " said Michael.

Whatever qualities Pamela possessed, effrontery
was the chief of them.

" Only two," she answered calmly. " One at
Brighton and the other under the shadow of Westminster Abbey." And she got away with it. By
some lucky chance Michael, during his three years
in London, had never heard of the one or the other.

" But to build even two was most meritorious,"
said he. " On the other hand, to build a pagoda
and a tiny monastery beside it for myself ? No man
may do so overweening a thing. A monastery for
others—yes. A pagoda, too—for the greater glory
of Gautama. But to feed a man's conceit, to sit by
the side of it and hear men say : ' That is U Wisaya
who built it, sitting there in the shade '—no, a
thousand times. It is forbidden. The mere thought
of it a sin—one amongst many to be atoned for.
And the recovery of this sapphire is for me the way
of atonement."

If Crowther had used one false note or one fantastic phrase which suggested that his little speech
had been made up to deceive us, if he had licked his
chops over his bygone wickedness or dished up his
repentance with a garnish of oil, I should have been
very much obliged to him. We should have been

free of him. But he was so simple and direct and effortless that no one could misdoubt him.

"It's laid upon me, as a task, a penance. I would much rather go back to that safe harbour I had found at Pagan and sit down there and meditate until I got at the truth of the eternal laws and became blended with the ultimate soul. But it seems to me that all the passions and desires of that earlier life of mine, of which you, Mr. Legatt, know, are buried in the heart of that sapphire and may wake again unless I hang it once more high in its consecrated place."

He looked so forlorn that I was not surprised to hear Imogen encouraging him.

"We will all help if we can," she said.

"But what can we do?" I cried. "Tell us!" Yes, I too had somehow fallen under the old compulsion. "The sapphire has gone."

"It will reappear," said Crowther. "It will be sold again—not in Kandy, I think, but in Colombo."

"To a passenger on a ship," I added, and Crowther nodded.

That, without doubt, was the likeliest way of disposing of it. To offer it for sale for a second time in Kandy within so short a period might easily provoke enquiries. Colombo, with the great tourist liners coming in and going out, flinging ashore for a few hours their cargoes of wealthy sightseers eager for mementoes of their voyage—Colombo was the place now where the sapphire must be looked for.

"The first thing to do, then," Pamela argued, "is to inform the police at Colombo."

This was the common-sense point of view, but it

ignored Crowther. The brotherhood of Buddha had nothing to do with the social framework. It brought no actions, fought in no wars, asked for nothing at any time from anyone. How in the world Crowther now hoped to get his sapphire back I could not imagine.

But it would not be by prosecuting a criminal.

" No," he said.

Then he rose from his seat and inclined his head.

" As a man, I thank you all," he said with a smile. " As a monk, I do not thank you. But I say that by your goodwill you have acquired merit which will surely be rewarded."

He turned away from us more abruptly than any of us had expected. I think that he was alarmed by Pamela's suggestion that we should call in the Civil power. Vague as, in many of its details, the creed he followed was, this, at all events, was clear. He could pursue no criminal and bear no witness against one. According to the immutable laws, the criminal would be punished without his puny help or ours. He walked across the terrace to the door of the first shrine, wherein lies hidden in the darkness the vast, recumbent image of Buddha the Saviour as he entered into his eternal rest.

But Michael Crowther was not the only one of the party to disappear. A group of visitors was clustered about the entrance to the Great-King Cavern, the glory of Dhambulla, and Pamela Brayburn joined herself on to it. In another moment the great double-doors were opened and Imogen and I had the terrace to ourselves. It suddenly occurred to me that this might, perhaps—after all—not be my unlucky day. I stood up.

"Imogen!" I said.

"Yes?" said she, and in her turn she stood up.

I looked at her and she looked at me.

"Imogen!" I repeated.

She nodded her head. Then she laughed with a lovely lilt in her voice, a lilt of pure joy.

"I've got to be told," she said. "Even in these days that's necessary."

"I love you," I said. "I love you very dearly"—and she was in my arms. I could feel the throb of her heart against my breast and the sweetness of her lips upon mine. Blue mountains and green forest, the great pebble of Sigiri and the high terrace of Dhambulla—it *was* my lucky day.

Some time afterwards, how long I cannot tell, Pamela rejoined us. She looked at Imogen and she looked at me.

"My mother used to remark——" she began, and I interrupted her.

"I have my doubts about your mother," I said, nodding darkly.

Both the girls rounded upon me at once.

"Oh!" cried Pamela.

"For shame, Martin," said Imogen.

"He's calling me a war-baby," exclaimed Pamela.

"I never heard anything so ridiculous! I said nothing of the kind."

"Practically you did, Martin," Imogen reproached me sorrowfully.

"I couldn't have. Pamela's too old. Much too old. Years and years too old."

They did what they always did when I refused to be brow-beaten. They turned their backs on me and made derogatory allusions. This time it was about jungle-folk and how they must be uncouth. "But, of course," said Pamela, "if he'd go up into trees and swing from branch to branch by his arms, he'd be too fascinating."

I rose and walked down the slabs to the car. But they caught me up before I reached the bottom.

"Your Crowther's a darling," said Pamela. "He's the first man I have ever heard say that it was meritorious to build the Westminster Aquarium."

We lunched at the rest-house, drove over to Sigiri and came back to Dhambulla for the night. Imogen slipped her arm under mine as we sat in the car.

"What fun we're having, Martin, aren't we?" she cried. "A lot of foolish little jokes, silly to other people, lovely to us, because behind them there's the great peace."

CHAPTER XV

THE LAST OF THE PEAK

IT was curious to notice how deep an impression upon so small an acquaintance Michael Crowther had made upon the minds of my companions. It was disturbing, too. For however loudly I might crow over our present freedom from the tyranny of his sapphire, I had all along a secret presentiment that its shadow would run out over our heads again ; and this presentiment was, willy-nilly, strengthened by the clear recollection which the two girls retained of its owner.

We arranged to sail for home on the same ship in a fortnight's time, and during the fortnight we travelled together, wandering from marvel to marvel of that glossy and multifarious island. But nothing that we saw effaced the picture of Uncle Sunday in his mufti; he was surrounded with so visible an aura of loneliness and disappointment.

We played a round of golf on the English-summer land of Nuwara Eliya, and as we sat at luncheon in the hotel, Imogen, after a few moments of silence, cried out in a little voice of exasperation :

" I never saw a face so thin."

Pamela Brayburn explained it.

" Fastings and vigils and visions."

" You're all wrong," I protested.   " I once made

that mistake. Pongyis don't fast. They mustn't fast. They mustn't eat after midday—that's true. But they can make up for it in the morning. They've got to keep fit."

" To get their Blues, I suppose," said Pamela sardonically.

" Well, Michael has got his, anyway," I exclaimed.

" Oh, Martin ! "

" Oh ! "

Again those shocked interjections reproached me. I was not nice. But I didn't care. I went on:

" And as for vigils, they don't keep them. They have long, lovely nights of sleep without fatigue from yesterday or anxiety for to-morrow. They don't even have the bother of undressing and no one knows better than two girls dolled up like you, how long that takes. And as for visions, if any one of them saw a ghost he'd be drummed out of the monastery in the morning."

" Yes, darling," said Imogen soothingly.

We drove down from Nuwara Eliya and bought tortoise-shell presents at Galle. And Imogen asked —and this, too, after an interval of two days :

" Why, then, *is* he so thin, Martin ? "

" Because he's like Martha," I answered, " if it was Martha. He's troubled about many things."

" One of those things we ought to have helped him to get back," said Pamela ; and that was that.

Towards the end of the fortnight we returned to the Galle Face Hotel outside Colombo, and went over, one afternoon, to bathe at Mount Lavinia amongst the catamarans. We were drinking tea in the garden of the hotel afterwards when I said :

" We could only have helped him to get it back by going to the police, and that he wouldn't have at any price."

Both girls burst out laughing with sheer pleasure.

" Now you've begun it, Martin," cried Imogen; and to my surprise I had, indeed.

I had been wondering, now that we were again in Colombo, whether we should run across Michael and hear whether or no he had brought the thieves to bay and recovered his treasure. I had a sneaking hope that we should and an outspoken prayer that we should not. It was the prayer which was answered. We were in and out of the town for a couple of days and not one of us set eyes on him or the Indian or Nga Pyu or Nga Than. We embarked on the Motor Ship *Rutlandshire* of the Bibby Line and moved out of the harbour late in the afternoon. Imogen stood by my side on the upper deck. We saw Adam's Peak rising up into the sky in a cleft of the mountains. We watched the evening clouds swathe it about and withdraw it from our eyes. Once I used to watch for it with a ridiculous eagerness. Now I was glad to see the last of it. For it seemed to me that with its shadow went the shadow of the sapphire.

There would be many years now before either Imogen or I saw it again, if ever we did see it.

" Yet we owe it a farewell," said Imogen waving her hand towards it. " You saved my life upon that mountain, Martin."

I shrugged my shoulders.

" Since I was up there with you, I was bound to do the little I could to look after you."

Imogen slipped her hand under my arm.

" Those who look after people sometimes find that looking after ends in loving," she said gently.

What she said was true, I think—at all events, so far as we were concerned. I looked back. I had seen her in London at dances, at dinner-parties, at theatres. I had never been in her immediate circle, but there had been a word or two here, a smile only, perhaps, there, a moment when her hand had rested on my arm as it did now. I had always known her for a friend as, I think, she had known me. But it had needed that moment above the precipice of Adam's Peak, when she hung in my arm and her life depended upon the strength of it, to warn me that my great need was the need of her.

" Ends in loving," I said.   " And in being loved ?"

Imogen laughed and said the most lovely thing which a man could hear.

" Oh, me ?   You were a little bit blind, Martin. I, on the other hand, used always to know you were about, when you were about."

The island disappeared.   The lights blazed forth upon the deck.   The water, sparkling with points of fire, swished past the ship's sides.   The stars were strung like lamps across the sky.

" You and I, Imogen," I said.

I thought with pity of the man who sought only to replace his offering on the spire of his pagoda and then meditate in a hopeful solitude upon the extinction of his soul.

We were four days out from Colombo.   It was,

and I suppose is, the practice of the Bibby Line to convert its fore-deck into a skittle alley. We were starting upon a competition which must end before we reached Suez. It was my turn and, owing to a happy lurch of the ship at the right moment, I knocked all the ninepins over with one shot. There was applause and I looked upwards to the higher deck as eager as any champion in a tourney that my lady should smile her acknowledgement of my prowess. But, alas! though many ladies hung over the forward rail, watching us for want of something better to do, my lady was not one of them. My first thought was :

" What a pity. I shall never do that again."

My second had a touch of grievance.

" Imogen, darling, you might somehow have been there."

My third was one of sheer amazement and dejection. The ship, I should say, had its full complement of passengers. Apart from the usual tourists, there were young men from the Burma Oil Corporation Settlement at Yenangyaung going home on leave, servants of the Forest Company, judges and barristers and Civil servants and commercial men with their wives ; so that even now one had not got them all definitely recognised and named. Moreover, there was but one class so that we all had the run of the ship and it was possible for a passenger to find a corner upon one of the decks where he could remain unnoticed even by those assiduous people who go conscripting for the games. So for the first time since we had left Ceylon I saw Michael Crowther. He was leaning over the forward rail in a line of spectators and watching the players in the skittle-alley with a friendly amusement.

I did not seek him and I was careful not to say a word about him, but I had no hope that neither I nor my companions would remain free of him. He was my Old Man of the Sea and I began to think of him as clamped on to my shoulders for the rest of my life. I should have liked to have run across him in Colombo and to have learned that he had recovered his sapphire and was on his way back with it to Pagan. But since he was on our steamer he had not recovered it and he was chasing it certainly as far as Suez. And a day later Imogen ran across him. He had a cabin on the small after-deck and for the greater part of the day remained in his chair beside it. Imogen found me leaning over the forward rail.

" Martin, guess who's on board ? " she cried.

" I know," I answered gloomily. " He saw me knock all those ninepins over with one shot."

", When I didn't," Imogen added remorsefully. I suppose that I had told the story once or twice to her and had managed to suggest in telling it that a world could not be really well organised where such achievements were not inevitably witnessed by one's womenfolk.

" You must come and talk to him," said Imogen.

" I suppose that I must," I answered.

" And shall we do it gracefully and with good manners, or shall we not ? " said Pamela.

We did it at all events with what grace we could. We sought him out the next morning.

" I'm the bad ha'penny, Mr. Legatt," he said.

" You're going as far as Suez, I suppose," I remarked.

" I'm going to England," said he.

Michael Crowther, however, took no more pleasure in his destination than I did.   England was another word in his vocabulary for failure and loneliness and cold.

" I have got to," he said.   " I ran those men down at Colombo.   I did a bad thing.   I threatened them with the law.   They described to me, boastfully, how they had climbed the pagoda, failed to loosen the diamond and in the end must content themselves with my chaplet of gifts."

" They had the sapphire still, then ! " I cried.

" No," Crowther answered.   " They had sold it. A girl—very young—not twenty I should think— came off a ship on one of the Round-the-World voyages with a man—I should think a little older than you.   They went along to the Galle Face Hotel for luncheon.   Just outside the hotel the thieves offered them the sapphire with its platinum chain, and after the usual bargaining the man bought it and gave it to his companion."

" You found out who they were ? " I asked.

" One of the porters remembered them."

" And you are following them ? " Pamela asked. " Yes."

" Like the Saracen girl who only knew her lover's Christian name," I observed.   " It doesn't sound to me a likely proposition."

" But didn't the Saracen girl find him ? " Crowther asked.

" One for his nob," said Pamela softly.

G

" London was smaller in those days," I returned.

" And we don't even know that they were going to London," said Imogen.

I was grateful to Imogen for her support against Pamela's quite uncalled-for jape, but I definitely disliked the " we." Imogen had obviously decided that we—she and I, at all events, and probably Pamela—were, upon our arrival in England, to spend our time and our efforts in searching through the country for a man and a girl who had bought a sapphire in Colombo.

" You know their names, perhaps ? " Pamela asked.

" Yes, that's about all I do know," Crowther replied. " I got them from the hotel.

" What was hers ? " Imogen enquired.

Crowther looked doubtfully at Imogen. He was disinclined to answer. He shook his head.

" From what I could gather you wouldn't be likely to know her, Miss Cloud," he said rather stiffly.

It seemed a curious consequence of adopting the yellow robe that a devotee to American slang should become the primmest of Victorians. But he little knew Imogen who had a catholicity in her friendships which was apt to stagger even her own generation.

" You never can tell," she remarked. " What's her name ? "

" Jill Leslie," said Crowther.

" No, I don't know her," said Imogen.

" And what's his ? " I asked.

" Robin Calhoun."

None of us knew a Robin Calhoun.

" Of course," said Pamela, who really could leave nothing alone, " he might have been the girl's uncle."

For a second or two Michael Crowther tried desperately not to smile. But he failed. And having begun to smile he went on to laugh. There were moments when Michael became very human.

" He might," he answered. " On the other hand he wasn't. As I told you, I made discreet enquiries at the hotel. I did not, after all, navigate the Irrawaddy River for nothing. If I didn't acquire merit I acquired knowledge, and you can take it from me that Robin Calhoun is not the uncle of Jill Leslie."

The luncheon-gong was beaten at that moment.

CHAPTER XVI

THE SILENT ROOM

WE travelled straight through upon one ship to the Port of London, arriving there on the morning of the last day of April. Then we scattered with the usual indifference of our race to the fellow-passengers with whom accident had cooped us for a month ; and comfortably confident that in a week's time we should not recognise one another in the street. I drove with Imogen and her cousin across London to Paddington, saw them off to the West of England and returned to my own lodging in Savile Row. I had not seen Michael Crowther that morning, and what with a press of work and the arrangements for my wedding which we had agreed should take place at the end of the Season, for some time I hardly gave a thought to him at all. Moreover, Imogen's parents opened their London house in Hill Street, and taking one thing with another I was a thoroughly busy man.

I made it a rule, therefore, whenever it was possible, to walk to and from my engagements for the sake of exercise ; and it happened in consequence, on a good many occasions when returning from a supper-party or a dance, that I passed on foot along Savile Row. There was a house in the row which intrigued me ; to be more correct, there was an upper part of a house. For the ground floor and basement were occupied by a tailor, as, of course, was the case with most of the houses. But at whatever hour I returned home, the first floor was usually alight, and discreetly alight. I mean that the blinds and curtains were carefully drawn and the light only leaked out at the sides or the tops of the two large flat windows. But it was burning. I do not indeed remember more than two or three occasions when late at night that first floor was dark. Several times, however, I saw people arrive in small groups, women and men, and all of them dressed as though they had come from a theatre or an entertainment. I do not remember that I ever saw anyone going away. At my latest I was still too early for the homing of these gay pigeons.

But the most singular circumstance in connection with this mysterious apartment was its silence. No noise whatever broke from it, no sound of music, no babble of voices, never a song, never a cry. I did not notice that peculiarity for some time; but once I had noticed it, it forced itself upon me afterwards each time that I passed the house. I wanted to hear something—anything; a signal that the company assembled behind the curtains and the blinds was enjoying its presence there and was associated in some pleasant fellowship; or even in some fantastic conspiracy. But I never did, and the quiet of the place became to me in the end sinister and a little alarming.

By this time May had turned London into a garden of lilac and sunlight and it was, I think, during the third week of the month and at seven in the evening when my servant told me that a Mr. Crowther would like to see me.   He was shown up, of course, at once.

" Michael, have a cocktail," I said.

Michael shook his head with a smile.

" In a little while I shall have to, Mr. Legatt, I expect," he said. " But to you I am still a monk."

" Well, sit down and watch me."

As I drank mine, he laughed.

" Do you remember, Mr. Legatt, how angry you were when I insisted on paying for your drink on the *Dagonet* ? "

" How I hated you ! " I cried.

" I reckon that I was hateful," he replied with equanimity.

Michael had now a thick growth of hair *en brosse*, flecked with grey, which gave to his thin, ecclesiastical face an incongruous and comical finish.

" I wonder whether you will do something for me," he asked, and I smiled rather sourly.   I knew that question was coming, just as I knew that I should help him if I could and that there would be no possibility of doubt that I could.   The pertinacity of a man with a single end in view would twist the stars from their courses.

" Of course I will," I answered, with more of acquiescence that I should than of eagerness that I would.

" Do you know a Mr. Jack Sanford ? "

" I don't, Michael."

It seemed astonishing to me that I didn't, since Michael obviously wanted me to know him.

" He lives in this street."

" He might live in Mandalay for all that means."

Crowther got up from his chair and wandered about the room, touching an ornament here and a book there.   He was very restless.

" What you want, Michael, is a Watson Number One," I said.

Michael laughed.

" I shall have, some day, to tell you what happens to Tempters.   It is not pleasant."   He turned and planted himself in front of me.   " So you can't help me."

" I can't introduce you to Mr. Jack Sanford, if that's what you mean."

He nodded his stubbly head.

" I thought that since you run about London at night you might have the right of entry there," he said, and I sat up in my chair.

" Oh !   Has he got the upper part of a house about six doors down ? "

" He has."

" Rather a mysterious place, isn't it ? "

" No," said Crowther simply.   " It's just a gambling hell."

I was not surprised.   I had not been able to see what else it could be.

" Something like Schwegu, in fact, when they are burning an abbot ? " I said.

Happily Imogen and her cousin were not present. Had they been, I should have had to listen to a chorus of : " Oh, Martin ! " and reproaches that I was not nice.

" But I suppose," I continued reluctantly, " that

if you gave me a little time I could get myself presented."

Michael's face lit up with hope.

" And me, too ? "

" Really, really," I began, and stopped abruptly. Michael was looking at himself in the mirror above the mantelshelf, with a wry smile upon his mouth.

" I should look odd," he said.

I was stricken with remorse. It was obvious that he wanted immensely to go to Mr. Jack Sanford's, as obvious, indeed, as the difficulty I should have in explaining him.

" Oh, dolled up in our best gent's dinner-jacket with trouserings to match, you'll look fine, Michael," I said. " Where can I find you ? "

He gave me the address of a private hotel in Bayswater, shook me by the hand and went out of the door. He did not thank me for the trouble I was going to be put to. I was serving myself by any act of kindness I might do to him, though what kindness there could be in introducing a monk into a London tripot I was not at this time able to imagine, except, of course, that by some means or another he hoped there to get on to the track of his stolen sapphire.

However, I was taking Imogen that night to dinner at a restaurant and a theatre and I put the problem to her. She overleaped in a second the obstacle of an introduction and cried :

" I can manage that all right, and I am coming, too ! "

" Imogen, it's no place for you," I protested.

" It's more a place for me than it is for Michael,"
she replied.

" Damn Michael ! " said I heartily.

" Oh, Martin ! " said she, and for the moment that
was the end of the matter.

But two nights later she brought up to me at a
dance an infinitely kind young man who regarded
my elderly bufferdom of thirty years as something
which demanded from him every consideration.
He called me " sir," and the title cut me to the
quick.

" This is Lord Salcombe," said Imogen.

" Imogen tells me, sir, you want one evening to
trot along to Jack Sanford's," he said.

Did he look down at my legs wondering whether I
should need two sticks to get me there ?

" I should love to," said I.

" Well, we might make a party, what ?   The three
of us ! "

" But there's to be——"   A fourth, I was on the
point of saying when a look of incredulous amazement from Imogen brought me to an inconclusive
stutter.   Lord Salcombe, however, put it all down
to senility, if he noticed anything out of the way at
all.

" We'll dine and go to a cinema.   Then we'll drop
round to Savile Row and try to draw the Muses.
Pretty good, what ? "   And since I looked puzzled :
" No ?   Cryptic, perhaps.   I mean the nine."   He
seized—really seized by both elbows, a very pretty
astonished girl who was passing him.   " Our dance,
Esmeralda !   Not your name ?   You don't say !
Never mind !   Our dance, what ? "

And in a moment they were half-way across the room. Imogen and I went downstairs to supper.

" You see, darling," she said sweetly, " what was wanted was a little finesse. Oh, of course, you have lots of finesse, really, and I am sure when you were out in the jungle there wasn't an elephant that could match you. But the noblest of men drop a brick from time to time, and if I hadn't stared you would have dropped St. Paul's."

" How ? " I asked humbly.

" The Salcombe boy wouldn't have thanked me for Michael. When he had seen Michael he would probably have suggested that we tour London by night in a charabanc. But if we go with the Salcombe boy by ourselves or with Pamela, we shall get the entrée to Jack Sanford's and then we can take Michael."

" Imogen, you're a marvel," I said. " You ought to be an Ambassador."

Imogen turned over a menu card and pushed it towards me.

" Please write that down and sign it," she said. " I'd like to show it to father."

If I have chosen too often to present Imogen in her laughing mood, I beg your pardon. The prolonged and viscous kisses of the films teach me that reticence is out of the fashion and I shall try to amend. But, in fact, we did keep a public reticence which was the very salt of our private meetings. Passion and a lovely comradeship went hand in hand with fun in Imogen, and if my picture of her lacks those deeper qualities, set the blame upon the painter rather than upon his subject.

We went to the house in Savile Row one evening of the next week—a party of four after all. But the fourth was Pamela Brayburn. Salcombe had no doubt prepared the way, for we were admitted without question into a dark hall and thence to a lighted one where we left our hats and coats. A large and portly butler—Crowther in other days would have called him an oldy Englishy butler—ushered us up a short flight of stairs into a beautiful oblong room. The inner wall of this room was broken by double doors which stood open, disclosing a second room at the back with a long buffet. At once the silence which had so perplexed me was explained. For although there was a buzz of talk from Mr. Jack Sanford's guests, it was contained within that inner room. The outer one with the windows on the street was the place of business, and there quiet and decorum reigned, broken only by the phrases of the tables—" *En cartes,*" " *Baccara,*" " *Rien ne va plus,*" " *La main passe.*"

Mr. Jack Sanford stepped forward and Salcombe presented us in turn. Mr. Sanford was a plump, sandy little man with a few long fair hairs running from front to back of his head. He had a white face, a button for a nose, a heavy chin and a pair of shrewd small blue eyes.

" Lord Salcombe's friends are very welcome," he said. " There is a buffet, as you see, and you will play or not as you feel disposed. There are two tables, you will notice, one for baccara and the other for a smaller game of chemin-de-fer. When I play myself, it is usually at the smaller table "—and with that he left us to our own devices.

We watched the big table for a little while where the play certainly ran high. I recognised one or two racing men, a proprietor of theatres, some well-known figures from the City, a Cabinet Minister and a young Frenchman who was seated by a pretty girl with a rope of pearls about her neck and some valuable rings upon her fingers. The banker was a dark, good-looking fellow with a thatch of black sleek hair and a quick eye, and it seemed to me that the luck was running against him. But I had no great opportunity of making sure, for Salcombe said :

" I think we ought to play a little at the shimmy table. I see there are some places vacant now."

We sat down, staked a little, took the bank in turn and did very little damage either to ourselves or our fellow-players. Imogen won twenty pounds; Pamela, after losing a five-pound note, wandered off with Salcombe to the buffet. I sat by Imogen's side, watching the clock and wondering what in the world Michael Crowther would be doing on this galley. The rooms certainly were as hot as Burma, but there must be some other attraction. But we couldn't see it.

It was three o'clock in the morning before Imogen and I discovered it. We discovered it at the same moment. Imogen was on my left hand and the shoe of cards had come round to her. She put five pounds in as her bank and I added another five, making the whole bank ten pounds.

" *Banco*," cried a voice across the table and both Imogen and I jumped as if we had been shot, to the amusement of the company. But we did not jump at the brusque voice across the table. Between the croupier's announcement that there was a bank of ten pounds and the challenge of the man across the table we had heard another voice, Jack Sanford's, and he was addressing the banker at the big table behind us.

"I think when you have exhausted those cards, Robin, we ought to close."

It was the name Robin which startled us. Robin was the key word to the enigma of Crowther's intentions. Robin must be that Robin Calhoun who had bought Crowther's jewel for his lady-love outside the Galle Face Hotel at Colombo. Here he was taking the big bank at Jack Sanford's little hell in Savile Row and no doubt Jack Sanford's partner. Imogen slipped the cards quickly out of the box.

"We'll go and look," she said quietly, "as soon as my bank's over."

I agreed with a nod of the head. We would go into the room with the buffet and look for a pretty girl with a beautiful sapphire on a platinum chain. But as chance would have it, Imogen's bank went piling up. It rose to sixty pounds and she thought it too mean a business to take her winnings and let the hand go, though she was now in a fever to have done with it. The bank ran four more times and then she lost when there was very little money staked against her. She passed the shoe, stuffed her winnings into her bag and got up. We crossed to the buffet, and with a sandwich and a glass of champagne as an excuse, we examined our fellow-guests. There were pretty girls certainly, but not one of them wore a sapphire on a platinum chain.

"We may have better luck next time," said Imogen. She led me by the sleeve to Mr. Jack Sanford, thanked him and asked: "May we come again?" in so wistful a voice that no man could have resisted her.

"We have a little chemin-de-fer game every evening," said Jack, his white, plump face dimpling with smiles. "And three times a week we have a table of baccara—Sundays, Wednesdays, and Thursdays. I shall be happy to see you and Mr. Legatt whenever you have the time."

I drove Imogen to her house. As she took leave of me at the door she said:

"Your Michael's a clever old bird. I wonder what he's up to?"

We were both inclined to imagine that Michael had devised some subtle scheme by which his sapphire was to be restored to him without the commission of any crime. But we were quite out of our reckoning. Michael had the simplest scheme in the world, if scheme it could be called at all.

CHAPTER XVII

THE MAN FROM LIMOGES

"YOU must see that he's properly dressed, Martin! And pay attention to his shoes! If he looks like a policeman out of uniform, we shall be asked to go. I think you had better take him to your bootmaker. And then you must give him a few lessons in chemin-de-fer. He'll have to play a little, else why did we bring him? And he must have a few pounds to play with. And above all, whatever he's after, he must promise not to make a scene."

Thus Imogen under the trees by the Row, on a morning in the first week of June. We had returned twice to Jack Sanford's apartment since Salcombe had introduced us. We had not seen any girl wearing the sapphire or one answering to the name of Jill Leslie. We had learned that the young Frenchman was the Vicomte de Craix and that he had been losing heavily. We had struck up a sort of gambling-room acquaintance with him and with a few of the other habitual visitors—the pretty girl with the rope of pearls amongst them. She seemed to have a large circle of friends, for she brought a new one each time, and everybody called her Robbie. In a word, we had established ourselves and acquired the right to bring a visitor.

I followed out my instructions dutifully, and on the Wednesday appointed, Michael, dressed by my tailor and shod by my bootmaker, with his hair now long enough to lie down upon his head, met Imogen and myself in the grill-room of the Semiramis Hotel at half-past eight of the evening. We dined together and Michael was the least excited of the three of us. I think that those of us who had willy-nilly fallen under the compulsion to help him in his quest of the sapphire always found him an exciting personage—yes, even when he was most still.

"You must have no fear on my account, Miss Cloud," he said with a smile. "I shall make no scene, and I can play chemin-de-fer and baccara, and I have money enough."

"You are sure of that ? " Imogen insisted.

"Quite. Don't forget that I had money enough to build a pagoda. And I think that I am not so far now from the end of my search but that it will last me out."

We were curious to know how he had discovered the whereabouts of Robin Calhoun and he told us as we ate.

"I went among my old acquaintances in the City. They were of the flashy kind, I regret to say, Miss Cloud, and I had an idea that it was possible that I might pick up a line on Calhoun amongst them. I was lucky. They knew quite a lot about Jack Sanford and his partner and how well they were doing."

Imogen was a little restless throughout the dinner and it was not until we were half-way through that she explained her restlessness.   Michael was drinking water.

" Don't you think that a glass of champagne would be helpful ? " she asked ; and Michael beamed at her.

" I might just as well, Miss Cloud," he said, " since I am eating at this forbidden hour. I have laid aside my yellow robe for the time being, as I have quite a right to do, and I am committing no fault, whatever I eat and drink. But I claim the right of our race to be illogical and I'll go on drinking water."

He insisted that there was no demand to be made upon any of us that evening, no scandal in which our names would figure.

" I want to see my man, perhaps the lady too, so that I may know them again. I want to scrape an acquaintance with one of them at all events, if I can. I haven't a gun or a mask or a car to make a getaway. There'll be no thrills, Miss Cloud, to-night."

But he was wrong. There were to be thrills, though they were not caused by Michael Crowther, and no man was more surprised than he when they occurred. The quest of the sapphire indeed was proceeding on the ordinary plane of human affairs. Sometimes chance helped him, sometimes it thwarted him ; and on this night it was unexpectedly to help him, although at the time not one of us was able to recognise any signs of his good fortune.

We went early to Savile Row in order to give Michael a chance of finding a seat at the big table.

It was eleven when we entered the room and the table was being actually made up, so that Michael could only find a place at one end. There had been no trouble about his admission; and once in the room he did not even provoke the least curiosity. The play was the thing and, anyway, odder birds than he had found a welcome at Jack Sanford's little casino. Imogen and I stood behind Crowther's chair and watched. We noticed that Monsieur de Craix had brought a couple of friends with him, one a thin, finicking, timorous, dilettante person whom I heard addressed as Mr. Julius Ricardo, and the other a burly middle-aged Frenchman with a blue shaven skin, inclined to be a trifle boisterous. Both of them seemed to me astonishing companions for so obvious a member of the French Jockey Club as the spruce young Vicomte de Craix. Or rather, they would have seemed astonishing companions in any other gathering. But if misfortune makes strange bed-fellows, a gambling-house makes stranger. Monsieur de Craix, who was seated next to the croupier, introduced the Frenchman to Robin Calhoun across the table.

"This is my very good friend, Monsieur Chaunard. I marked the place for him next to you, Mr. Calhoun," and he laughed, adding: "He likes a game, I can tell you."

Robin Calhoun bowed to this new-comer upon his right, smiled, ran a shrewd eye over him and was content.

"You are of Paris?" he asked, and Monsieur Chaunard shook his head vigorously.

"No, no, my friend, look at me! I am of the

Provinces. I make the china pots at Limoges. Now I take my holiday from the business." He sat down in his chair and rubbed his hands together loudly. Close by my side I heard a little prim voice:

" Vulgar ! Vulgar ! " and I saw that this new Mr. Ricardo was standing at my side and in quite a twitter lest the man from Limoges should misbehave.

The cards were brought in to Robin Calhoun who tore the wrappers from the packs and handed them across the table for the croupier to shuffle. By the side of the croupier on the one side, as I have said, was the Vicomte de Craix, and on the other, exactly opposite to Monsieur Chaunard, sat a man in the early forties whom I had seen and talked to once or twice before, a partner in a famous firm of stockbrokers named Arnold Mann and a very level-headed person. Chaunard turned to his neighbour on his right.

" You have the good fortune ? Yes ? No ? For me, I think you shall see something to-night. Yes. I feel that I am in my veins."

" Oh, dear, oh, dear," murmured Mr. Ricardo. " In the vein."

The murmur reached Monsieur Chaunard's ears, and he smiled blandly at his twittering Ricardo.

" No, no, you are wrong, my friend," he said simply. " It is a phrase. I am in my veins. It means I am not the weathercock which turns South and East and North and West. No, I go plong for the nine," and he slapped his hand down on the table as though he pinned the famous card down there for good. Mr. Ricardo was, I think, dazed by that wondrous confusion of veins and vanes. He had no words and we no eyes for him. For the game was beginning.

We saw the cards, now one thick pack, passed back to Robin Calhoun. He held them tightly between his thumb and his fingers and extended them to the right and the left across the table, offering at the same time with his left hand a blank red card so that anyone could slip it into the pack and make a cut wherever he or she chose. I think the pack was cut six times. There was an air of expectation in the room that night which passed from one to the other of us and held certainly those who stood about the table in a curious suspense. We waited for a great *duello* between the manufacturer from Limoges and Robin Calhoun. Imogen at my side, for instance, was standing with her lips parted, her eyes fixed on Robin Calhoun. There was something in her gaze which reminded me faintly of the afternoon in the rest-house on the road to Anuradhapura, when I had seen her upright against the wall. Mr. Ricardo on the other side of me was breathing hard and lifting himself ridiculously on his toes and so down again. I, too, was waiting for a curtain to go up. Or, rather, the curtain had gone up and I was waiting for the action to begin. There were the characters brightly illuminated ; Jack Sanford looking on comfortably with a big cigar between his lips ; Robin Calhoun glancing round the table once with a question : " Is that staked ? " when a chip was a little too near the line ; the impassive croupier opposite with his long broad blade of very thin black wood ; the young

Vicomte de Craix next to him with his eyeglass ; and opposite, the big black man from Limoges, his thumbs in the armholes of his white waistcoat, at his ease, completely in his veins, with a vast smile upon his face as though he wanted to kiss the world.

"I begin with the moderation," he said and pushed a ten-pound chip over the line. Mr. Ricardo gulped audibly. It might have been his money which was pushed over the line. " Afterwards we shall see."

We did see. The man from Limoges took the cards for the right-hand tableau, a financier from the Argentine those upon the left. I did not notice the value of the cards, but I remember that the bank won from the first or right-hand tableau and was on an equality with the second. At the second coup he won from both tableaux. The bank had started with five hundred pounds and it must now have amounted to double that sum. As Robin Calhoun began to deal the third coup, the man from Limoges began his antics.

Calhoun dealt two cards to each tableau and two to himself. He dealt them one by one, face downwards in the usual way, one to the right, one to the left, one to himself, and so again. It was the croupier's business to lift the two cards for the right and left tableaux in turn on his long blade, still face downwards, and present them to the player whose turn it was to hold them. The two cards for the right hand were thus in the first instance dealt in front of Monsieur Chaunard, although it was the second player to his right who would handle them. Monsieur Chaunard did not touch them. It was not his right. He was leaning back in his chair perfectly correctly. But he looked at the backs of them and said gently but clearly, so clearly that the croupier who had already stretched forward his blade to pass the cards on, stopped in the middle of his movement :

" Aha, we lose again. We have a *bûche* and a one. And our friends on the left they have an eight and three, also making one. And the dealer he has a *bûche* and a six. We must draw a card on our side, by the law." He looked round at an assemblage outraged into silence. " We shall draw again the one, making us two. Our friend on the left, he too must draw. He will draw a two making him three. And the dealer having six will not draw. So, as I say, he will win."

The silence was broken by the indignant voice of Mr. Jack Sanford.

" Really, Mossoo le Vicomte, your friend——"

" He has the bad flavour—yes," said the man from Limoges genially, and at my side Mr. Ricardo in a sort of agony :

" Taste ! Taste ! "

Robin Calhoun turned with a smile to Chaunard.

" You agree ? " said he. " Not quite out of the top drawer, what ? "

Chaunard moved his head forward quickly, and there was for a second a flutter of alarm about the table. But it seemed to me that as yet, at all events, there was no chance of trouble. Chaunard was not so much goaded by the insult as interested in the phrase. He, in fact, and Robin Calhoun were the coolest people present. Robin was marvellous.

" It is, of course, impossible to continue the game. I beg you all to withdraw your stakes."

He reached his hand out to the stack of cards leaning against the rest in front of him. It was like good acting, quicker than life and very neat but without any appearance of hurry. In a fraction of a second he would have picked up the pack and scattered it in confusion over the table. But he did not get that second. Monsieur Chaunard who, with his blue chin, really looked like an actor, was by a fraction of a second quicker. A very strong hand pounced upon Robin's wrist.

" Let the cards stay as they are," said Chaunard, and such authority rang in his voice that we were all taken by surprise—even Robin Calhoun. For he shrugged his shoulders and sat back in his chair. Then from the opposite side of the table, where, in fact, we were standing, another voice, very cool and quiet, was raised, Mr. Arnold Mann's.

" Yes, let the cards stay as they are, and, Jack, perhaps you had better close the doors to the buffet."

I never saw anything more sinister than the aspect of that table, with the company still as a set of images and their eyes watching lest Calhoun's fingers should touch the stack of cards in front of him or the croupier's blade the four cards still face downwards upon the table. In the other room voices were being raised, questions were being asked, there was an excited surge of people towards the double doors. Mr. Jack Sanford was just in time to prevent a rush into this quiet room.

" Just a moment ! " he cried. " It is a little question. Stand back, please. In a moment I open again."

He managed to close the doors but he did not open again. The stockbroker with the cool voice continued:

" Let us see whether this gentleman is right. You said that your cards were a ten and a one. Will you turn them up ? "

Monsieur Chaunard obeyed. They were a ten and a one.

" And the second tableau was an eight and a three. Let us see them."

He reached across the table and turned them up himself.

" Yes, they are an eight and a three. Now let us see the dealer's."

But Calhoun did not move. To upset the big stack now would have been a confession of guilt to a charge which no one had formulated. With his own two cards he was not concerned.

" They may be any two out of the pack," said he.

" And what do you say they are, Monsieur Chaunard ? " Arnold Mann asked.

" A *bûche* and a six."

Arnold Mann himself took the scoop from the croupier, and using infinite care not to touch the big pack stacked against the rest, lifted daintily upon the blade the two cards in front of Robin, and turning them over dropped them in the middle of the table. There they were, a King and a six.

Again there was a stir about the table. I wondered that Robin Calhoun sat in his place so still. If he scattered the big pack even now, we should take it as a confession, no doubt, but we should have no proof. But I think now that he was afraid. The stir was no longer to be put down to fear. There was anger—yes, even amongst those well-dressed unobtrusive people of good manner, the dangerous anger of the mass.

" And the next cards to be turned up ? " Mann asked, looking at Chaunard.

Chaunard looked round the table.

" With your consent . . ." he said, and with such light fingers that one could hardly believe they belonged to such big strong hands, he picked up the stack of cards and held them out to the stockbroker.

" The first card for our tableau here will be an ace and for the left-hand tableau a two," he said.

Amidst a deadly silence Arnold Mann exposed the two top cards, an ace and a two. Here and there a cry of anger rose. It looked as though the storm must burst. But the stockbroker and the man from Limoges between them held the gathering in control.

" I think you should explain," said the stockbroker.

" I will do better. I will make you an experiment first. I will tell you the cards you hold one by one, and one by one you shall turn them up."

No one had eyes now for either Jack Sanford who stood by the door as white as a perspiring ghost, if so strange a thing could be, or for Robin Calhoun who sat in his place with a mask for a face, a mask without an expression. Chaunard gave the value of a card and a card of that value the stockbroker turned up. So it went on in a monotonous exactitude until the pack was exhausted.

Our admiration of such a feat was immense, but Monsieur Chaunard did not wait for its expression. He beamed on us. He handed himself bouquets on the instant—Caruso after singing " *La donna è mobile* " to an Italian audience.

" That was good? Yes? Worthy of the bravos? I think so. Aha, Mister Banker," and he swung round upon Robin Calhoun. " Me—it may be—I do not come out of the top of my drawers, but the memory, he does ! "

" Revolting ! " twittered Mr. Ricardo.

Imogen leaned forward right across me.

" Nonsense ! He's an absolute darling ! "

" Silence, if you please," said Mr. Mann.

" Yes, the silence, whilst I talk," Chaunard agreed enthusiastically. " Monsieur de Craix, he comes to see me in Paris."

" At Limoges," said the stockbroker.

" I make the apologies. We are the mugs here to-night but I do not make us at Limoges. No. I inhabit Paris. At times I come to stay with a friend in London "—and here Mr. Ricardo shifted his feet uncomfortably—" just to keep myself fresh in the idioms of your language. But that is all. M. de Craix, he says to me : ' There is a game of baccara. Often it is—oblong.' "

" Square," said Mr. Ricardo.

" Well, square or oblong. ' But now and then there is a big killing.' So having a holiday I come and I am lucky. For the first time I come there is to be the big killing—the 705 system, as the old chief

of my establishment used to call it. I beg your
attention."

He rose and walked across the room to a desk upon
which some packs of cards lay in their wrappers.
As he rose Robin Calhoun rose, too, and at once
Arnold Mann, the stockbroker, spoke sharply.

" You will wait, if you please, Mr. Calhoun."

" Yes," said the Frenchman over his shoulder.
" Certainly the gentleman should wait. Both the
gentlemen should wait. For there may be restitutions."

Decorous as the whole conduct of this scandalous
affair had been, that one word restitutions sent a
wave of brightness and hope throughout the company. Mr. Robin Calhoun resumed his seat with a
shrug of the shoulders and a contemptuous face.
Mr. Jack Sanford, holding tight to the handles of
the double doors, looked as if he were going to
faint.

Monsieur Chaunard, no longer of Limoges, brought
a pack of cards to the baccara table and resumed his
seat. He stripped the wrapper from the pack.

" I will arrange the cards in an order," and he
turned over the top card. It was a seven. He
looked at the second—it was a ten. He laughed and
looked at the third—it was a five. He rose and
bowed with great ceremony to Jack Sanford.

" I thank you. My work is done for me, and then
the wrapper replaced."

He laid out the cards face upwards in four lines of
thirteen cards to a line. Counting the Court cards
and the tens of no value, the object of the game
being to get nine or as near to it as possible, the

values ran as follows. For I made a note of them
as the cards were turned up.

$$7 \; 0 \; 5 \; 9 \; 0 \; 2 \; 6 \; 0 \; 4 \; 1 \; 3 \; 6 \; 0$$
$$8 \; 0 \; 1 \; 2 \; 6 \; 9 \; 0 \; 8 \; 7 \; 0 \; 9 \; 7 \; 0$$
$$4 \; 9 \; 0 \; 2 \; 5 \; 0 \; 4 \; 8 \; 0 \; 3 \; 2 \; 0 \; 8$$
$$1 \; 1 \; 3 \; 5 \; 5 \; 3 \; 4 \; 0 \; 0 \; 0 \; 6 \; 0 \; 7$$

Monsieur Chaunard contemplated the cards with
a smile.

" This is the combination known to a famous chief
of my establishment, Monsieur Goron, as 705.
You see the very good reason," and he pointed to
the first three cards of the top row. " Yes, it is all
correct. I have him by the heart. Now I gather
the cards all up in that order, beginning at the top
row and working from left to right like the grousers
from the moors in your illustrated papers. So ! "

I had never seen a man so completely savouring
the enjoyment of the leading part. He was Mounet-
Sully and Coquelin and Henry Irving and Lucien
Guitry all rolled into one. He beamed, he—I find
no other word for it—he listened to the deep silence
of the room, he watched the eyes riveted upon his
hands. He was happy.

" So ! "

He had the pack in his hand, the cards now face
upwards and the last card picked up showing a
seven of spades. He turned the pack over so that
now the backs were uppermost and the top card, of
course, was the first seven.

" Now," he said, " in that order, which was the
order of the pack when it lay upon the desk there,

the banker cannot lose one coup. Once or twice there may be an equality. Every other time he wins."

Robin Calhoun laughed sarcastically.

" I think our unusual visitor is forgetting that the cards were shuffled," he said.

To my amazement, and to Mr. Ricardo's disgust, the big visitor became playful. He turned and dug his long middle finger into Robin's white waistcoat at the level of his waist.

" That is the good one ! "

" Ah," murmured Mr. Ricardo. " A good one."

" No, no, my friend," Chaunard continued, taking no notice whatever of Mr. Ricardo. " It is you who do the shuffle now with the words, and your croupier who did not do the shuffle with the cards then. I watch him. With my eyes, I watch him."

" Well, I don't suppose you watched him with your feet," said Robin sourly.

" Yes, I watch him. And he shuffle as a hundred tenth-rate conjurers can shuffle, without altering the lie of one card."

" But I cut the pack afterwards," cried a woman towards the end of the table.

" So did I ! "

" So did I ! "

Other voices joined in but they left Monsieur Chaunard quite unmoved.

" And so you shall again, madame. And you ! And you ! And you ! "

With an excellent mimicry of Robin Calhoun, he daintily extended the pack held tight between the fingers and thumb of one hand, and the red card for the cut with the other. " As many as will. The cut, it makes no difference. The 705 is a work of genius. Now you, monsieur! Now you!"

I think that he had the pack cut seven times.

" Will someone sweep those old packs off the table ? " he asked, and as soon as that was done he moved the rest across from in front of Robin to in front of Arnold Mann.

" You are the banker. And you cannot lose ! "

Arnold Mann slipped the cards off the pack to right and to left and to himself, turned them face upwards, refused cards or drew cards as the hands required, when the pack was exhausted sat back.

" It is true. The banker wins every coup." He looked steadily for a moment or two at Monsieur Chaunard. " And what is this establishment of yours of which you spoke ? "

Monsieur Chaunard shrugged his shoulders.

" The Sûreté of Paris,'' he replied, and a movement rippled swiftly about the table like a flaw of wind about a pond. " You have an establishment of the same kind here. You call it the Q.E.D."

" No, no ! " Mr. Ricardo was of too precise a mind to endure so ridiculous a variation. " The C.I.D.," he cried like a man suffering grievously from the toothache. " The C.I.D.," and he repeated the initials, spacing them, so that never such a mistake might occur again.

Monsieur Chaunard was charming, not at all annoyed by the unnecessary interruption, just dignified and firm, if I may use his admirable phrase, a man in his veins. He looked rather sorrowfully at Mr. Ricardo.

" My friend, you overstep a little.   In the social-
ities I am at your feet.   But in the matters of police,
I know.   I read your papers.   I see great riddles
solved and at the end—what ?   Q.E.D.   Ah, a fine
tribute !   The Press—it gives us no such recognition
in France."

" Very well," said Arnold Mann a trifle impatiently, " you belong to the Q.E.D. of France."

" It is so."

" And your name ? "

" I am Hanaud."   The reply was made with a
superb simplicity.   " In every generation our police
has a Hanaud.   I am he of this one."

There seemed to be nothing further to be said and
Hanaud rose from his chair.

" You will understand, Mr. Sanford, Mr. Calhoun,
that I am not here officially.   If ever you came to
France that would be another matter.   But here I
am the friend of Monsieur de Craix and all that I
can do is to repeat one little word—restitutions."

He bowed ceremoniously and in a dead silence he
went out of the room with Mr. Ricardo at his heels.
He had hardly closed the door behind him before
the spell was broken.   A veritable clamour broke
out.   Those imprisoned in the buffet added their
voices and their strength.   The double doors bent
and broke.   Jack Sanford was swept aside ; a wave
of curious, angry people surged in to mingle with the
others.   And all at once that decorous assemblage
became a mob, ugly, raw, deadly.   Jack Sanford,
shaking with fear, cowered against the wall.   In
front of him a throng of hysterical women and
excited men threatened him.   Fine clothes went for

nothing. It was mob-passion working up to the fling of the first stone; and of the two sexes it seemed to me that the women were the more alarming.

" Ladies—gentlemen—we will put all right. It was a mistake—someone has tricked us all," Jack Sanford screamed in a high shrill feminine scream which made me feel sick. And at once jeers and cries interrupted him. But amongst them all was one in the room who kept his head. I caught Imogen to my side and drew her away towards the windows upon Savile Row. I looked about for Michael Crowther. He had disappeared. I said to myself bitterly : " He has bolted. Pongyis don't fight even to protect the women they are with," and as the thought flashed into my mind, the door on to the staircase was thrown open and Michael stood upon the threshold. He cried in a voice which overtopped the tumult so that not a man nor a woman but must hear him :

" The police ! "

It was a word of magic.

" The police ! " he cried again and his voice rang with authority. He was again as in old days the captain of a ship and the ship in danger. The shouts were hushed, the abuse and the threats died away in growls. No one wanted the police brought into the affair. All turned towards the door ; and with a spontaneous single movement the women fell back, the men ranged themselves in front of them. A bare space of floor littered with fragments of lace was left between the men and Crowther at the door.

"You?" said Arnold Mann.   "You are of the police?"

Michael shook his head.

"There are no police," he answered quietly. "But in five minutes there would have been."

A gasp of relief followed upon his words. A woman here and there even began to repair her face and her toilet. There was suddenly a sense of shame. In the midst of the silence Crowther stalked across the room.   He looked at Imogen and myself.

"You and I, at all events, have no reason to stay."

We followed him down the stairs without a word. Imogen and I got our coats from the cloak-room and went out.   Even in that quiet street a tiny crowd had gathered.   For once the silent room had spoken but it was silent again now.   I had parked my car a few houses away.   Crowther was still in command. We drove away.

H

CHAPTER XVIII

IMOGEN ASKS QUESTIONS

AT the corner where Clifford Street runs into Bond Street Crowther asked to be put down. I stopped the car but Imogen said:

" Please wait a moment, Michael."

It was a small car and we were all together on the one seat with Imogen between Michael and myself. She turned her face towards him.

" Didn't you feel to-night that you had a place in the world ? " she asked.

Michael was silent.

" In this world—here ? "

Michael moved his legs uncomfortably.

" And rather a fine place if you chose."

" I think I'll get down," said Crowther.

But he did not open the door. Imogen was still looking at him. I was remembering small, long-forgotten things—not his bumptiousness nor his dishonesty—but how completely he was master of his ship amongst the swirls and sandbanks of the Irrawaddy and with what neatness and certainty he had edged her into the one tiny vacant space in the line of steamers at Mandalay. Thus we sat without speaking for a few moments. Then Imogen continued her questioning.

" How old are you, Crowther ? "

" Forty-three," he answered.

" Not too old," said Imogen.

" To lose one's soul again? No. Not too old for that," he replied. His hand moved towards the catch of the door, but Imogen had not done with him.

" You were sure of yourself to-night, Crowther. One could tell it from your voice. You had authority, You were the Centurion who says unto one, Go, and he goeth and to another, Come, and he cometh."

Crowther's hand fell to his side again. It seemed to me that Imogen was pressing him rather cruelly.

" You enjoyed your moment to-night, Crowther."

Crowther did not answer, but Imogen pressed him.

" I could hear that, too, in your voice. You enjoyed it."

" Yes, I did."

Crowther made the admission reluctantly, remorsefully.

" Well, then ! " cried Imogen.

" The more blame to me," Crowther answered. " It was vanity."

" It was power."

And with his next words Crowther's calmness broke up like the face of a pool in a sudden storm. His voice was low but vibrant with passion.

" No ! I tried here. I failed here. I was more unhappy here than I believed it possible that a man could be."

Imogen caught him up.

" You tried . . . you failed . . . you were unhappy. . . ." She repeated, weighing his words. Were there ever reasons so feeble ? They sounded all the more lamentable in that there was no contempt in Imogen's voice. A note of surprise, perhaps, that the man who had dominated a room full of hysterical and violent people should use such excuses, but no more than that.

" Service means nothing, then," she said gently, and Crowther started as though she had slapped his face.

" I have only one thing to do here and then I'm through. Through! Do you hear that?" And in a gust of bitterness he added : " I hope I won't see you again."

He snatched at the handle of the door and flung himself out of the car. He banged the door to and stood for a moment on the kerb. The light of a street-lamp showed us his face. It was white and his eyes were smouldering with resentment. Then he turned on his heel and went back by the way we had come—up Clifford Street towards Savile Row.

Imogen looked straight in front of her with her face set. She was hurt, and deeply hurt. I felt a swift unreasonable stab of jealousy. Why should Imogen be so concerned? Why should Crowther so disquiet us with his lost sapphire?

" It might be the Kohinoor," I grumbled.

Imogen shook her head.

" It isn't a jewel at all. It's an idea," she answered.

It was at all events the symbol of an idea. But the idea had given us nothing but trouble and to Imogen had brought actual danger. It stretched over our heads as the shadow of Adam's Peak stretched over Ratnapura. I drove on slowly, wishing that I had never set foot on the gangway of the *Dagonet* nor made the acquaintance of her Captain.

Suddenly Imogen laid her hand upon my arm.

" Do you mean that, Martin ? " she asked.

" I never said a word," I answered.

" You didn't have to. I knew what you were wishing and I don't want you to wish it. For I think we found our way to one another sooner than we otherwise should have done because of Michael's sapphire."

I had no answer to that. The morning on Adam's Peak, the day at the rest-house in the jungle, the meeting on the terrace of the Rock-Temple at Dhambulla—they had made a whole world of difference to both of us.

" You're right, sweetheart," I said, and since at this time of night I could drive across Mayfair with one hand, I slipped my left arm about her waist. " We'll do what we can."

But I never looked upon Crowther with the same eyes afterwards, nor thought of him with the same regard. A little while ago he had grown into an aloof and romantic figure—the man who must recognise no ties, be moved by no love, and owe no duty. But four words spoken by Imogen had stripped the romance from him. " Service means nothing, then ? " I wanted to be fair. I knew that the monks taught and taught well, but there was no obligation upon them to teach. Their monastery grounds were school-rooms but they need not keep them open. Service was no part of their creed. Service meant nothing and I could not remember anything worth devoting a life to into which service did not enter.

And Crowther bristled with anger. For he had no answer.

CHAPTER XIX

JILL LESLIE

THE establishment of Jack Sanford was open for the last time on the night when the man from Limoges had the bad flavour to demonstrate the 705 formula. I might go home as late as I would, I saw no light slip past the edges of the curtains into Savile Row. All was dark in that upper apartment. A board announced that a commodious flat was to let and one day the big vans of an auctioneer carried all the furniture away to a sales-room. Robin Calhoun had vanished. Michael Crowther and his troubles passed for a little time out of my knowledge and might, perhaps, have done so altogether but for one of Imogen's idiosyncrasies.

It was one of her pleasures to discover a new restaurant, and the smaller the better. At once all her friends must try it. The cooking was the best in London, the cellar stocked with unparalleled vintages. There never had been a restaurant so choice, though there was certain to be another one just a tiny bit better when in the course of a month or two another discovery was made. Late in June of this year Imogen discovered such a paragon of a place in that capital of little restaurants, Soho. It was a long, low, frenchified room with cushioned benches against the wall and scrubby menus written out in copying ink, and it was called Le Buisson. Two little green trees in two little green tubs stood outside the window upon the pavement. There was a patron and several *spécialitiés* of the *maison* which were quite marvellous ; and, in fact, it was quite indistinguishable from half a dozen similar restaurants within a radius of a hundred yards. To Le Buisson I was accordingly taken on the very last day of June. We dined there at eight o'clock intending to go to a cinema afterwards, and as we took our seats I noticed, a little way down the room, a young singer who was beginning to make her mark in the world. Letty Ransome. She was of a quite lustrous beauty with black hair and a pale, clear face romantic in repose. She gave an entertainment single-handed with a piano to help her.

" Won't she be late ? " I asked of Imogen.

" No. She comes on late nowadays. I saw her at the Corinth a couple of days ago," Imogen answered. " You see who's with her ? "

I had not seen more than the back of her head, for she was talking earnestly to Letty Ransome, but she turned her face towards us at that moment.

" Why, it's the girl who was with De Craix at Jack Sanford's——" And then I stopped with a gasp. " Do you see what she's wearing ? "

" Yes," said Imogen without any surprise whatever.

The girl carried about her neck the platinum chain with the sapphire pendant. " Yes, that's Jill Leslie." And as she spoke the names she smiled at the girl and gave her a nod of recognition.

"How in the world did you learn that?" I asked. "She was never with Robin Calhoun."

I remembered, indeed, that on the last evening she had come to the house at the same time as ourselves, with a stranger.

"Yes, I know," Imogen agreed. "But she always had a word or two once or twice with Robin Calhoun, a look or two more often. So I guessed even before the night when Ricardo and his detective appeared. But that night made me certain."

Jill Leslie, meanwhile, had opened her big eyes with surprise at Imogen's recognition of her, had flushed up to the top of her forehead and then returned a little bow and a smile of thanks. Taken feature by feature she could not have answered to any canon of beauty, I suppose, except for her eyes, which were big and clear and dark as pools in a wood. Her hair was the most ordinary brown, her nose a trifle tip-tilted, her mouth generously wide. But she had beautiful teeth and a Madonna-like oval of a face. What gave her charm was the contrast between this placid contour of a devotee and her humour and high spirits. She was quick in the uptake and had enjoyment ready at her fingers' ends. The right word, and the demure face was a tom-boy's—with a sparkle of champagne. At this moment in the restaurant, it was grateful and a little bewildered.

I asked Imogen what she would eat.

"Grapefruit, a trout *meunière* and a cheese *soufflé*," said she. "I told you, Martin, darling, didn't I, that she was the one I was sorry for?"

"You did, Imogen," I answered. "You have a

catholic heart and the most narrow-minded appetite I ever came across."

" You see all her rings are gone."

I looked again at Jill Leslie.

" Now I see.   There was a rope of big pearls, too, wasn't there ? "

As we ate our dinner I began to be curious.   I asked :

" You guessed that this girl was Jill Leslie pretty quickly ? "

" Well—I don't know about that," Imogen replied.

" Sooner than I did, anyway."

" Darling, you didn't guess it at all.   I had to tell you.   You hadn't the slightest idea.   Oh, I'm not disheartened about it.   I've no doubt that you were thinking of higher things—how many elephants can push how many logs into the Irrawaddy, if there was Summer Time in Burma.   No, I am delighted that you shouldn't see what's under your nose.   It gives me great hopes for our married life."

" When you've done," I said, " I should like to ask you a question."

" My other name's Sibyl," said Imogen.   " My spiritual home is Delphi."

" Very well.   You want Michael to get back his sapphire and hang it up on his pagoda ? "

" I certainly do," Imogen answered firmly.   " I had a foolish moment or two when I tried to argue him out of his plan.   But I was wrong.   He has got a belief and that's much too tremendous a thing for little people to meddle with.   I've got an idea that Michael without his belief would be very like a Pekinese dog close shaved, nothing very much to

look at anyway.   But with his belief he's the milk
in the cocoanut.   I shouldn't wonder if that big voice
of authority which brought us all to our senses in
the house in Savile Row was nothing more than—
what shall I say ?—a by-product—I know that's a
good word—of his belief.''

I had not been prepared for this treatise on faith.
I had to revise my own views a little by the light of
it.   I had lightly put down that voice of authority
to a renascent habit of command, a readiness for an
emergency which the Captain of a ship must have.
But, after all, the swirls and shallows of the Irrawaddy did not make such very heavy demands upon
the quality of a Commander, whilst the manœuvre
of edging a steamer into a vacant space against the
bank at Mandalay must fall within the routine of
every voyage.   No, I must look to something else
than the command of a river steamer for the power
which had come out of Michael Crowther in volume
enough to stop a riot.

" Very well," I said.   " Then here's my question."

" Yes, darling ? "

Imogen spoke indulgently like a schoolmistress
encouraging the first signs of intelligence in a pupil.

" You didn't tell Michael which of the young
women at Jack Sanford's was Jill Leslie ? "

" No, darling."

" But you want Michael to get back his sapphire ? "

" Yes, dear."

" Then why didn't you tell him who had it ? "

Imogen looked at the wall across the room.
There was a short silence.   Then she said :

" Is not the peacock a beautiful bird ? "

I expected that there would at all events be the picture of a peacock painted on the opposite wall. But it was quite blank. Then I remembered my own attempt at general conversation after dinner at Hatton.

" The Socratic method of enquiry seems unpopular," I reflected aloud.

" And unreasonable," said Imogen. " Women are often right but seldom logical."

At the table further down the room a waiter was presenting a bill, and Letty Ransome was redecorating her lips with the help of a little hand-mirror. Imogen wrote a few lines on the menu, folded it, wrote a name upon it and handed it to our waiter.

" I've asked Jill Leslie to have coffee with us. You don't mind, Martin, do you ? I'm curious about her—rather moved by her." Imogen laughed as she added : " Besides, I'd like to find out for my own satisfaction why I didn't tell Michael that she was the girl who had his sapphire."

The two girls walked down the room towards the door. As they reached our table I stood up and made a place for Jill Leslie by the side of Imogen on the bench against the wall. Letty Ransome said : " Good night ! I must hurry," and passed along and out. The waiter brought a chair for me which he placed at the end of our little table. And Jill the next moment was seated between us. I think that she had not meant to sit down. She had intended to make an excuse and go away with Letty Ransome. But she had been taken by surprise and she looked from one to the other of us with a wild fear. She was between us, she had been captured, she half rose and sat down again.   She cried out in a sharp, low voice :

" It's no good.   There's nothing more.   The others stripped us to the skin."

" We want nothing at all.   Neither of us ever played at the big table," I said.   " Imogen would like you to have coffee with us.   That's all."

" Why ? " asked Jill Leslie.   She was still looking from one to the other of us, less afraid but more bewildered.   She gave me the impression of an animal caught in a trap.

" Why ?   Why ? " she repeated, and for answer Imogen laid a hand upon her arm and ordered the coffee.   Jill Leslie set her elbows on the table and buried her face in her hands.

" All those people there—most of them, anyway —they were horrible.   They threatened us.   Prison ! Oh ! " and her shoulders worked.   " And lots of them had won. . . .   It was only now and then that Robin . . .   Oh, why be kind to me ? "   She turned to Imogen.   " I brought people there. . . . Yes, you guessed it. . . .   But they had it all back . . . and more, too.   They had everything."

" Your pearls, too ? " said Imogen gently.

" Of course," answered Jill Leslie.   " You see, there was Robin. . . .   They threatened him. Everything had to go."

" Except the sapphire," said Imogen, and Jill Leslie's hand darted up to her throat to make sure that the chain was still about her neck.

" I meant to keep that if I could," she said in a low voice.   " You don't know.   Oh ! "——

Jill Leslie was labouring under an excitement

which I did not understand. Her hands fluttered, her eyes shone unnaturally bright. The little restaurant was almost empty now, and Jill Leslie, moved by Imogen's tenderness, poured out the strangest story to us, the strangers of an hour ago.

" I was in a convent school in Kensington—it's only two years ago. I was studying music. I can sing—I can really sing. I was eighteen. I used to go out, of course, for my singing lessons. A girl at one of my classes introduced Robin to me. It wasn't just the sort of thing a schoolgirl dreams about. At once it wasn't. From the first I knew that this was my man. He might be anything—all that the fine people in the room at Savile Row called him—it didn't matter. I belonged to him if he wanted me. And he did want me."

She had been talking under her breath with her hands pressed to her forehead and her head bent. But she lifted it up now. There were tears upon her cheeks, but the glimmer of a smile about her lips.

" We had no plans. I suppose we felt that the world would fall down on its knees and make a path for us. I was allowed to go out at night every now and then to concerts and the opera with my singing mistress. She was a darling. One night, without telling her anything—I used a concert at the Queen's Hall as an excuse and said that some friends had invited me. I went with Robin to a musical play at the Hippodrome. It was divine to me. I had all the colour and the bright dresses and the dancing and the music in front of me, and Robin at my side. I was off the earth altogether. There are times, an hour, a moment, when you live." She looked again from one to the other of us, but no longer in fear. " I expect both of you know—something like music itself—beyond words, beyond even thought which you can understand. We went on to a supper club afterwards, Robin all fine in a white tie and shiny shoes, and me in a little schoolgirl's evening dress. The waiters knew him. My, but I was proud ! There were lovely grown-up women in gorgeous gowns and jewels. I had to keep hold of Robin's arm, I was so sure one of them would snatch him away from me. And my heart kept thumping away until I thought I'd die. We danced. I was afraid to get up in my little white silk frock amongst all those goddesses. But Robin said that they'd all give me their jewels and gowns in exchange for my youth and freshness and have much the better of the bargain. So we danced. Oh, dear !—the moment we danced there was nothing anywhere but us two dancing. No supper-room, no people, just a sort of lovely swooning music and we two dancing to it in a mist. When we went back to our table . . . there was a clock over the door exactly opposite to us—a big clock like a sun with gold rays sticking out all round it. I looked at the clock. It was two in the morning."

Jill Leslie stopped to take breath. She had been pouring out her story in a seething jumble of words. She had to tell it to the first pair of sympathetic ears she met with ; and here was Imogen, her friendly soul inviting confessions, her frank and lovely eyes promising at once secrecy and understanding. I offered a cigarette to Jill and handed to her a red lighter out of my pocket. The little flame lit up the girl's face with its odd look of strain and wildness. Her hand so shook that she could hardly hold her cigarette still and the flame wavered so that I thought she would never light it at all.

" Could I have something to drink ? " she asked.

There was still a glass of champagne left in our bottle. I poured it out for her.

" Will that do ? "

Jill Leslie nodded her thanks and drank the wine down, throwing up her head as though her throat were parched.

" I was frightened out of my wits for a moment. I couldn't go back to the convent. It was too late. If I had gone, I might not have got in. If I had got in I should have been expelled the next morning," Jill resumed. " But the next morning I was glad. It was up to Robin, you see. He took me home with him. The flat in Savile Row was his then. He had lots of money. I suppose he had made it in the same way. I didn't know. I didn't care. I was with him. He sent out for clothes for me the next morning. We went to Paris. He gave me my pearls there. In the autumn we started off round the world. We went to the West Indies, Panama, the South Seas, Tokio, Java—it was wonderful. We were two years on the journey. Imagine it ! No school, no nuns, colour and heat and light, and new amusing things to see every day. And at Colombo he bought me this sapphire——"

She broke off at this point abruptly.

" You brought a man with you to Savile Row," she said.

" Michael Crowther," said I.

" I didn't like him."

" Why ? "

" He was "—Jill searched for a word—" secret. He was thinking all the time of one thing but you weren't to know what it was until he sprung it on you."

I laughed.

" That's a pretty good description of Michael."

" I like people to be natural and friendly. I don't want them to crab other people or be sarcastic or mysterious. I like them to fit in and take their part with the rest. They needn't be clever so long as they're bright. But that man ! He was an iceberg."

" But, my dear," said Imogen, " you hardly spoke to him. He went away with us."

" But he came back," said Jill.

I was startled.

" That night ? "

" Yes."

" But he had lost nothing. One small stake, perhaps."

" He didn't come back for money," said Jill. " I didn't at that time know why he had come back. He made an excuse downstairs that he had left his hat and coat behind. Otherwise the door-keeper wouldn't have let him in again. When he came upstairs I was standing by Robin. I couldn't leave Robin to face all that riot of people with only poor Jack Sanford. Jack was just like a suet pudding, wasn't he ? So I stood by Robin and whilst the others were demanding their money your friend asked me if I was Jill Leslie, and when I said that I was, he thought that if I gave him our address he might be able to help us. I was sure there was a snag somewhere, but we were up against it, anyway. Jack Sanford owned the flat. We two were living in Berkeley Street and I gave him the address. Of course, we have moved since. We are down and out."

She turned to Imogen.

" Do you know what he wants ? "

" Yes," said Imogen.

" What ? "

" The sapphire."

Jill nodded her head.

" Funny, isn't it ? He offered quite a price for it. But it'll be the last thing I'll let go. I never took it to Jack Sanford's because I was afraid that I might lose it. I have only got to take it in my hand and I can go all round the world again. And I'm hoping now that I shan't have to let it go at all."

" So things are better," I suggested.

" A little. I told you I could sing, didn't I ? I've got a small part in a new comic opera called *Dido*."

The newspapers had during the last week or two been discreetly peppered with details of that stupendous production to be. We were all on edge for it, or supposed to be. We certainly should be when the night of the first performance came. We knew of the famous comedian who was to play the pious Æneas, of the great producer already on his way from Berlin, of the witty libretto which had actually arrived from Hammersmith, of the dresses and scenery to be designed by the modish young artist from Chelsea. We had heard of the music— we were to have melodies instead of a rhythm with a saxophone—and how all Europe was being ransacked for a singer who would graft on the wildness of lovely Dido the sparkle of an exquisite gaiety.

" You're to be in *Dido* ? " I cried. " We'll come on the first night and cheer you."

" You won't notice me," said Jill. " I've a little bit of a part and just enough of a salary, I think, to allow me to keep my sapphire."

She got up ; and all at once the life had gone out of her. Her face had lost its colour, her mouth drooped, her eyes were dull.

" I must go," she said. She held out a hand to each of us. " You have been very kind. I thank you both very much. You have been sweet to me. But we begin to rehearse to-morrow, and I must go home and rest."

She went off with a listless step and passed out by the door into the tiny porch. Through the upper glass panel of the door we saw her open her hand-bag. She spilled something upon her thumbnail and then raised it to her nostrils.

" I was sure of it," said Imogen.

" Cocaine ? "

Imogen nodded.

." Poor little girl ! " said she.

Imogen was silent for a few moments afterwards. We were quite alone in the little restaurant now and rather in the way. For a waiter in his shirt-sleeves was removing the table-cloths and piling the tables one upon the other with a quite unnecessary noise. Imogen, however, was unaware of these resounding hints. She said :

" You'll understand now, Martin, why I didn't tell Crowther that she was the girl who had the sapphire. I wanted to have a talk with her."

" And now that you have talked with her ? " I asked.

" Yes, there we are," said Imogen.

And there, indeed, we were. On the one side Michael and his far-away pagoda and the compulsion we were all under to help him in his quest. On the other hand this little unhappy girl who had only to hold the sapphire in her hand to live again in the warmth and joy of her tropical adventure.

" What are we to do ? " cried Imogen. " I believe that she's the sort of girl who wouldn't sell but would give that sapphire back, once she knew Michael's story. And then be heart-broken because she had done it." She was troubled. " What are we to do, Martin ? "

I looked at the wall opposite and said :

" Is not the peacock a beautiful bird ? "

CHAPTER XX

THE FIRST NIGHT OF *DIDO*

JILL LESLIE had gone before it struck either Imogen or myself how much of her story she had left out. Her life might have begun at her convent school for all that she had told us. There had not been a word of a home or of parents or of other friends that she had made for herself. After she had gone off with her Robin, no enquiry seemed to have been made for her, and certainly no search. It was not as though she had been deliberately separating one phase of her youth for us, and keeping the rest secret. She had been talking without control. We could speculate about it as we chose, but I was persuaded that Jill knew no more than what she had told us, that outside the school she had no home and was acknowledged by no parents. And we never did know any more. Jill stood in a solitary relief against the social web with its infinite threads. She must make her own path and find her own counsellors. It was this circumstance, dimly surmised at once by Imogen and only now understood by me, which so keenly enlisted our sympathies and rather dulled our enthusiasm in Michael Crowther's behalf. Jill was no doubt a wayward and wicked little girl, but she was a good fighter, she was constant to her lover through good fortune and through ill, and for whatever harm she did, she paid.

Jill, then, went off to her rehearsals, Imogen and I to the settlement of our affairs and Michael Crowther dropped once more out of sight. Our marriage was to take place towards the end of July.

" You see, if we arrange that," said Imogen, "we might go to Munich, mightn't we, for the first fortnight of August and the Wagner Festival and then run down to Venice ? "

" We might certainly do that," said I.

" Martin, why don't you suggest something ? " she asked.

" Because, my darling, if anything goes wrong with our honeymoon, I want to be able to blame you and not you me," I answered.

" I think I shall have to turn Pamela on to you," said Imogen thoughtfully. " She knows the right words."

Pamela was to be a bridesmaid, so I was not alarmed. I had the whip hand of the bridesmaids. One word of insolence—even the right word—and they got a bouquet instead of a diamond buckle.

It was just a week before the wedding when Michael Crowther paid me a visit. He was looking thoroughly discouraged. It was seven o'clock in the evening. He would take nothing but a seat, and he dropped into that as if he would never get up out of it again.

" You're tired," I said.

He nodded his head.

" Walking about." He bent forward with his

hands clasped between his knees. " I don't know what I am going to do."

" I can tell you one thing you can do," I replied briskly. " You can come to my wedding."

Crowther shook his head.

" No, I can't do that."

His answer was immediate and decided.

" Oh, indeed ! My mistake ! " said I, and I suppose that my face and voice both showed that I had taken offence. For he hastened to add :

" You're not misunderstanding me, Mr. Legatt. If I were to go to a wedding it would surely be to yours. But, of course, it's out of the question that I should go to any."

That, for a moment, puzzled me. Here were we in London with the sunlight pouring into the room and the low roar of the streets floating through the open windows. Here was Michael dressed in a dark lounge suit like any other man of my acquaintance. It was difficult for one so full of his affairs as I was to realise that half a world stood between us two and our creeds. I sat down opposite to him.

" Wait a moment, Michael."

I transported myself to Burma. The priests of his creed were in no sense ministers. Their concern was with their own souls and the smoothest path to extinction. They neither sat by the beds of the sick nor shared in their rejoicings. And of all festivals to be avoided a marriage was the first. They looked forward to the cessation of life that is and not the creation of life to be. Of course Michael would never come to my wedding.

" Yes, I understand now. But I am sorry."

Ever since the night when Imogen had tempted him to renounce his purpose I had had a suspicion that he might do so. He had so brusquely and definitely fled from her questions and her company. I am sure that he was shaken, that he had savoured his moment of authority with a thrill of keen pleasure. But the weakness had passed. He was the man of the yellow robe masquerading as a denizen of the world and seeing his corner in his monastery at Pagan still barred away from him like a harbour behind a reef.

" You tried to buy back your sapphire," I said.

" And I failed. To-day I am farther away from it than ever."

" How's that ? " I asked.

He drew out of a pocket a folded evening paper. He unfolded it and handed it to me.

" Read ! "

The first item of the issue which leaped to my eye was a picture of Jill Leslie. Side by side were the pleasant chubby features of the famous manager who was responsible for the production of *Dido*. Across the top of the two columns of letterpress which these pictures adorned was printed in large capitals :

DIDO DISCOVERED.

AN INTERVIEW WITH MR. DAVID C. DONALD.

I read that the discovery had really been made some while ago. Miss Jill Leslie off the stage had all the qualities which the leading part required, a lovely voice, humour, liveliness, a note of passion and a grace of movement. If she could reproduce these gifts behind the footlights Mr. Donald would have earned the gratitude of the public by presenting to it a new young *prima donna*.

" ' But,' said Mr. Donald smiling, ' to quote a manager who has preceded me, there was the rub. Would Miss Leslie come over the footlights ? If so, I had the ideal representative of Dido. In order not to alarm her by too big a task and perhaps dishearten her in the end, I engaged her for a small part. Then I asked her to oblige me, whilst I was negotiating for a leading lady, to read Dido's part at our rehearsals and in return I would give her the understudy.' "

Miss Leslie, it appeared, obliged with the greatest success, triumphed over the nervousness natural to one in her position and gave Mr. Donald confidence that he need look no further.

" ' Yesterday evening, just before our first dress rehearsal,' Mr. Donald continued, ' I told her that she was to play the part and, of course, receive a salary commensurate with its importance. We open at Manchester on Monday night, play the opera for a month in that town and come to London early in September.' "

I folded the paper again and handed it back. Jill Leslie was to have her chance and I was delighted, as Imogen would be when she heard the news. I was anxious, indeed, that Michael should go away so that I could telephone to Imogen. But on the other hand, if Jill made a success of it, Michael was further from his sapphire than ever. I saw again

Jill Leslie clasping the jewel tight in the palm of her hand. It would only be dire want which would induce her to sell it.

"Of course," I said—I did not think it, I did not want it ; but with Crowther's woebegone face in front of me I said what I could to comfort him—"Donald may be wrong. Jill Leslie may fail——"

"But I don't want her to fail," cried Crowther, lifting up his face towards me. "That would be an evil wish."

He was very energetic in his repulsion of the idea and very sincere. It might mean a dozen more lives in a degraded form, for all he knew, were he to let that meanness creep into his soul.

"I want her to succeed, of course," he exclaimed. "But what am I going to do ? I daren't fail again."

I did not like that phrase at all. Nor the look upon his face. He was living over again the three years of loneliness and defeat, his confidence and self-esteem draining from him like blood from his veins. No, he daren't fail again—lest he should find himself face to face with a way out which he must not follow. For he must take no life, not even his own.

I thought for a little while what answer to make to that question. There was an answer, but I felt more and more certain that it must not be given now.

"I'll tell you what I think, Michael," I said. "You must wait. Jill Leslie won't listen to you at the moment. She'll be taken up with her part. She'll probably hate you for your persistency if you approach her again. You are very likely to persuade her that she has got a talisman in that sapphire and you are trying to take it away from her. You have just got to lie low until she has made her appearance in London. I reckon that Imogen will want to go on the opening night. So we shall be back in town. We haven't got a house yet and we shall stay at some hotel. But we'll let you know. After all, if you remain another two months in England you'll miss the whole of the rains in Burma."

Michael Crowther took himself off and I rang down the curtain upon the Quest of the Sapphire for an interval of two months. At least, I thought I did. But that night there were still some words to be spoken which were to throw an unexpected but a most illuminating light upon one of the minor characters in our play.

Imogen and I dined in the grill-room of the Semiramis Hotel—a corner where all the tides of London met. At one table you might see the leaders of Finance bending their heads in unison like the Mandarins of a nursery. At another would be a party dining on its way to a theatre. At a third, men from the north who had backed a play, with managers, all smiles, who meant that they should never see again one farthing of the capital which—let us use the blessed word—they had invested. There would be authors with a play in their pockets, and actresses and actors on the top of the flood, and people who just enjoyed a good dinner and the to-and-fro of famous persons and infamous persons, and the vivid enjoyment of country folk up for a few nights in town. We had a table near to the entrance with a pillar at our backs,

and we had hardly taken our seats before a
voice which had a vague familiarity reached our
ears.

"It's just one of Donald's stunts."

Certainly the words could not provoke my
curiosity. Donald's stunts were a normal element
in the Londoner's life. If the lady had said:
"Donald can't think of a stunt," then the metro-
polis would have held its breath until he did; and
I should have looked up . . . as I did. But it was
the sharp indignation in this faintly familiar voice
which made me do it. I looked up and saw a pale,
lovely, dark-haired girl standing by a table near
to ours. Of course . . . Letty Ransome. I had
heard her performance only yesterday. She was
wrapped to the throat in sables and was speaking
to the table's occupants.

"It's absurd, of course," she went on. "Jill
will never play the part in London. You can
take it from me."

Imogen had spoken of Letty Ransome as Jill
Leslie's friend when we had seen them dining
together in Soho. Not much more than skin-deep,
that friendship! But however frail, it did not
account for the rancour in Letty's voice.

"You finished last night, didn't you, Letty?"
asked the lady at the table who was being addressed
and in a voice which, perhaps, was a trifle too sweet.
So there were claws at the table, too.

"Yes. Just for the moment. I am working
out a new sketch." But the new sketch was not
in her thoughts. "Yes, Jill opens in Manchester
on Monday. It's rough on her, really. What can

she do, with her inexperience, except something too tragic for words?" She suddenly swept round. "Oh, darling," she cried enthusiastically, "I was afraid that you had forgotten."

Jill Leslie had just entered the big room.

"I couldn't get away," said Jill, and she saw Imogen. Her face lightened and as I stood up to greet her, I noticed with satisfaction the discomfort which showed on Letty Ransome's face. She was probably not aware of the malevolence which had made her face ugly, and of the jealousy which had sharpened her voice till it rasped like an old saw. But she could not but know that we had heard every word that she had spoken.

Meanwhile Jill had moved forward to our table and was speaking to Imogen.

"If I can do it!" she said in a whisper.

"You will," answered Imogen. "I'll send you a telegram on Monday. I am really, really delighted. So is Martin."

"You're good friends," said Jill Leslie. "I shall love to think that you are wishing me a little of your happiness."

She looked from one to the other of us and shook our hands.

"Letty, I've had nothing to eat all day," she said.

We heard Letty Ransome answer: "Poor darling, you must be starved!" and as they moved away: "Miaow!" said Imogen.

A few days afterwards we were married. We went to Paris, Fontainebleau, Munich, Venice. I am not to be blamed. Imogen must carry all the reproaches. She was definite.

" Forests, tigers and panthers are for bachelors," she declared. " If they are clawed it's their affair and serves them right. Adam's Peak is for matrimonial possibles. But for honeymoons luxuries are required and luxuries are conventional."

So we travelled on Blue Trains and occupied royal suites in Grand Hotels, and bathed in tepid seas from fashionable beaches, and knew ourselves to be incredibly blessed. But all the more we were visited with twinges of remorse on account of the two troubled ones we left behind—Michael Crowther obsessed by his idea, Jill Leslie with the ordeal of her début in front of her. We returned to London, indeed, before our time in order to be present at the first performance of *Dido*.

There are many who will remember that first night. It was a riot—a riot of colour, of melodies, of dancing and broad comedy. From the opening chorus which began, so far as I can remember, thus :

Pious Æneas took his Daddy on his back—
　　Bless my soul what a lad !
He groaned : " It's too bad
　　My infernal old Dad
　　He swears that he's Troy
　　But he's avoirdupoy
And I'd dump him on the sand for a drach—
　　Ma ! Ma ! Ma ! "

to the finale of the fireworks at the Carthaginian

Crystal Palace, it was a tumult and it ended in a tumult of an audience wild with enthusiasm.   As Imogen and I made our slow way from the auditorium to the street, on all sides we heard:

" It'll run for a year."

" Sure thing."

" Wasn't that little girl good ? "

And indeed from all the riot Jill Leslie had stood out daintily demure and exquisite, a Queen Dido without majesty, an Offenbach Dido, a Dido in high-heeled shoes.   Whatever her faults she could sing, she appealed and she came right over the footlights with something oddly virginal about her which took her audience by storm.

" Did you see ? " said Imogen as we sidled this way and that through the crowd which had gathered about the doors.   I had seen very distinctly.   All through the performance Jill Leslie had worn, shining darkly against the satin of her breast, the blue tablet of the sapphire.

" She'll never sell it to him," said Imogen.

" Not after to-night," I agreed.

There rose in front of me a picture of Michael Crowther's tortured face.   I heard him saying: " I daren't fail again."   Absurd ?   Yes.   One particular dark sapphire.   Whether it hung round the hti of a pagoda in Burma, or round the throat of a charming, vivacious little *prima donna* of Comic Opera in London—what in the world did it matter ?   But it did matter and enormously.   It mattered to Michael, for it was an expiation.   It mattered to Jill, for it was the token of her passion and the epitome of her happiest days.

"I remember what you once said about it, Imogen," I observed.

"That Michael's only chance was to ask for it as a gift?"

"Yes."

"But I am a great deal less confident that Jill would give it to him now," said Imogen thoughtfully. "You see, Martin, now it's an idea to her, too."

I did see—and I was afraid. For if Michael did not repossess himself of it, he was as likely as not to destroy himself. Yes, I faced that contingency honestly for the first time. There was no adequate reason, to be sure. But is there ever an adequate reason? Adequate, that is, to you and me who stand apart and look on. I had once asked Michael what he did with himself during these months of waiting.

"I take long walks in the City late at night, when the City's empty and the streets are as hollow as a cavern," he had answered.

I could see him tramping restlessly along those narrow corridors so thronged by day, so silent by night that every footfall would reverberate and deride; trying to tire brain and muscle; trying to numb the dreadful temptation to draw a razor across his throat and have done with it.

"Yes, Michael might kill himself," I reflected, but I reflected aloud and Imogen turned to me with horror in her eyes.

"You don't mean that!"

"I do."

"Martin!" she whispered; and she stood in the

side street whither we had gone in search of our car, jostled by the passers-by and unaware that she was jostled. That tragic possibility had not occurred to her till this moment, but now that it did it frightened her almost as much as it did me.

I say almost. For I was haunted by an odd sort of conjecture. Suppose that each man's creed were true for him, if he really believed in it ! Suppose that belief actually created truth instead of coming out of it ! Suppose, for instance—we had found our car now—that just at this junction where Whitehall and the Strand, the Mall and Northumberland Avenue flung their traffic into Charing Cross, some huge machine bore down on us and I believed, as I did believe, that we should still be together—why, it would make very little difference. The finding of a path in a new world. The work of adapting ourselves to new surroundings. But if for Michael his creed were the truth, and he killed himself—there would be ten thousand degraded lives to be lived through as an expiation.

" We have got to stop that," I said with a shiver, and the next morning I sent for Michael.

" You have got to tell your story and ask for that sapphire as a gift," I said to him. " It's your only chance."

Michael Crowther looked at me gloomily. He was so worn with sleeplessness and anxiety that his skin had something of that transparent look which the dying wear.

" Imogen once told me that you might very likely succeed. She thought Jill had just that generosity which would give when it wouldn't sell."

I did not tell him that since last night her confidence had diminished. Michael's face lightened wonderfully.

" She thinks that ? "

" She thought that, when she spoke to me," I said correcting him ; and hurried on to add : " But you must wait for the right moment. You can only ask once."

Michael drew in a deep breath.

" Yes, I can only ask once. I understand that." He stood in a thoughtful silence with his eyes upon the floor. " Yes, I'll choose my time. Will you thank her from me ? "

CHAPTER XXI

A SUMMARY

I NEED only summarise now the weeks which elapsed before a swift succession of events brought the history of this sapphire to a remarkable conclusion. After the resounding success of *Dido*, Robin Calhoun slowly emerged from his hiding-place. At the first he was rather like a turtle which pokes its head out from its shell, watching on this side and that for an enemy. But he took courage in the end and sat sleek and debonair by the side of Jill Leslie in public places. She was the bread-winner now and in the more honest way. There was a small group of people amongst whom Jill Leslie, Letty Ransome and Robin Calhoun were, if not all the most prominent, the most frequent. Letty Ransome had made a success with her new sketch, and seemed to have quite reconciled herself to the idea that her friend might have a success, too. They made their headquarters at the grill-room of the Semiramis Hotel, and more to my amusement than my astonishment, I saw Michael Crowther enrolled in their group. They were obviously not difficult. It was a society of gay spirits and light hearts rather than of brilliant wits. If you were noisy, that helped a little, but you might sit quiet if you chose. You must do your share of the entertaining—no great matter, anyway

—you must not put on any airs and above all you must not be mordant at the expense of your companions. They hated sarcasm like a British soldier. Amongst them Crowther sat, kindly and gentle. He became something of a pet.

I remember that one day in early October, when Imogen and I were taking our luncheon in the grill-room, Jill Leslie drifted across the room to us. Imogen asked her how Michael got along with them and her face dimpled into smiles.

" He's a lonesome old dear, isn't he ? " she said. " Whoever of us makes him laugh counts one."

" And the play ? " I asked.

" Fine," said she, and she went off to her matinée.

Michael was very wisely taking his time. He had made friends and in that sort of company, generous and accustomed to incomes with lengthy inter-mezzos, friendship had the predominant claim. Michael was at that moment paying the bill. He was sitting against the glass screen in the inner part of the grill-room and he had as his guests Letty Ransome, Robin Calhoun, Jill Leslie who had run off to the theatre and a young author who this year had risen out of the waters.

" I wonder," I said as I looked at Michael.

" So do I," said Imogen. " I have been wondering some time." ˙

" That settles it, then," said I, and I scribbled a line on the card which had reserved our table and sent it across the restaurant. Michael looked towards us and nodded, and when the little party had broken up he came over and sat down with us.

" We are both a trifle worried," I said.

" Yes ? "

" You've been in England some time now ? "

" Five months."

" Longer than you expected ? "

Michael saw now the drift of these questions. He smiled at us with a sweetness of expression—I can find no other phrase, though I gladly would—which wiped away as though with a sponge the customary gravity of his face.

" Not longer than I was prepared for," he said.

" You are quite sure of that ? " Imogen asked—I think that I should say pleaded. " You see, we can help in that way."

Michael raised his eyebrows and wrinkled his forehead and said with a whimsical air :

" If I stay in this country much longer—I shall fall into the gross error of thanking you. That would be altogether wrong. You are acquiring so much merit that you may be a king and a queen in your next life."

" Or we may even never marry at all," I cried enthusiastically.

" Or, if we did, we may by this time have got our divorce," cried Imogen with an even greater fervour. " Any of these great blessings may be ours, Michael. Therefore, if your bowl is empty, you need only hold it out behind you."

" But it isn't empty, Imogen," said he.

" Thank you, Michael," said she very prettily.

It was the first time he had called her by her Christian name, and she was very pleased.

" It is still just full enough," he continued, " to last me out and carry me back to Pagan. For now

I think that I shall not be long." He drew in his breath with a gasp as he pictured to himself the moment when he must put all to the test of a girl's generosity and whim. " One way or another, I shall know very soon."

He spoke with so much certainty that I cried out to him :

" I believe that you have fixed a date."

" I have," he answered. " I could hope for no more likely moment for my petition to succeed."

There was a confidence in his manner and a tiny note of boastfulness in his speech. I must suppose that such trifles soothed my vanity, as indicating that we poor humans lived on a plane not so noticeably lower than Michael's. For indications that Michael was really one of us always amused and delighted me. Imogen, however, was of the more practical mind. She leaned across the table very earnestly.

" Take care, Michael ! There's one amongst your new friends who won't let you get away with that sapphire as a present, if she can help it."

" Letty Ransome," said Michael, pressing his thin lips together.

" Yes, Letty Ransome," Imogen agreed. " She's not quite the type to let a sapphire as good as Jill's go out of the family without making a fight for it. I don't fancy that you could persuade her that Jill was acquiring merit by letting it hang round the top of a spire two hundred feet from the ground."

" I have not mentioned the stone to her," Michael answered, " although she has spoken of it to me."

" Oh, she has," Imogen said slowly. " She admires it ? "

" Yes."

" Then more than ever I beg you to take care."

Nothing could exceed the earnestness with which Imogen spoke.   We had both learnt to love Michael Crowther, queer as it must appear to anyone who remembers him when he strutted the deck of the *Dagonet*.   But we loved him with the kind of love which one gives to a child.   We did not expect his mind to work along the ordinary lines nor his heart to long for the ordinary things.   And since, to fulfil a penance which no one but himself had imposed, he wanted this sapphire of Jill Leslie's, he must have it as a child must have a toy.   Otherwise there would be—yes, there, as Mr. Donald's predecessor had said, was the rub.   In the case of a child there would be a crumpled face, clenched fists, a torrent of tears and a wailing as of sea-gulls about an island of the Hebrides.   In the case of Michael we could not even conjecture.   We could only fear.   He had said : " I dare not fail."   We knew no more than that of what was passing in his mind, but it was enough to light the way to some very dark and terrible conjectures.

" I am glad that we don't know exactly when he is going to ask," said Imogen as she watched him depart from the grill-room.

It was a cowardly thought.   Then I was a coward, too.   For I shared it whole-heartedly.   I had the apprehension which one feels for a dear friend who must suffer the surgeon's knife.   I was glad not to know the moment when the patient would be stretched upon the table, or to linger in the waiting-room until the result should be announced.

CHAPTER XXII

AT THE MASQUERADE BALL

BUT we were present when the moment struck. On the last day of the month a ball for some charity was held in the Albert Hall. It was a masquerade ball, and those who attended it were bidden to dress in the Waterloo period or wear a domino. Imogen had a mind to return some of the hospitality which had been showered upon us during our engagement. So we hired a box and arranged for supper to be served in it. At three in the morning she was leaning over the edge of the box watching the throng below and she turned round and called to me :

" Martin !   Come here ! "

She was excited by some incident happening upon the floor. I went to her and she caught me by the arm.

" Look !   Look !   Do you see ? "

I saw many things and many people, and amongst the things, that people dressed anyhow in the Waterloo period. I am all for liberty myself and if a warrior likes to wear plates of armour in a day of cannon-balls, by all means. Nor did I mind Henry the Eighth coming to life again and multiplying himself six times, so long as none of him tried to snatch my Imogen. I never saw such a medley of dresses. There were Greek goddesses and Sultans with scimitars; Mandarins who should have been nodding upon mantelpieces danced with girls from Alsace in satin clogs; Crusaders and Tyrolese mixed amicably with Zulus and Cossacks.

" There ! There ! " cried Imogen, twitching my sleeve, and looking, I perceived Letty Ransome dressed as a *vivandière* dancing with Thomas à Becket.

" It seems to me a very happy combination," I said.

" No, no, darling, I don't mean there. I mean there," cried Imogen, as she nodded vigorously in exactly the same direction. I moved my eyes to the right and then I moved them to the left, and at last I took in the tiny point in that huge scene at which I was intended to look. I saw Jill Leslie with a man in a yellow domino. They were not dancing, nor was Jill talking. She was listening with a puckered forehead to something impossible to understand. They were standing, and every now and then they took a few steps towards us and stopped again. Once I laughed and Imogen asked :

" What's amusing you, Martin ? "

It would have taken days to explain. Jill was dressed in an impossibly dainty frock, Marie Antoinette down to her knees—or rather Madame de Lamotte—her pretty shoulders already bared for the branding, the sapphire a great blot of blue fire upon her breast, and below the knees her own slender and twinkling legs. And just at that moment she jumped up and down on her toes with her feet together and with her hands clasped, just as little Miss Diamond had done long since on the beach of Tagaung, to this same man who was so eagerly talking to her. He was wearing a yellow domino now. He had been wearing the uniform of a Captain in the Flotilla Company then. But it was he. For he had looked up and I had seen his face. Miss Diamond had been trying to detain him. Miss Sapphire was trying to understand him.

" Crowther," I said. " Crowther at a masked ball at the Albert Hall ! "

" He has chosen this time of all times—why ? " Imogen asked.

It did seem unreasonable. Yet without a doubt he had Jill's attention.

" He has some queer reason at the back of his head," I answered, and, remembering a word he had dropped here and there : " This was a date he had planned."

They came to a halt just beneath our box. I leaned over, but there was such a hubbub of voices that not one word of what Crowther was saying rose as high as our ears. Something of real significance occurred, however, for we saw Jill lift the blot of blue fire from her breast and look at it, and from it to Michael. And then a fisherman or an ice—anyway, a Neapolitan, ran forward to claim her for a dance. She nodded her head and had actually started to dance. But she stopped, and running to Michael laid a hand upon his arm. She spoke a few quick words, waved her hand at him with a smile, and was off with her partner across the floor. Imogen leaned over the edge of the balcony.

" Michael ! "

In a momentary lull her voice reached to him, and he looked up.

" Come up, Michael," and she gave the number of our box. Neither of us dared to put a question to him when he did come. Was that parting smile of Jill's a consolation or a promise, or a vague encouragement to hope ? Michael for a time gave us no enlightenment. He sat, his chin propped upon his hand, his eyes roaming over the fantastic scene, and every now and again his breath catching in his throat as though he saw—what ? The white spire of his pagoda across that foam ˙ of dancers, or death stalking amidst them with his scythe.

Imogen filled a glass of champagne and took it to him. He smiled and put it aside.

Imogen thrust her small face forward—and I knew that Michael was going to add an extra life or two to his tally, however earnestly he might resist.

" Drink it ! " said Imogen. She took the glass and put it into Michael's hand.

" It's a sin," he answered.

" Commit it ! " said Imogen.

" I disobey the Law," he pleaded.

" Well, I get fined for leaving my car about," said Imogen. " Drink ! "

Michael looked at the glass winking invitingly in his hand, and looked at Imogen, and his face broke up in a smile.

" Imogen, here's your very good health." And he drank the glass dry. A little colour came into his face and the tension of his body relaxed.

" Now, Michael, we want your news," said Imogen, and she took a seat beside him.

" There isn't any," Michael returned. " But there will be to-morrow. I don't think Jill Leslie understood what I meant quite. I mean I don't think she understood the reason why I made a petition so unusual."

" I'm sure she didn't," I interrupted. " I was watching you both from this box."

" It was my fault," Michael continued. " When you have had for a long time one idea in your head, you begin to think other people are familiar with it. You leave out the necessary details. I expect that writing a book must be always presenting that sort of difficulty."

" But Jill didn't turn you down ? " Imogen asked anxiously.

" No ! " Michael returned. " But she couldn't hear me out. There was too much noise and too much whirl for her to give her attention. I can understand that, can't you ? "

" What I can't understand is why you ever chose a time and a place like this," said Imogen.

" Perhaps I was wrong," Michael replied slowly. " But I thought, to-night she will be at her happiest. She has her success, her love, all this colour and light and gaiety, and she'll look a picture in her pretty frock and know it and she is kind. With all that dark hard time just behind her, within reach of her memory, she'll be in the most likely mood."

" What's the result then ? " asked Imogen.

" She said that I was to call upon her to-morrow

afternoon at half-past three and she would have no one there. I wonder whether——" And all his fears came back upon him and he looked from one to the other of us, his eyes as wistful as a dog's.

" Where does Jill live now ? " Imogen asked.

" She has for the moment one of the small flats in the Semiramis Court."

" Very well," Imogen continued. " You shall lunch with us at half-past one at the Semiramis Grill Room."

" Wait a moment," said I. " Let me look at my diary ! "

" Darling," Imogen observed gently, " don't be absurd ! Michael will lunch with us at half-past one at the Semiramis Grill. Afterwards, at half-past three o'clock, you might go up with Michael to Jill's flat, and I'm quite sure that your tact will tell you at once whether you may stay and help Michael or not."

Michael stood up with every expression of relief upon his face.

" That's what I wanted desperately. Thank you ! "

He shook us warmly by the hand and went off. I looked grimly at Imogen.

" Coward ! " I said.

" Well, you wanted to get out of it, too. You go about in forests and shoot harmless little tigers. You're the strong man and very persuasive, dearest, too."

Thus mingling sarcasm with flattery Imogen had her way. It was not quite so unusual as you might think. We were to give Michael luncheon on the morrow, and afterwards he would learn his news.

Our work was done. We went down on to the floor, danced, and Imogen disgraced herself. We were waltzing and approached the steps of one of the gangways to the floor. On the second of these steps a fat, red, pompous, bald man stood, dressed elaborately as a Roman Emperor—golden greaves upon his legs, a purple toga with the end flung across his shoulder and a wreath of laurels upon his crown. He had come in state, for two lictors with the paraphernalia of their office stood behind him. One could not imagine a man more conscious of the perfection of his dress or of his fitness to wear it. The Emperor surveyed the Albert Hall with a placid satisfaction as though he had just built it with slave-labour brought from a successful campaign upon the Danube. As we came close to him Imogen stopped. She was dressed as Columbine and in white from the flower in her hair to her feet. There were others in the hall pretending to be Columbine —that was to be expected—but Imogen was Columbine.

" Just wait a minute," she said, and leaving my arm she ran up to the Emperor with the most eager expression upon her face.

" You'll excuse me, sir," she said very clearly, " but can you tell me at what hour you're to be thrown to the lions ? "

The fat man who had begun to listen with a smile, turned away with a snort of disgust. He was furious at the gibe. On the other hand it made Imogen's evening for her. She gurgled with pleasure as we resumed our broken waltz and her anxieties for the morrow were forgotten.

CHAPTER XXIII

LETTY RANSOME'S HANDBAG

THERE were, after all, four who took their luncheon the next day at our table in the grill-room of the Semiramis. But we began as three, assembling in our proper order of unpunctuality: Michael Crowther to the minute, myself next, Imogen last. We sat for five minutes or so in the lounge, I with a Bacardi cocktail, Imogen drinking it and Michael looking on benevolently. Then, through the swing doors Letty Ransome burst in. She was in a fluster but there was nothing discomposing in that. A fluster was as much a complement of Letty Ransome as her skirt. She could not move about in public without either. She swung into the grill-room and out again, she jingled some bracelets at Michael and poured out some ecstatic words to another group. Imogen whispered quickly:

" Ask her to have a cocktail, Michael!" and since he hesitated, she added an imperious: " Be quick or I'll make you drink one yourself."

Michael rose and, blushing—he who had once been Michael D., the Captain of the *Dagonet*!—said timidly: " Letty, will you join us? "

Letty was at the age which thrives on long nights in dusty rooms. She was radiant of face, and for the rest of her, shiny as lacquer from her smooth hair to the points of her shoes. She was introduced to Imogen and myself and was kind to us ; and I ordered a large clover-club for her.

" I saw you both at the ball. Wasn't it wonderful ? " she cried. " I never enjoyed myself so much. Have you seen Jill ? "

" No," said I.

" I thought that Jill and I might lunch together," said Letty.

" I don't think that she's coming down for luncheon," Imogen observed.

" Oh ? " Letty was a trifle put out. She looked about the small lounge, and Imogen said :

" Won't you lunch with us ? We're going in now."

" I'd love to," said Letty. " But I must run up to Jill's flat." A shadow of annoyance flitted across Imogen's face. It was just to avoid such a contingency that Imogen had asked her to lunch with us. Once let Letty Ransome offer her advice about the destination of the sapphire and Michael Crowther went out at a hundred to one. Ideas, the vitamins of the soul, meant nothing to her practical mind. Imogen might call a sapphire an idea, if she were crazy enough to think it one. Letty knew it for a colourful piece of corundum with a definite market value.

" You see," Letty explained, " a party of us drove back to Jill's flat at seven o'clock this morning. Jill had a bath and went to bed and then we all had breakfast in her bedroom. I left my handbag there when we went home. I won't be a second."

She sprang up and ran out into the hall ; and she was away a longer time than we expected. We all watched the hands of the electric clock jump as a minute elapsed, then wait ever so long, then jump again.

" Oh, I do hope——" said Imogen and stopped there lest Michael should be distressed by her fears. But, oddly enough, Michael was the least troubled of the three of us. He had ascended to some plane of faith whither neither of us could follow him.

" If I were to describe Letty Ransome and Jill Leslie," he said with a smile, " I should quote Monsieur Chaunard's difference between himself and his memory."

He made us laugh, anyway, and got us over one of the clock's jumps.

It was a quarter to two when Letty Ransome left us and ten times the minute hand made its tiny leap before Letty reappeared and when she did we were all a little shocked at the change in her. She was breathing as though her lungs were choked, she was distracted with the effort to breathe. Her colour was patchy ; where the rouge did not flare, her skin was the hue of tallow and the scarlet of her lips was not an ornament but a parody. She dropped into her chair.

" I was a fool," she said with a gasp. " The lift was up at the top of the building. I didn't want to keep you. I ran up the stairs. It's only the third floor but I've been warned against stairs." She smiled appealingly. Her beauty had all gone, so it was, perhaps, the more natural that she should pray :

" Will you give me a moment ? "

" Take your time, of course," said I. " We're in no hurry. Michael has an appointment at half-past three—— Oh!" My grunt was due to a lusty kick on the ankle delivered by the small but capable foot of my wife.

" This is the bag ? " she asked. " It's pretty."

It was lying on the small table between them. Imogen was not at all interested in the bag nor did she think it especially pretty. But she had to keep her blundering husband quiet if she could. She reached out her hand and took the bag up just a second before Letty Ransome reached out hers ; though Letty's movement was a swift dart made in a spasm of fear. She drew back her hand at once when the movement had failed, but the fear remained in her eyes. " It's just an ordinary bag," she said with a little catch in her voice. But it was not quite an ordinary bag. It was a charming affair of old tapestry, and a medallion of blue enamel was let into the centre of it on each side. Imogen turned it over, admired it, and put it back on the table again.

" Shall we go in now ? " she asked, and she led the way into the grill-room. She turned round at the door and looked at Letty. " Ah ! " she remarked. " You haven't forgotten it this time. I was afraid that you had left it on the table."

She nodded towards the bag which Letty was now carrying clasped tightly in her hand.

" Not twice in twenty-four hours," Letty returned with a laugh. " I am too helpless for words without it."

I asked them in turn what they would like for luncheon.

" Something simple," said Imogen.

" Me, too, please," said Letty.

" Quite so," said I, and knowing the sort of simple food which would appeal to Letty, I ordered blinis, Homard à l'Americaine, cold grouse with a salad and an apple flan. Letty had by now quite recovered her spirits and she rattled away about the ball and how much she had enjoyed it. I could not bring myself to believe that in reality she ever enjoyed anything. Spite was so large an element in all her thoughts. Every comment must carry its little stab, planted viciously with however little dexterity. We were told that Carrie Baines looked lovely, and if she had only dared to smile she would not have given everyone the impression that her loveliness was a mask of enamel. As for dear old Lord Pollant, wasn't he a marvel ? When he danced his *râtelier* so chattered that the castanets in the orchestra weren't wanted at all, were they ? And having had my fill of this talk, I broke in rather abruptly :

" Did you find Jill awake when you went up ? "

Letty Ransome was in the middle of saying : " Minnie Cartwright—they tell me she used to be lovely," and she repeated with a stammer : "—used to be lovely—" and then the clatter of her voice died away altogether and once more her face was as patchy as a Spanish shawl.

Something had happened then up the stairs in Jill's flat whilst the minute hand of the clock jumped ten times. All that agitation under which Letty

had laboured when she re-entered the lounge was not
due to hurry nor to any malady of the heart. For
here it was, renewed. Something terrible had
happened. Silence for a little while held us all.
We tried not to look at Letty's terror-stricken face.
Then I repeated my question.

"Was Jill awake?"

"I don't know," Letty Ransome answered
sullenly. "I had left my bag in the sitting-room on
a chair by the door. I snatched it up and ran down
again."

But she had been ten minutes away. Three
would have sufficed for all that she had done; even
if she had not hurried. Letty was lying.

"Had the maid who let you in called her?"

"Nobody let me in," Letty replied. "The outer
door was on the latch. Jill told the maid to leave
it like that and asked us to see to it, when we left
her this morning. The waiters don't have keys.
Jill said that she might need something and didn't
want to get out of bed to unfasten the door. I
fixed the bolt back myself."

Letty was on surer ground here. She spoke with
a growing confidence. It was eight o'clock, or near
to it, before Jill's friends had left her. She was very
likely, at that hour of the morning when the servants
would be about the corridors, to leave her door so
that she should not be disturbed to open it if she
wanted anything. Letty was speaking the truth
now. We were all certain of it—and all the more
certain, therefore, that we had been right in believing
that she had lied before. Suddenly Letty began to
babble in a low, quick voice:

"I want you to do something for me. I shall have to go in a minute. I have a matinée this morning—and I think something of importance is coming along. Someone is coming to see my show and I want a little time alone before I appear. If it comes off it's going to make a great difference to me. And I want to keep myself up, if you understand." She was fairly babbling now. "If people hear that you're running about all night and get home at eight in the morning, you lose it again. You lose their respect. They won't take you seriously. That's what I mean. They won't believe you're a serious actress."

She was asking us to believe her now. I had no idea of what was coming but she was speaking or rather pleading very earnestly. It was clear that something was at stake for her—something important ; just as it was clear that something terrible had happened during her ten minutes' absence from the lounge.

"What do you want us to do ? " I asked.

"I want you not to mention to anyone that I left my bag up in Jill's flat this morning," she said.

The prayer sounded rather an anticlimax to the careful preparation for it. None of us was likely to go about advertising that the brilliant young actress, Letty Ransome, had left her handbag behind her in a girl-friend's flat at eight o'clock in the morning after a ball. Nor could I see that it would have done her all the damage she feared if we had. I told her that she was exaggerating but she would not have it.

"No," she argued. "The suburbs for one thing

and the managements for another, would say at once : ' Oh, she's just like the rest. Anything for a good time.' I should lose caste. It would do me actual harm if it was known that I had left my bag behind me in Jill's flat at eight o'clock this morning."

I disbelieved every word she was saying. She had not been at all disturbed by any such fears as those which she was now expressing when she had announced in the lounge her intention of running up to Jill's flat. It was only since she had come down from it that we had been showered under with these excuses. It seemed to me better to be clear about it all.

"What you want is that we shouldn't say you had run up for it at a quarter to two this afternoon," I suggested.

Letty Ransome got suddenly very red. She shrugged her shoulders impatiently and turned a pair of dark eyes on me which were hard as steel and as angry as a wild-cat's.

"Of course," she said pettishly. "It's the same thing. If I hadn't left my bag upstairs this morning I couldn't have run up to fetch it this afternoon, could I ? I should have thought anyone might have seen that."

She got up as she spoke. She was holding her bag in her hand. She composed her face to a semblance of civility as she turned to me.

"I thank you for my very good lunch," she said.

"But you have had no coffee," said I.

"I can't wait. I daren't."

She was now in a hurry to be off.

"Good-bye!" And as she moved she turned again towards us.

"You'll remember what I asked—won't you? It's nothing, of course, but still—you'll remember."

Fear and an effort to make light of her fear—a not very successful effort—then she was gone. The waiter brought coffee for the three of us who were left and we sat wondering what we should do. I was uneasy and inclined to go up at once to Jill Leslie's flat. On the other hand, Michael's appointment was for half-past three and it was only a quarter past now. If he went up before his time he might very well seem a trifle too importunate and receive in consequence a blank "No" to his petition. On the other hand—there was Letty Ransome's face as she came back into the lounge and again as she appeared towards the end of our luncheon. I think we were all of us in a quandary. Meanwhile the minutes passed. I called the waiter and ordered the bill and paid it—and meanwhile the minutes passed. I turned to Imogen.

"We might go up now," I suggested. "Michael and I?"

Imogen looked at the clock on the wall. There were still eight minutes to the half-hour.

"Yes," she said, "but wait outside the door until the exact time."

Neither Michael nor I had thought of that most excellent device. Michael, indeed, was thinking of nothing but his petition. All through luncheon he had been framing sentences and selecting words. I had seen his lips moving at other moments than when he was eating and drinking.

" Very well."

I got up and touched Michael on the shoulder.

" Let us go ! "

We went through the lounge into the hall.   I said to the porter :

" Mrs. Legatt's car, please."

He ordered a chasseur to fetch it and Imogen bade us go upon our errand.

" But I'd like to see you afterwards," she added. " I shall expect you, Michael.   You'll bring him along, Martin."

" Right ! " said I.

Michael and I turned to the lift in the corner.

" The third floor, please," said I.

The liftman looked sharply at each of us in turn. But he said nothing.   He ran us up to the third floor and we walked along the corridor.

At the door of Jill's flat stood a policeman.

CHAPTER XXIV

THE FOURTH THEFT

THE policeman barred the way.

" I am sorry, gentlemen."

We were utterly taken aback. Of all the possibilities which had crept in and out of my mind during the last hour and three-quarters, that we should be stopped by a policeman was certainly not one.

" We have an appointment with Miss Leslie," I said.

The policeman looked at us for a moment or two without speaking. He was slow rather than suspicious and it was impossible to infer from his expression whether the reason for his presence at the door was trifling or serious.

" Will you give me your names ? "

We gave them and he continued :

" If I take them in I must rely upon you to see that no one enters while I am away."

" We promise," I said.

" Thank you."

Beyond the door a narrow passage stretched to another door. An electric light burned in the passage. The policeman passed in and closed the outer door upon us. He was away for five minutes at the least. Then he opened the door again, admitted us, and himself went out, once more to stand on guard. In the sitting-room a man in a black frock-coat with a white edge to the opening of his waistcoat was looking out of the window. He turned as we entered and bowed to us.

" I am the manager of the hotel," he said. But the explanation was hardly necessary. His dress declared him.

" Mr. Walmer," said I.

" Yes."

He was a young man, distressed but not flurried.

" This is a dreadful business," he said quietly. " If you wouldn't mind waiting for a minute, the inspector would like to speak to you."

" Inspector ? " I cried in dismay.

" Yes."

It was clear that he meant to answer no questions. So I put none. I looked at Michael. He, too, was completely at a loss. But I think that he was harassed by a doubt whether after all he would be able to make his carefully rehearsed petition. We remained thus in the greatest uneasiness for the space of five minutes, and then the inner door, which I presumed gave on to the bedroom, was opened just wide enough to allow a complete stranger to pass through. He was a thick-set, middle-aged man with a rugged face, dressed in a double-breasted blue suit, and he spoke with a note of culture in his voice which I had hardly expected from his appearance.

" Mr. Legatt ? " he asked looking from Michael to me.

" Yes," said I.

" Mr. Crowther ? "

" Yes," said Crowther.

" I am Inspector Carruthers."

We bowed and waited.

" I understand that you gentlemen had an appointment here with Miss Leslie."

" At half-past three," said I.

" Will you tell me when the appointment was made ? "

" Last night at the Albert Hall."

" Can you give me any idea of the nature of the appointment ? "

" It was of a private nature."

The inspector nodded his head as if he found that statement quite sufficient.

" I am afraid that the appointment cannot be kept," he said gravely.

Michael made a startled movement.

" But it was of the greatest importance," he protested.

" Death cancels even appointments of the greatest importance," said the inspector.

" Death ! "

It was Michael who repeated the word. I must do him the credit of stating that though his cry had the very note of despair, the selfish fear that he had thereby lost his sapphire had nothing to do with inspiring it. It was too deep and true. And just because it was deep and true it astonished me. For I seemed to hear the very abnegation of his creed. Here was the man who, by the annulment of his own life, had proclaimed louder than words could do that existence was misery and death release, now bewail-

ing death as the immitigable ill. But I was wrong.
I looked more closely into that tortuous mind.
Grief at the elimination of a life young and bright
and generous accounted for not the smallest element
in his distress. But that she should not have done
the good deed of repairing a great sacrilege before
she died—that, indeed, was matter for tears. By
your good deeds you cease to live.

For my part, I was thinking of Jill as we had seen
her last night, a gay and sparkling little figure.
Then another picture rose in front of me, one rather
sinister and not to be obliterated—the picture of
Letty Ransome's haggard face when she had joined
us in the lounge below after running up to these
rooms.

" When did Jill die ? " I asked.

" Half an hour ago, perhaps. Not more," the
inspector answered. " Miss Leslie gave orders that
she should be called at half-past two. The maid
found the door ajar at that hour and went into the
bedroom. She was alarmed, and telephoned to the
manager here, Mr. Walmer. Miss Leslie was still
alive when the doctor arrived. You would not wish
to make any statement about the nature of your
appointment ? " Inspector Carruthers repeated his
question almost casually.

" I don't think so," I answered.

" No, I suppose not," Carruthers agreed.

" Of what did Jill Leslie die ? " I asked.

" The doctors will tell us. There is a police-
surgeon in with the hotel doctor. Meanwhile, do
you know who are her relations ? "

" No," I said.

" She will have friends who might know, I suppose."

" I rather doubt it," I replied. " Her nearest friend is Mr. Robin Calhoun."

The inspector held a pencil poised above a little note-book for an appreciable time. Then he wrote the name down.

" Thank you ! I think we know that name, don't we ? "

" I shouldn't wonder," said I.

" His address ? "

I looked towards Michael, for I had not an idea where Robin Calhoun lodged now that Savile Row knew him no more. Crowther, however, knew and he gave the number of a house in a street of Bloomsbury.

" A friend of his ? " Carruthers asked.

" An acquaintance," answered Michael.

Carruthers turned to the manager.

" Perhaps, Mr. Walmer, you would telephone and see if you can get hold of him."

" I'll see to it at once," and Mr. Walmer went out into the corridor. Inspector Carruthers took his place at the window and drummed with his knuckles on the window-pane. " Curious that the maid found the front door open, isn't it ? " he asked of the world in general. " Curious, and one would have thought a little dangerous, eh ? A big hotel. All sorts of people staying in it. Asking for trouble, what ? "

I made a tiny movement with my hand to check any impulse to reply which Michael might be feeling. For if ever I had seen the net spread in the sight of the bird, it was now. Let one of us answer : " The door was left open at eight this morning by Jill's own wish," and round the inspector would swing. " Yes, I know that, because I asked the maid who attended to Jill Leslie when she got back to the Semiramis at seven o'clock this morning. But how did you know ? " and out must come the story of Letty Ransome's handbag and all the complications which that might involve. I was not prepared to tell that story yet. I was not sure that it would ever be necessary to tell it. I wanted to know a little more as to how poor Jill Leslie died, before it was told ; so I made my little signal to Michael Crowther to walk delicately.

The indolent inspector at the window noticed it, however. He strolled across the room and planted himself in front of Michael, legs apart and hands behind his back.

" Could you explain that to me ? " the quiet, cultured voice pleaded. " It would be so helpful if you could. A girl in a big hotel or apartment-house going to bed and leaving her front door open all night—yes, all night, mark you, Mr. Crowther. Odd, eh ? Yes, and risky ? "

He lifted himself on to his toes and let himself down again. His eyes rested upon Michael's face hopefully. He was asking for help from a friend. Every moment I expected Michael to answer eagerly and helpfully : " Yes, but Inspector, the door wasn't open all night. Jill Leslie didn't get back until seven, when the servants were about." But Michael was not such an innocent as I was assuming him to be. Imogen and I had fallen into the habit of construing Michael as a child. But we were wrong. He had moments, such as this one, when he was once more the Captain of the *Dagonet*. He looked quite stolidly at Inspector Carruthers.

" Young people, Inspector ! They don't take the precautions which we elders do. They don't expect danger."

" No, I suppose not," Inspector Carruthers agreed.

If he was disappointed he betrayed not a sign of it.

" We shall be clearer about the position when the doctors have finished," he added.

The doctors nearly had finished. We heard the water running into the wash-basin in the bath-room a minute or two afterwards, and after a minute or two more they came into the room—the hotel doctor, a small dapper fellow, the police-surgeon, a tall loose-limbed man with a grey moustache and a powerful, clean-cut face.

" Dr. Williams," Carruthers introduced to us the hotel doctor, " and our surgeon, Mr. Notch."

I was very interested to see Mr. Notch. He was one of my heroes, a pioneer in the early days of Alpine exploration, to whom one of the great Aiguilles of the Mont Blanc range had fallen on his nineteenth attempt.

" We shall have to make a post-mortem," said Mr. Notch. " But we have very little doubt as to the cause of death."

" Very little," Dr. Williams agreed.

" Yes ? " said Carruthers.

" It seems to be a clear case of cocaine poisoning," said Mr. Notch.

Carruthers nodded his head.

" In that case the question of the open door ceases to be of importance, doesn't it ? " he remarked, his eyes sliding carelessly from my face to Michael's. Did he look for a sign of relief ? He certainly did not get it.

" There will have to be an inquest, of course," Mr. Notch continued. " And it may as well be held as soon as possible, if you agree, Inspector."

" Certainly."

" The day after to-morrow, then. I'll arrange with the Coroner and send for an ambulance at once. If you don't want me any more I'll go down and tell the manager now."

He was already at the door. As he opened it I repeated a question which I had already put to Inspector Carruthers.

" At what hour did Jill Leslie die, Mr. Notch ? "

" She was dead before I arrived," and he looked at Dr. Williams.

" About a quarter past three," Dr. Williams declared.

" And up to what hour could she have been saved ? "

The surgeon and the doctor both shook their heads.

" That's too difficult for us," Mr. Notch replied. " There are no fixed rules, you know. It depends on a number of things. I have known some who were certainly dying three or four hours before they died. Some, on the other hand, have been brought back to life certainly within an hour and a half of the moment when they would have died if they had not been attended to." He stood for a moment or two. " Poor little girl ! What a waste, eh ? I saw her the other night in her comic opera. She was so pretty in it, so engaging ! "

He nodded to the inspector and went out into the passage. I was disappointed. It was ridiculous to be disappointed, especially at this moment. But the ridiculous, unsuitable idea always does seem to occur at moments made for tears. I certainly did not expect Mr. Notch to open a window and climb down a rain-pipe. None the less, for him, a hero of the high Alps, just to go out by the door like all the rest of us earth-clinging people, seemed to me an insufficient exit. I was roused from this foolish reflection by Inspector Carruthers.

" I wish you would tell me why you asked that last question—up to what hour could she have been saved ? " he said.

I replied :

" I was uneasy, you see. I was wondering whether Jill could have been saved if we had come up to this flat before our time. We had an appointment at half-past three. We have been kicking our heels downstairs with nothing to do. We were just marking time until half-past three."

Certainly that possibility had crept uncomfortably into my mind. But it was the recollection of Letty Ransome with her face as patchy as a Spanish shawl which had prompted my question. Letty Ransome had been in this room at ten minutes to two—an hour and a half before Jill Leslie died.

She had just snatched up her bag, she had said, from a chair by the door . . . only the knowledge that the indolent inspector seemed indolently to remark every ripple of my muscles stopped me from an obvious jerk. For there was no chair by the door. More, there could have been no chair by the door. The room was rectangular, and the door at the end of a wall within the angle. Open it and at your right elbow a side wall ran straight forward to the windows. There was no place for a chair there. It would have blocked the entrance had it stood there. Behind the door on the other side stood a long sideboard which occupied the whole space of the wall. Letty had lied. She had not picked up her bag from a chair by the door. From the table in the centre of the room, then? If she had, wouldn't she have been contented just to say that and no more? Why embroider and falsify so natural and likely an action? I began to suspect that the bag had not been left behind in this room at all, but in the bedroom where Jill now lay dead and had then lain dying.

" You gentlemen did not breakfast here with Miss Leslie, I suppose," said Carruthers.

So he knew about the breakfast-party! Then he knew, too, that Jill had not left her outer door open during the night. He had undoubtedly been setting a trap for us.

" No," I answered.

" Several people did, and I want their names. For they will have to give evidence at the inquest."

" Mr. Calhoun is the most likely person to be able to give them to you," I said.

K

" But you both saw this young lady at the ball ? "
the inspector continued.

" Yes."

" Well, then—I don't like to ask it—but there is
something which troubles me in spite of the doctors,
who seem very confident." Carruthers opened the
door of the bedroom and looked in. Then he came
back to us.

" Yes. I must trouble you, I am afraid. I want
you to remember what Miss Leslie wore at the Albert
Hall and to tell me anything which you notice."

He led the way into Jill Leslie's bedroom. The
doctors had drawn a sheet up over her head. For
the rest the room was in disorder. Jill's gay frock
and underclothes were thrown on to a couch, her
stockings were tossed on to a chest of drawers, her
shoes lay on their sides and apart as she had kicked
them off, and about her bed chairs had been thrust
aside as though the doctors had found them drawn
up for the breakfast-party and had pushed them
away. I looked at the dressing-table. There were
pots of cream, a great crystal powder-bowl with a
big puff on the top of the powder, bottles of scent,
combs and hairbrushes all in disarray ; and one
open, empty, jewel-case. But what I, and no doubt
Michael, looked for upon that dressing-table was not
there. Inspector Carruthers made no suggestions
and pointed to nothing. He left us to survey the
room for ourselves, and when we had finished he
took us back into the sitting-room.

" I wonder," he said, " whether you gentlemen
noticed what I noticed."

' There were no ornaments," said I.

" Exactly. Not one piece of jewellery however small or inexpensive. It doesn't seem to me reasonable."

" But there is a reason," I explained. " Jill Leslie had a good deal of jewellery a few months ago. But Calhoun got into difficulties and she sold it."

" Did she indeed ? Calhoun was her lover ? "

" Yes."

" I remember something of Mr. Calhoun's difficulties. We heard of them officially. You relieve my mind, Mr. Legatt, when you tell me that she sold everything to get him out of his scrape."

The inspector laid just enough emphasis upon the " everything " to make sure that I could not disregard it. The question I had been anxious to avoid ever since I had looked about the bedroom was actually put to me and I had to answer.

" I didn't say everything, Inspector."

The inspector smiled.

" No, I did."

" She kept one thing back."

. " Only one ? "

" So far as I know, only one," I replied.

" There was only one jewel-case on the dressing-table," Carruthers agreed. " What was it she kept back ? "

" A large square sapphire on a platinum chain."

" Did Miss Leslie wear it last night ? "

" Yes."

Carruthers turned to Michael Crowther.

" Did you, too, notice it ? "

" Yes," said Crowther.

" And it has gone now," said Carruthers.

There certainly had not been a sign of that blue stone on Jill's dressing-table.

" I don't like that," said Inspector Carruthers. " Not one little bit."

" Jill may have lost it," I suggested. " At the ball, or on the way home."

" Do you think she did ? " the inspector asked.

I wished that he would not ask me questions like that. I expected him to say : " Yes, that is a possibility," or " As an advertisement, isn't that played out ? "—something, at all events, which would lead us away on to the safe ground of general conversation. But he would not thus indulge me. We were not to ride off on the method of : " Is not the peacock a beautiful bird ? " No—he must put the most inconvenient and direct question, and wait dumb until he got his answer.

" No," I answered. " I do not think she did. I heard her once speaking of it. I saw her as she spoke of it. I am certain that if she had lost it she wouldn't have gone to bed until she found it."

" It was a valuable stone ? " he asked.

Now, since my marriage I had learned a good deal more about the value of jewels than I had known previously. It was natural, therefore, that I should put on a few airs. One's prestige as a man can be more or less measured by one's knowledge of the value of things which women love. So I preened myself and answered :

" In the order of stones the sapphire stands below the pearl and the emerald and the diamond. It is nearest to the ruby. But if it is big enough and flawless, it can compete with any of them. Now, this particular sapphire was very big and quite flawless."

" And of a beautiful colour, I suppose," said Carruthers.

I smiled importantly.

" It was. But I must point out to you, Mr. Carruthers, what you with your experience must, indeed, already know, that the synthetic sapphire worth a shilling a carat may have a lovelier depth of colour than the genuine stone."

" Oh ! " said the inspector. I hoped that he was going at once to take out his pocket-book and make a note of that valuable fact. But he did not. He lifted himself once or twice upon his toes.

" It was valuable, then," he said, " and Miss Leslie wore it last night, and Miss Leslie is dead this afternoon, and the valuable thing has disappeared."

" And from that you infer——" I said.

" That we mustn't infer," he replied. Then he flung out his hands and slapped them against his thighs. " Only we must hope that the doctors' post-mortem confirms their first examination, and that we have only to deal with a case of theft."

I was in one respect like Carruthers. I could say : " I don't like that. Not one little bit." For if the sapphire had been stolen again, I knew quite well who had stolen it.

CHAPTER XXV

THE CROWN JEWEL

CARRUTHERS opened the door of the sitting-room and went out to the uniformed police-man in the corridor.

" Armstrong ! "

" Yes, sir."

" I shall want to see the man who was in charge of the lift when Miss Leslie and her friends came back from the ball, and, if he was relieved afterwards, the liftman who has been on duty since. I shall also want to put a few more questions, now, to the chambermaid in charge of this room. Will you get those people here as soon as possible ? "

" Very well, sir."

Armstrong hurried off upon his errand and Carruthers turned towards us. A subtle change had come over the man since this plain and simple case had been complicated by the certainty of a theft and the possibility of a murder. His move-ments were quicker, his eye brighter, he was vitalised body and mind. He looked dangerous now.

" I want to know from you two gentlemen——" he began briskly, but we were spared the question. For the door was burst open and Robin Calhoun tumbled rather than ran into the room.

My first sensation was one of relief. I felt sure
that I could put into words the inspector's interrupted demand. "I want to know from you two
gentlemen whether you know of anyone else besides
yourselves who had an appointment with the dead
girl or any reason to visit her this morning." It
was not that I had any desire to spare Letty Ransome the consequences of what must have been on
the most lenient view, a cruel and beastly crime.
But I saw tremendous difficulties ahead for Michael
Crowther and I wanted to talk them over with
Imogen before I was forced into a decisive statement.

But when I saw Robin Calhoun's face that sense
of relief vanished altogether. It was ravaged with
grief. He was unshaven, unwashed, and the colour
of lead. His clothes were all tumbled as though he
had jumped out of bed and slung on to his body the
first habiliments which were handy. Of the sleek
and debonair adventurer, neatly trimmed for the
trimming of mankind, nothing was left. He was
just an ordinary poor devil of a lover struck down
by the death of his mistress. His words, too, were
the words of melodrama.

"I can't believe it. If such things can happen,
there's no God! But it's not true, is it? This is a
joke, of course. Jill's played me up. We shall have
a laugh over it—in a minute—shan't we?" And he
broke away from his pleading. "My God, how can
you three stand staring at me like mummies?
Hasn't one of you a tongue?"

The inspector looked at me.

"Mr. Calhoun?"

"Yes," I answered.

There was a good deal of curiosity in the inspector's glance as his eyes turned again to Robin Calhoun. He obviously knew more than a little about Robin Calhoun and expected to find in his relations with Jill Leslie a business partnership rather than a union of passion.

" I am sorry to say that it's true, Mr. Calhoun," he said gently.

Calhoun dropped into a chair at the table and buried his face in his hands. Then he drew his hands down until his eyes looked over the tips of his fingers at the bedroom door.

" Jill's in there? " he asked, and now very quietly.

" Yes."

" Can I see her ? "

The inspector opened the door and Calhoun rose and walked towards it. In the doorway he swayed a little as he caught sight of the small, shrouded figure upon the bed.

" Will you leave me here alone, please ? "

"For a little while, Mr. Calhoun," said Carruthers, and Calhoun went into the room and closed the door behind him.

By this time Armstrong, the policeman, had assembled two liftmen and the chambermaid in the corridor ; and at a word from Carruthers he brought them into the room. But their evidence from the inspector's point of view was unhelpful. One of the liftmen had come on duty at seven in the morning. He remembered taking up Jill Leslie and a party of friends soon after seven, to the third floor. No, he did not know any of their names, but one of the gentlemen he had taken up several times before and one of the ladies. He had been on duty until one o'clock. Although he had, during the six hours, taken up several people to the third floor, he had taken up no one who gave the number of Jill Leslie's flat or asked in what direction it lay.

The second liftman had come on duty at one. He knew Miss Leslie by sight, of course, and some of her friends by sight and by name. Mr. Calhoun, for instance, Miss Ransome the entertainer, and this gentleman here, Mr. Crowther. He had brought none of them up since he had come on duty until just now.

The chambermaid, as she had told Mr. Carruthers already, had left the outer door open at Miss Leslie's request. As far as her work had allowed her, she had kept an eye upon it, and she had seen no one at all enter it. But she had a number of flats to attend to and it was only now and then that she was within sight of it.

" Did you go in at all ? " the inspector asked.

" No, sir. Miss Leslie did not wish to be disturbed."

Inspector Carruthers nodded his head.

" That all seems clear enough. You will probably be wanted at the inquest. You'll receive a notice."

He dismissed the servants and sat down at the table and took his note-book from his pocket. He made a few notes in shorthand and looking up at Crowther, remarked :

" You said, I think, that you were not present at the breakfast-party."

" I was not," Crowther answered.

" Right," said Carruthers.

He continued to write, and as I watched his fingers and the hieroglyphics forming on the page, I took the courage to make a suggestion.

" The sapphire might have been hidden by Jill Leslie in the chest of drawers amongst her linen."

Inspector Carruthers observed :

" You are married, I take it, Mr. Legatt," and he went on writing.

I drew myself up a little.

" I am. And what, then ? "

" This, then. If the young lady had hidden it away in a drawer amongst her linen, wouldn't she have put it back in its case first ? "

The question stumped me.

" I suppose she would—unless she was too tired." I saw an argument there. " And she must have been tired after dancing all night."

" Tired enough, certainly, to take her bath and jump into bed before she had her breakfast. Where were her friends, do you think, when she was hiding her sapphire ? "

I shrugged my shoulders.

" All over the flat, I expect."

Carruthers smiled—a rare thing with him that afternoon.

" I should think that's just about the truth." He looked up at me. " Do you really believe that she hid the jewel and left the jewel-case out ? "

" I don't say that I do," I answered. " It's only a suggestion and if it's unwelcome, I withdraw it."

Inspector Carruthers leaned back in his chair.

" You may be right, Mr. Legatt. But neither you nor I believe it. I certainly shouldn't have left

Mr. Calhoun in there alone if I had," he said watching me shrewdly. " Anyway, we shall know very soon. As soon as that poor girl is taken away there will be the usual routine : search, finger-prints, photographs. If the sapphire is tucked away anywhere in that room it will be found this afternoon."

He turned a page of his note-book and became at once very businesslike and brisk.

" And now, gentlemen, if you will kindly sit down, I'll take from you a statement of the nature of the private business with Jill Leslie which brought you up to this flat at half-past three this afternoon."

There was no question any longer of whether we would like to make a statement. We had to make it. Michael Crowther recognised the necessity as clearly as I did. And with the utmost simplicity of voice and word, he told the story of the sapphire, tracing it from Tagaung to the pagoda at Pagan, through Ceylon from Kandy to the rest-house on the road to Anuradhapura, and from the rest-house to England and Jill Leslie. Inspector Carruthers took it all down in shorthand, filling page after page of his book and lifting his eyes from time to time with a wondering glance at Michael Crowther.

" That brings us down to three o'clock this morning when you last saw the stone hanging on the chain round Miss Leslie's neck." He looked at me. " You have nothing to add, Mr. Legatt ? "

" No. Michael has told you everything."

" Very well. I will have a copy of this statement made in longhand and I'll ask you to sign it, Mr. Crowther, and you to witness it, Mr. Legatt. I

have your addresses, I think.   Yes.   Then I need
not detain you any longer."

But we were not done with yet.   For Robin
Calhoun's voice spoke from the doorway :

" Wait a minute, please."

Crowther had been so occupied with the telling of
his story, I so attentive to check it, and Carruthers
at so much pains to keep his fingers up to the pace
of it that not one of us had an idea how long the
bedroom door had been opened and Calhoun listening.   Calhoun came forward and drew a fourth
chair up to the table.   He was very quiet now, and
his face a better colour.   The greatness of his distress
had draped him in a dignity which, I felt sure, he
had never worn before.   He commanded our respect.

He leaned forward on his elbows clasping his hands
together, and he spoke to Michael Crowther.

" I heard everything," he said.   " It's as queer
a story as I've ever heard.   But it comes out of
the East where our standards don't run.   And
hearing you we must know that what you said
is true——"

He looked down upon the table unwilling that we
should see his face, and distrustful of his voice ; and
none of us interrupted him or hurried him.

" If Jill had been alive she would have given you
her sapphire.   She was the loveliest little girl . . .
quick of heart . . . and too good for me.   But in
this one little thing which I can do, I shall do what
she would have done.   I shall give you her sapphire
very willingly."

And the man had not a farthing—and he had been
living on Jill's salary—and his prospects were of the

poorest. If there were truth in Michael's creed, surely Jill had earned the Great Release.

" But we think it has been stolen," said Carruthers.

" It must be recovered," Robin Calhoun replied.

The inspector folded up his note-book.

" Then Miss Leslie made a will," he said, and Robin Calhoun stared at him.

" A will ? "

" Yes, leaving all that she possessed to you."

" A will ! " Calhoun repeated scornfully. " Of course she made no will. I should have heard of it if she had." For a moment he smiled. " Jill making her last will and testament ! I can see her sitting on one foot with her tongue in her cheek, writing out her will like a schoolgirl writing an essay——" And as the picture which he described rose up in front of him, he broke off with a sob.

Carruthers, however, could not leave the matter there.

" If she made no will," he said, " the sapphire will go of necessity to her next of kin."

" She has no next of kin," cried Calhoun. " Who they are I don't know. She didn't know. Someone paid for her schooling in the convent—we don't know who it was. Since she came away with me none but the friends she herself made have had anything to do with her. Not a visit. Not a letter. She was alone."

Inspector Carruthers was troubled. He frowned, he drummed on the table with the butt of his pencil in a real exasperation.

" The position becomes more difficult than ever," he said.

"Why?" Robin Calhoun demanded.

"Because, you see——" I never expected to see Carruthers so uncomfortable as he was then. "You see, Mr. Calhoun, if Miss Leslie made no will and has no next of kin, the sapphire, with everything else which she possesses, belongs to the Crown."

We all sat back in our chairs. Michael's high, slender pagoda spire which had just begun to show white with a gleam of sunshine in a cavern of the clouds, faded again behind the mists.

CHAPTER XXVI

CROOKS ALL

MICHAEL and I walked away from the Semiramis in a gloomy mood and were near to the top of the Haymarket before either of us spoke.

" Do all the jewels left to the Crown go to the Tower ? " he asked.

" Oh, Michael ! Michael ! " I said. " Even Nga Pyu and Nga Than would fight shy of the Tower. The days of Captain Blood are past."

History was not Michael's long suit. Mundane history, I mean, for he was thoroughly well up in the history of the bo-tree and its ramifications.

" You haven't answered my question," he said simply. " Do all the jewels which fall to the Crown go to the Tower ? "

" No, Michael. Very few of them. Most of them go to Christie's."

Michael stopped.

" To be sold ? " he cried, his face lighting up.

" To the highest bidder," I answered, and gloom resumed its sway. " We'll go and talk it over with Imogen."

We were still living in the hotel by the Green Park, and whilst Imogen gave us some tea we told her of

Jill's death and the disappearance of the sapphire.
Imogen was shocked by our narrative.

" Jill was a child," she said, " and just when her
troubles, for the moment at all events, were over
——" She did not finish the sentence and was silent
until Crowther took his leave. She went with him
to the door of our set of rooms.

" You needn't be down-hearted, Michael," she
said as she let him out. " This is our affair now.
We'll see what we can do."

But though she spoke valiantly, there was something quite mouselike in her quietude when she
returned. She threw that off, however, very soon.

" Martin, let's push it all away for a few hours.
Couldn't we go out and dine together alone—not
too early—nineish ? And we could talk things all
over and hammer out what we are to do."

" Splendid, darling. Where shall we dine ? "
And I had a brain-wave. " Oh, I know ! "

" Where, then ? " Imogen asked.

" Le Buisson," I replied triumphantly. For was
it not at that little discovery of Imogen's in Soho
that we had first got to know Jill Leslie ?

But Imogen frowned. Le Buisson had ceased to
mean anything to her for many a week. It was just
one in a monotonous row of restaurants, all low-
roofed and narrow and frowsty, all with little green
trees in little green tubs at the door, all once, each
in turn, declared to be the last word of Bohemian
witchery, all now condemned as tedious and shoddy.

" Not Le Buisson," she said. " No, Martin."

I waited for her choice with some anxiety. There
was a new bar in Oxford Street, painted bright red,

with high stools and a counter. Imogen had lately been setting her friends up on those high stools and forcing them to munch sandwiches and drink dark beer. I was determined not to dine that way even if my refusal involved a divorce on the ground of mental cruelty. Happily Imogen was in a mood for fine clothes and chose the Embassy.

" Meanwhile, Martin, dear, before you sit down to lose money at your stuffy old Club, do you think that you could find out where Letty Ransome lives ? "

" I'll try," said I.

Periodicals and newspapers exist in which the people of the stage advertise their addresses. A dramatic *Who's Who* is published each year. If these means should fail me, Michael Crowther might help, and, indeed, in the end it was from Michael Crowther that I got the information. Letty Ransome had rooms in Cambridge Terrace.

I had this piece of news to my credit at dinner. We talked ways of using it through the meal and after it. We came to two definite conclusions. We must at all costs see Letty Ransome before the inquest and we must leave our line of argument to be settled after we knew whether we or one of us was to be called into the witness-box, or whether neither of us was wanted at all.

This latter question was settled for us the next morning. I received a letter from Inspector Carruthers, stating that the post-mortem examination proved conclusively that Jill Leslie had died from cocaine poisoning and that since the inquest was only concerned with the manner of her death, it was proposed to call only those who had been present at the breakfast-party.

"Letty Ransome, then," said Imogen.

"Yes, surely," said I. "Now, how to get hold of her?"

"I think that you had better leave that to me, darling," said Imogen.

"I will, indeed," I agreed fervently.

Leave the dirty work to the woman is the golden rule of married life, and I went off to my bath. I heard the telephone at work whilst I was soaking in hot water, and I was still wrapped in towels when Imogen began to shout through the door.

"Martin! Martin! Letty Ransome's coming here after her rehearsal."

"When's that?"

"At five this afternoon."

"But, Imogen, I'm not sure that I can get away."

"Don't be absurd," said Imogen. "Darling, if half a dozen old teak-trees stand up one day more, it can't really matter so very much."

Imogen's conceptions of the work of my very important Company were at once primitive and contemptuous. But I consented to be at home by five and actually Letty Ransome and I met on the stroke of the hour at the entrance to the hotel. It was an embarrassing moment for both of us but Letty carried it off the better of the two. She had more nerve or less shame.

"Come up and have some tea, won't you?" I said brightly as though we had met by the merest chance and this grand idea had suddenly dawned on me.

" But I can only stay for a moment, I'm afraid.
I'm so busy," Letty answered, all smiles and dimples.
She was looking pretty enough to melt an iron heart
and though her tailored suit, the fur round her neck,
her shoes and stockings and the rest of her dress
were just what other girls were wearing, she herself
made them different. She gave them a special
distinction. Imogen's judgement failed to recognise
the distinction although, believe me, it was there.
People turned and gazed when Letty passed.
Imogen used barbed words instead—words spoken
with the gentlest voice, but definitely barbed.
However, the barbed words were reserved for me ;
to Letty Ransome she was sweet. For instance, as
she poured out the tea, she said to Letty—she said,
her voice dropping sugar :

" You came up in the lift this time, I suppose."

Letty turned pale and pushed her chair back. If
I could have sidled unnoticed from the room I
should certainly have done so. The only one of the
three who was at ease was Imogen. And she had
battle in her eyes, and enjoyment in her face.

" You haven't mentioned that ! " said Letty
leaning forward, her face strained, her fingers
twitching.

" No ! No ! " said I.

" Not yet," said Imogen.

Letty chose to ignore the " yet."

At the same time she took no notice of me whatever.

" I was sure of that," she declared.

" Why ? " asked Imogen.

" You wouldn't have sent for me if you had,"

Letty replied rather shrewdly, I thought. The invitation would never have been sent had not some accommodation been contemplated. It was a threat and an offer to deal in one. Letty had scored a small point for what it was worth. But she must needs spoil it. For she added :

" Besides, you wouldn't break a promise."

" I hope not, if I made one," Imogen answered. " I remember that you asked for one. I can't remember that we gave one."

Letty now turned appealingly to me but before she could speak Imogen got in something very nasty.

" On important occasions, of course, my husband speaks for himself. On a trumpery little sordid affair like this, I venture to speak for him. He gave you no promise. Did you, darling ? "

" I did not, Imogen," I said stoutly in the tone of one who adds : " And God defend the right ! "

" No promise was made," Imogen resumed.

Letty changed her ground. She took the way of pathos but I cannot think that she was wise. If a woman wants to act pathos to anyone she should select a man. Letty's eyes filled with tears. She said in a voice of studious resignation :

" You must do what you think best, of course, but you can't have realised what this affair means to me. I am beginning to make a little position for myself——"

" So you told us," Imogen interrupted, never without a sweet kind smile.

" And if it's known that I was mixed up with a little singing-girl who doped—well, you can see the harm it must do me."

Imogen looked at once utterly perplexed.

" But I can't see," she said. She hitched her chair forward. She was just asking earnestly and innocently for a little information which—oh, she was certain about it—would clear away all her mystifications in a second. " You are going to give evidence at the inquest, anyway."

Letty stood up as though a spring had been released. But the spring had no strength and she sank down again.

" Oh, you know that ! " she said.

" Of course I know that," Imogen returned. " How could I help knowing it ? "

There was a delicate suggestion here that she was being called herself.

" You have to allow that you had breakfast with —what did you call her ?—the little singing-girl who doped. What additional harm to you could it do to admit that you left your handbag behind and went to fetch it at luncheon-time ? "

" I can't admit that," said Letty stubbornly.

" But why ? " Never was a woman at such a loss to understand. " You must see how awkward it is going to make it for me ! What am I to say ? "

Oh, Imogen, Imogen ! I admired her nerve and deplored her duplicity. So frank and ingenuous she was, Letty Ransome could not but believe that she was to be summoned as a witness.

" Say nothing," said Letty Ransome.

" To a coroner as busy as a little bee ? My dear ! And a jury of ironmongers sniffing at a scandal in theatrical life ? Not so easy to say nothing. I should just be seeing you in front of me as you joined us with your bag in the grill-room. You haven't an idea how strange you looked ! And on top of that, your asking us to promise never to mention it ! You see, they would be certain to ask why we hadn't told the inspector-man about it at once. Of course, if we understood—but as things are, it's bewildering."

All the natural colour ebbed from Letty Ransome's face. From a pair of frightened eyes she stared at Imogen.

" I see," she said slowly.

And we all saw. No one was puzzled any more. Imogen's last sentences meant nothing if they did not mean a threat. Letty Ransome, to borrow the jargon suitable to the subject, had got to come across with a history of what she did between a quarter and five minutes to two on the afternoon before at the Semiramis Hotel. If she held her tongue she must run whatever risk there was to run that we should inform the police and the coroner of her visit to Jill Leslie's flat.

Letty Ransome came across.

" I think that I had better tell you everything," she said, passing her tongue between her lips.

" It would be wise, I think," said Imogen.

" When I went into Jill's flat she was still living."

It was the statement which we expected, yet it shocked us both as if it had been some dreadful news flung at us unexpectedly over the wireless.

" Yes," said Imogen. " Then you went into Jill's bedroom."

" I had left my handbag there," Letty answered.

" Yes," Imogen agreed. " There wasn't any chair near the door of the sitting-room."

" I didn't look," said Letty Ransome. " I told you a chair by the door as, at that moment in the lounge, I would have told you anything."

" Except the truth," Imogen remarked.

" I was frightened out of my life," Letty pleaded.

" Naturally," Imogen explained to her, " since you had left your friend to die alone without calling for help."

Letty Ransome shrank back in her chair. I got an impression that the chair had widened and grown higher and that Letty had dwindled. She looked so small, so diminished from the arresting figure I had seen not half an hour ago on the door-step of the hotel.

" It would ruin me if that were known," she whispered ; and some comprehension of the abominable nature of her excuse entered her mind as she heard herself utter it. " Oh, there was nothing to be done," she cried. " Jill was unconscious. She was breathing—horribly. Her breath was roaring —yes, roaring in great long gasps, and her chest rose and fell beneath the bedclothes with a violence which I didn't think any heart could stand. I didn't dare to go near her. For a few moments, too, I couldn't run away. I was held there as if my feet were chained. It was awful. That room— the sun outside—and the horrible sound from the bed—I was frightened out of my wits. I was suddenly mad to get away. I snatched up my bag from the dressing-table——"

" Oh ! " Imogen interrupted. " It was on the dressing-table ? "

" Yes," Letty ran on, hardly noticing the interruption. " I snatched it up. I remember that I had seen no one in the corridor, that I had run up the stairs instead of using the lift. I wondered if I could get away. I looked into the corridor round the edge of the front door. It was still empty. So I ran—oh, I ran ! I didn't say anything to you. It couldn't have done any good."

" Why not ? " asked Imogen.

" Jill was actually dying."

" How do you know ? " asked Imogen. " How do you know that she wouldn't be alive now if you had called for help at once ? "

Letty did not answer. She sat and stared and stared at Imogen, and then a little sigh fluttered from her lips. I was just in time, I think. In another second she would have slipped off the chair on to the floor.

" We must get her some water," I said, and Imogen ran for it.

" She'd better have some brandy, too," said Imogen.

We had, therefore, an adjournment of the witness's cross-examination whilst the waiter was summoned, sent to fetch brandy and brought back with it. During that adjournment, Imogen and I both and quite separately came to the conclusion that Letty Ransome had not realised in the slightest degree that there might, by prompt action, have been a chance of saving Jill Leslie's life. I don't even know that there was a chance. The police-surgeon, with all his experience, would not commit himself.

I had no doubt that Letty, standing in that room with the sunlight coming in at the window and all the summer sounds of birds and insects, and with the shrouded figure on the bed gasping out its life like some overwrought machine, never dreamed but that Jill was actually dying and beyond recall. The conviction certainly made a difference in our judgement of Letty. We were able, if not to believe, to assume that had Letty imagined that Jill could have been saved, she would have roused the whole of the Semiramis Court rather than let her friend die. Letty's next words, indeed, strengthened our assumption.

" Do you mean to say that Jill could have been saved ? " she asked in a shaking voice.

" No one can say that," Imogen answered gently ; and at once our assumption began to lose its strength. For with the utterance of those words Letty's assurance began to return. Her eyes became less guilty and more wary.

" Then I don't think you ought to have suggested it," she cried on a note of indignation.

" Let's go back to the handbag," said Imogen coldly ; and the suggestion brought Letty Ransome low.

" Why the—the handbag ? " she stammered, and was lost.

" Because Jill's big sapphire was stolen from her dressing-table that morning, and the police know it," said Imogen, deftly mingling fact and probability to make one convincing indictment.

" Jill's big sapphire ! " Letty repeated with round, incredulous eyes.

"And the platinum chain," said Imogen.

Letty shrugged her shoulders.

"They had better search the chambermaid's trunks," she said disdainfully. I had been somehow quite sure that this would be Letty Ransome's reply. No doubt Imogen was prepared for it too, for she was ready with her rejoinder.

"And your handbag, Letty."

"You think I stole it!"

"I'm sure you stole it."

"You dare——" Letty Ransome rose to her feet. "I'll not stay here another moment." She whisked across to the door. "It's outrageous!" She laid a hand upon the door-knob, and then she stopped and looked round. She saw me drawing the telephone instrument nearer to me. It stood upon a side table and I had only to turn my chair to reach it.

"Who are you going to telephone to?" she demanded.

"Need you ask?" I returned.

"You see, Letty," Imogen resumed, "you fetched your bag from Jill's dressing-table and you came back to us in the lounge, not quite yourself. You told us that you found it on a chair in the sitting-room. That wasn't true. You asked us not to mention your visit to the room. You asked us very urgently, and you gave us a ridiculous reason. When I picked up the bag to admire it I could see you were so nervous that your fingers were twitching. You were afraid that I was going to open it, Letty. When we went in to luncheon you sat on it. When you went away you were clutching it—just as you are now."

Slowly and very sullenly Letty Ransome came back into the room.

" I didn't mean to leave the bag behind again," she answered. " It's my only one."

Neither Imogen nor I made any rejoinder. As a matter of fact we were not too comfortable. Now that the police were quite certain that Jill had died from an overdose of cocaine, a drug to which she was addicted, they were not really interested in the theft of the sapphire. No one had moved them to take any action. It had nothing to do with the inquest. A direct threat to raise it at the inquest might be beating the air. Our hope was that Letty dare not run the risk of allowing us to try.

" Why do you want the sapphire ? " she asked.

It would, of course, have been too ridiculous to have tried to explain to Letty Ransome the dreams and hopes which had gathered about that stone. She would not have understood them in a thousand years, and when she had understood them she would have thought us all liars. Imogen took the simplest way.

" That's our affair," she said, and I saw Letty Ransome's face change. She looked from one to the other of us with an easiness which she had not shown before. A smile glimmered on her lips and spread. She began to laugh with a real amusement.

" I see," she remarked. " Birds of a feather, what ? I must now have your promise."

" You'll have it, but you won't need it," I answered. " What can we say, if we've got the sapphire ? "

Letty Ransome thought that over and it seemed

to her reasonable. Thieves betray thieves, certainly, but not to convict themselves. She suddenly opened her bag, took out of it a twist of tissue-paper and laid it on the table. In the twist of paper lay the sapphire and its chain. Imogen's hand darted out and grasped it—oh, greedily enough to persuade Letty Ransome that she had nothing any longer to fear from us. She shut up her bag with a snap. She looked at us derisively.

"You make me tired, you two," she said, and she sauntered out of the room.

CHAPTER XXVII

THE LAST

I WAS indignant. Letty Ransome had hardly closed the door before I cried :

" Did you hear that, Imogen ? "

" Of course I did, darling," she answered.

" She thinks we are a couple of crooks," I said.

" Well, aren't we ? " she asked, playing with the sapphire.

" We are not. Just listen to me ! "

" I will. But, dearest, don't you think you had better have a whisky and soda first ? "

The advice was sound and I always take sound advice. But I was not to be diverted. I had lunched at my club which was conveniently placed between the officialdom of the West and the solid interests of the East. I had sat beside a King's Counsel to whom I had put our problem ; and now reinforced by his judgement, I was prepared to prove to Imogen that my capacities were not limited to cutting down half a dozen old teak trees in a forest. Over my whisky and soda I expounded the law.

" The sapphire is not the property of the Crown. If Jill died intestate and without kin, the property of which she died possessed would belong to the Crown. But the sapphire was taken from her whilst she was alive. Therefore she was not possessed of it when she died."

Imogen nodded.

" I was always certain that if we went down to the House of Commons and sent for the Chancellor of the Exchequer and told him that there was a sapphire for him to sell, he would be bored to tears," she said.

" I don't think you are quite following my argument, Imogen," I said.

" Word by word, darling," Imogen insisted.

" Very well."

I took a drink and Imogen sat with her eyes upon my face and her hands in her lap, suspiciously dutiful.

" The only person really in a position to take action is Jill herself; and she's dead. The sapphire's in the air. To establish ownership to it amongst the living would be impossible."

" I think you're marvellous, Martin," said Imogen. " It's such a comfort to know that we shall not be acting illegally when we do what we are going to do, anyway."

We took the sapphire with its chain to a jeweller the next day and got him to put a price upon it. Then we sent for Robin Calhoun and persuaded him to take the price. He made a little show of a fight against taking it, but Jill was gone and he had the cost of her burial to discharge and his circumstances were distressful. In the end he took it and went his way. After he had gone :

" I think," I said, " that we had better buy a passage to Rangoon and give it to Michael with the sapphire, don't you ? "

Imogen agreed.

"So you, too, noticed that his clothes were getting shabby and his shoes wanted heeling, and his face was longer every day," she said tucking her hand through my arm.

"I shouldn't think that there's much to spare in Michael's pocket nowadays," I said.

I think that Michael had actually a narrower margin than we imagined. We telephoned to his address in Bayswater the day after the inquest, asking him to call. I shall never forget the look upon his face when Imogen handed to him his sapphire and his steamer-ticket and he knew that his long pilgrimage was at an end. It was like a clean, clear morning after a hopeless night of rain. He could not speak. He made a few little whimpering noises of joy and the water stood in his eyes. I thought that he would burst into tears. He made a forward movement with his head towards Imogen and checked himself.

"You may, Michael," Imogen said with a smile, and she lifted her cheek to him.

But he passed the privilege by. He stood up straight, although with an effort. His face lost—not all at once but by subtle gradations—the warmer human looks which it had worn during his quest and our endeavours to help him. We saw Galatea returning to stone. He became not stern but aloof, an ecclesiastic set apart amongst his solitary imaginings. So I had seen him twice—once on the steamer at Schwegu and once on the terrace of the Rock Temple at Dhambulla. So Imogen had seen him once. Michael D. had gone long ago. Michael went now. Uncle Sunday remained. He did not thank us. Why should he? The little we had done in obedience to the inexorable Laws would be of immense advantage to ourselves. He just said: " Good-bye ! " and went away.

As soon as he had gone Imogen did what was for her the rarest thing. She sat down and cried—really cried, with the great tears rolling down her cheeks.

" I had an idea," she said between her sobs, "—I am too ridiculous and I am making myself hideous—I had an idea that we might have gone down to the docks and seen him off. But he doesn't want us." She turned and clung to me whilst I slipped an arm about her. " Oh, Martin, you must never go back to Burma. I can't have you sitting about any old pagoda and perfectly happy. No, I can't ! "

I reassured her as best I could. We did the wise thing we had learnt to do in conditions of stress. We went out and dined together alone in a restaurant gay with lights and lovely people. But in the midst of the gaiety and the lights we had glimpses of another and a distant world—the shadow stretching out over earth and sea from the summit of Adam's Peak, the bungalow in a glistening jungle where Imogen had crouched against a wall with the terror of death at her heart, and the high terrace above Sigiri where I had first held her in my arms.

THE END